BOOKS

Simply Learning, Simply Best!

Simply Learning, Simply Best!

倍斯特出版事業有限公司
Best Publishing Ltd.

老外都這麼說

超有梗...

日常英語 Talk Show

口語與幽默感一起飆升

陳紳誠、謝旻蓉 ◎著

情境喜劇&詼諧英語對話&超實用英文句式

邊聽邊看，邊笑邊學！開口就讓人OS：「這個人的英語好有梗！」

全書**68**個主題，包含所有『聊天的梗』與所有『喜怒哀樂』
204個欲罷不能的小對話，**204**個用了涮嘴好用句型

跟著MP3一起說，英語有梗達人就是你

外師
超有梗錄音

I broke my finger.
On the other hand,
I was feeling ok.
雖然我的手指頭骨折，
另一方面(另一隻手)我
感覺還好。

was drinking so much
nicknamed myself
Johnny Walker.
我喝很多酒，多到把自己取
名叫約翰走路。

Well, at least you don't have to
pay your mortgage anymore.
喔，老兄你再也不用付房貸了。

作者序 ☺

首先我們想感謝倍斯特出版的編輯群給我們機會創作這本書。

這本書原先的企劃案是文法句型書,但是,到書店去放眼一望,文法或句型的書籍比比皆是,怎麼寫應該都是大同小異吧。另外,外國人不了解本地學生為何要背文法,認為**多聽**、**多看**、**多講才是王道**,真實生活的英文對話是不可能像寫作文般套用文法公式。綜合了兩邊的意見,並與編輯溝通後,這本書順利轉型成以情境式的分類、以幽默的口語代替枯燥的文法造句來介紹單字、句型、和一些相關的文法。

筆者在協助撰寫這本書的過程中學習了不少英美的流行文化和脫口秀用詞,並且發現口語化的情境式英文要正確的翻譯而不破梗是有挑戰性的。當中觸及的層面包含文化差異和當地的習慣用語,翻譯成中文時還要考慮到有些字在不同的情境中所表達的意思可能不同。

希望各位讀者在利用這本書學習時,跟我們一樣開心快樂,並能從中學到一些實用句型及文法,在不同情境裡也能順利開口說英文。

陳紳誠、謝旻蓉

編者序 ☺

　　以前，我們認為英文有時就像公式一樣。但是，英文可不是數理化學，而是一個活生生的語言，我們必須用更「有趣」的方式來學習。

像美劇的會話情節

　　翻開本書你會發現裡面偷偷埋藏很多**笑梗**，有像美劇無俚頭的幽默與偷偷放冷箭的嘲諷。更重要的事，這些都是我們一直想用英文表達的意思。閱讀本書不但可以幫助你英文口語能力變好，還能學習西方人幽默的思考方法。

聊天的梗都在這裡

　　常常與外國人聊天會支吾其詞嗎？那麼你需要更多「靈感」。此書提供所有適合聊天的梗，與所有關於喜怒哀樂道地又自然的表達方法。讓英文跟上中文想要表達的感覺，自在地東聊西聊！

　　希望此書可以成為您英文學習路上的好朋友！一起跟著本書邊聽邊看，邊笑邊學吧！

倍斯特編輯部 謹上

Chapter **2**
喜怒哀樂都在這裡 ▌▌▌▌▌▌▌▌▌▌▌▌▌▌▌

Chapter 1
日常交際

打招呼

這樣說英文

Ⓐ Good morning, sir. How are you doing today?
Ⓑ Couldn't be better. A cup of iced café au lait to go please.
Ⓐ Here you are. That would be NT$50. Have a nice day.

Ⓐ 早安，今天好嗎？
Ⓑ 再好不過了。請幫我外帶一杯加牛奶的冰咖啡。
Ⓐ 好的，總共是 NT$50。祝您有個美好的一天。

Ⓐ Hello Joan, how's everything?
Ⓑ Great! How are you? I saw you at the infirmary the other day. Is everything alright?
Ⓐ Oh, I am ok. I went there with my friend. He sprained his ankle, so I had to drive him there.

Ⓐ 哈囉，瓊。一切都好嗎？
Ⓑ 好得很。你呢？我那天在醫務室看到你，一切還好吧？
Ⓐ 喔，我沒事。我是跟我朋友去的。他扭傷腳踝，所以我需要開車帶他去。

Ⓐ There you are, John. I have been looking all over for you.
Ⓑ Ditto! I have been looking all over for you too.
Ⓐ That's a coincidence. What's up?

Ⓐ 原來你在這裡，約翰。我到處找你。
Ⓑ 同樣的，我也到處在找你。
Ⓐ 真巧。有什麼事嗎？

Vocabulary

Café au Lait   ph. 【法】加牛奶的咖啡
Infirmary [ɪnˋfɚmərɪ]   n. 醫務室
Sprain [spren]   vt. 扭傷

Ditto [ˋdɪto]   adj. 同樣的
Coincidence [koˋɪnsɪdəns]   n. 巧合

這樣用句型 002

> _____, sir. How are you doing today?

- Good afternoon　午安，先生。您今天好嗎？
- Greetings　哈囉，先生。您今天好嗎？
- Good evening　晚上好，先生。您今天好嗎？
- Long time no see　好久不見了，先生。您今天好嗎？
- Nice to see you again　很高興再次遇見您，先生。您今天好嗎？

> He _____, so _____.

- is almost late for school... he asks his dad to give him a ride to school
  他上學快遲到了，所以請他父親載他去學校。
- ate too much during lunch... he entirely skipped dinner
  他午餐吃太飽了，所以完全省略晚餐。
- fell asleep last night... he didn't finish his homework
  他昨晚睡著了，所以作業沒有寫完。
- likes to help others... he decides to join a volunteer organization
  他喜歡幫助別人，所以他決定加入志工團體。
- is a great singer... he has fans all over the world
  因為他是個很棒的歌手，他在世界各地都有粉絲。

 句型！ …, so … 這個句型是用來說明前因後果的。就如同中文裡的「因為…，所以…」。

11

There you are, John. _____.

- Everyone's looking for you　原來你在這裡，約翰。大家都在找你。
- Where have you been　原來你在這裡，約翰。你去了哪裡？
- We were worried about you　原來你在這裡，約翰。我們都很擔心你。
- You are late for the wedding ceremony
  原來你在這裡。約翰，你趕不上結婚典禮了。
- Who are you hiding from　原來你在這裡，約翰。你在躲誰呀？

用這句話更厲害！

003

❶ Hello. It's been a while! I didn't expect to see you.
哈囉，好久不見！我並沒預期在這裡看到你。

❷ Fancy meeting you here! When did we last meet?
想不到在這遇見你！上次我們見面是甚麼時候的事？

❸ What's up? Tell me, how have you been?
你好啊！告訴我，近來如何呀？

❹ You again? Didn't I just see you just now?
又是你？我不是剛剛才看到你嗎？

❺ What's going down? The boys are coming over now.
有什麼事嗎？孩子們現在要過來。

❻ Hi. My name is Garfield. What's yours?
嗨，我名叫加菲爾，你呢？

❼ Are you available this afternoon? Why don't you join us?
你今天下午有空嗎？為何不加入我們？

❽ Good day, Mr. Peterson. Wonderful weather we have here!
日安，彼得森先生。今天天氣真好。

❾ Howdy. Have you eaten yet?
您好，吃過飯了嗎？（呷飽沒？）

⑩ How do you do? I don't believe we have met.
您好，我們應該還不認識彼此。

⑪ How are you doing? You look fabulous!
近來如何？你看起來好極了！

⑫ How have you been? It's been awhile!
最近好嗎？已有一陣子了吧！

必背單字片語

☑ **Expect** [ɪkˋspɛkt]　vt. 預料; vi.〔用進行式〕懷胎
She is expecting a baby. 她懷孕了。

☑ **Fancy** [ˋfænsɪ]　vt.【口】想像；想不到
Fancy spending an afternoon at the beach!
想想整個下午在海邊度過的感覺吧！

☑ **Available** [əˋveləbl]　a. 有空的
There is still space available for the next train to Taipei.
下一班往台北的列車還有空位。

☑ **Howdy** [ˋhaʊdɪ]　n.【美國德州方言】您好
Howdy partner. Are you ready for the road trip?
夥伴你好，準備好要上路了嗎？

☑ **Fabulous** [ˋfæbjələs]　a. 驚人的；【口】極好的
Such a fabulous evening! Let's take a stroll at the park.
今晚真棒，我們到公園散步一下。

☑ **Awhile** [əˋhwaɪl]　adv. 片刻；一會兒
Please wait awhile while we process your paperwork.
請在我們處裡您的文件時稍等片刻。

Unit 2 見到很久不見的朋友

這樣說英文

004

Ⓐ Hey Peter, long time no see. How's everything?
Ⓑ Yeah, everything is great. I've worked overseas for the last few months. What's up with you?
Ⓐ I am doing ok. Welcome back. Let's catch up this weekend.

Ⓐ 嘿彼得，好久不見了。一切都好嗎？
Ⓑ 是呀，一切都很好。過去幾個月我到國外出差。你呢？
Ⓐ 我很好。歡迎回來。這個週末我們敘敘舊吧。

Ⓐ Wow, is that you John?
Ⓑ Who wants to know? Do I know you? You look familiar.
Ⓐ It's me, your ex-girlfriend Jane from high school. What happened to you?

Ⓐ 哇！是你嗎，約翰？
Ⓑ 誰在問？我認識你嗎？你看起來好面熟。
Ⓐ 是我，你在高中時的前女友珍。你發生什麼事啦？

Ⓐ Hi Jane. You look so different! What happened to you?
Ⓑ Five babies, two divorces, unemployment for a decade and a foreclosure.
Ⓐ That's rough. But, you are one tough cookie.

Ⓐ 嗨，珍。你看起來真不同。發生甚麼事了？
Ⓑ 五個小孩、兩場破碎婚姻、失業十年、房子還被法拍…
Ⓐ 真是苦了你，但是你是個很強悍的女人。

Vocabulary

Catch up　ph. 趕上；敘舊
Overseas [`ovɚ`siz]　adv. 在海外；在國外
Ex-girlfriend　ph. 前女友

Unemployment [ˌʌnɪm`plɔɪmənt]　n. 失業
Foreclosure [for`kloʒɚ]　n. 法拍

這樣用句型

> **Hey Kate,** _____

- it's been awhile　嗨,凱特,已有好一陣子沒見了。
- how long has it been　嗨,凱特,有多久沒見了?
- it must have been years　嗨,凱特,應該已經好幾年沒見了。
- when was the last time we met
  嗨,凱特,上次我們見面是甚麼時候呀?
- I never expected to meet you here　嗨,凱特,我沒預期會在這裡見到你。

> **Wow!** _____

- Could it be you, John　哇!是你嗎,約翰?
- You look familiar. Are you John　哇!你看起來很面熟。你是約翰嗎?
- Are you who I think you are　哇!你是我所認為的那個人嗎?
- Are my eyes playing tricks on me　哇!我的眼睛正在騙我嗎?
- I cannot believe this. Is that you, John
  哇!我真不敢相信。是你嗎,約翰?

> **Hi Jane. You** _____

- look just the same　嗨,珍,妳看起來都沒變。
- haven't aged one bit　嗨,珍,你一點都沒變老。
- look like a million dollars　嗨,珍,妳看起來格外的漂亮。
- are really here? How has it been　嗨,珍,你真的在這裡?最近好嗎?

1 日常交際

15

・ surprise me! Long time no see 嗨，珍，真是驚喜，好久不見了！

註 look like a million dollars 字面上的意思是「看起來像百萬元」，暗指像是用百萬元治裝打扮出來這麼的漂亮，所以用來形容他人看起來很帥或是很漂亮。

用這句話更厲害！

❶ Look who's here! Where have you been all these years?
看看是誰在這裡，這幾年你都到哪去了？

❷ Well, well, well! If it isn't John the man himself!
哎呀呀，這不是約翰本尊？

❸ Oh my goodness! Is that you, Jane?
我的老天，是你嗎，珍？

❹ Wow. I couldn't recognize you!
哇，我認不出你！

❺ Hello stranger! Look at you! You look great!
哈囉，陌生人，看看你，你看起來好極了！

❻ Oh my! You haven't aged a bit.
哇！你一點都沒變老。

❼ Gosh Jane, you look so different!
哇，珍！你看起來不一樣！

❽ Oh my goodness! What happened to you?
老天，發生甚麼事了？

❾ It can't be you!
這不可能是你！

註 雙方許久不見後，對方變得跟印象中大不同而說的驚歎語

❿ Are my eyes deceiving me?
我的眼睛在騙我嗎？

⓫ I never thought I'd see you again.
我以為不會再見到你了。

⑫ Hi. It's certainly been awhile.

嗨，確實過了一段時日沒見面了。

必背單字片語

☑ **Recognize** [`rɛkəg͵naɪz]　vt. 認出；承認
I couldn't recognize most of my high school classmates at the reunion.
同學會時我無法認出大部分的高中同學。

- -

☑ **Stranger** [`strendʒɚ]　n. 陌生人
Kids need to be cautious talking to strangers on the street.
小孩在街上與陌生人講話要很小心。

- -

☑ **Aged** [`edʒɪd]　adj. 舊的；陳的
This bottle of aged wine is very rare.
這瓶陳年的酒非常稀有。

- -

☑ **Different** [`dɪfərənt]　adj. 不同的；特別的
She acts differently around the boy she adores.
她在喜歡的男孩面前表現不同。

- -

☑ **Deceive** [dɪ`siv]　vt. 欺騙；蒙蔽
I wanted something a bit different.
我想來點不同的東西。

- -

☑ **Certainly** [`sɝtənlɪ]　adv. 無疑地；確實
This restaurant is certainly the most popular around the neighborhood.
這家餐廳確實是這附近最受歡迎的。

1 日常交際

超有梗 日常英語 Talk Show
Daily English Talk Show

Unit 3 想認識做朋友

這樣說英文

007

Ⓐ Hello, I don't think we've met. My name is Jane. Nice to meet you.
Ⓑ Hi there. My name is John. I am the host of this evening. Would you like to sit with me?
Ⓐ My pleasure. Lovely evening, isn't it?

Ⓐ 哈囉，我們應該還不認識，我是珍，很高興認識你。
Ⓑ 嗨，我叫約翰，是今晚的主辦人。你願意跟我坐在一起嗎？
Ⓐ 樂意之至。今晚很美，不是嗎？

Ⓐ Excuse me. I am wondering if you can tell me how to get to the botanical garden?
Ⓑ I'm sorry I'm not a local. I'm also trying to get there myself.
Ⓐ Really? Let's find out together.

Ⓐ 打擾一下，不知你能否告訴我怎麼去植物園？
Ⓑ 真抱歉，我不是當地人。我自己也在找要去那裏的路。
Ⓐ 真的嗎？那我們一起找吧。

Ⓐ Hi beautiful. Are you alone? Can I buy you a drink?
Ⓑ Sure. I drink scotch. Have a seat.
Ⓐ Bartender, bring us one scotch and a glass of Vodka with coke, please.

Ⓐ 嗨美女，妳一個人嗎？我能請你喝一杯嗎？
Ⓑ 好啊，我都喝蘇格蘭威士忌。請坐吧。
Ⓐ 酒保，請給我們一杯蘇格蘭威士忌和一杯伏特加可樂。

Vocabulary

Host [host]　n. 主辦人；主人
Pleasure [`plɛʒɚ]　n. 愉快；樂意
Botanical garden [bo`tænɪkl̩ `gɑrdn]　ph. 植物園

Local [`lokl̩]　n. 當地居民；本地人
Bartender [`bɑr͵tɛndɚ]　n. 酒保

18

這樣用句型 008

> Hello, _____.

· I haven't seen you around here before　嗨，我之前不曾在這裡見過妳。

· are you looking for something　嗨，妳在找什麼嗎？

· you look familiar　嗨，妳看起來很眼熟。

· you seem lost　嗨，妳似乎迷路了。

· I think we're in the same class　嗨，我想我們在同一班。

> I am wondering if you _____.

· can help me out　不知你能否幫我的忙。

· have the time　不知妳是否知道時間。

· are single　不知你是否單身。

· have a boyfriend　不知你是否有男朋友。

· know where the library is　不知你是否知道圖書館在哪。

😊 句型!　**wonder if + 子句** 是指不知是否…的意思，也可用 wonder whether + 子句來代替。

> May I _____?

· sit here, please　請問我可以坐在這裡嗎？

· accompany you until you feel better　我可以陪你直到你感覺好一點嗎？

· invite you to dinner　我可以邀請你一起吃晚餐嗎？

· ask you out for a movie　我可以約你出來看電影嗎？

· offer you a suggestion　我可以提供你一個建議嗎？

用這句話更厲害！

009

❶ They have so much in common. Can they make friends?
他們有好多共通點喔。他們能成為朋友嗎？

❷ Do you want to be my pen pal? Can you give me your email?
你要當我的筆友嗎？你可以給我你的電郵信箱嗎？

❸ Let me give you my number. Call me when you're available.
我給妳我的電話。妳有空時打電話給我。

❹ Text me if you need anything.
如果你需要任何事情，傳簡訊給我。

❺ My name is Peter, what's yours?
我名叫彼得，你的名字是？

❻ Can you add me on Facebook?
你可以將我加入你的臉書好友嗎？

❼ Would you like to join me for a stroll?
你想跟我去散散步嗎？

❽ Would you like a drink?　你想喝點甚麼嗎？

❾ Do you want to get a bite at recess?　你想去吃點東西嗎？

❿ I love your dog. What's her name?
我好愛你的狗，她叫甚麼名字？

⓫ I cannot believe we are alumni of the same college.
真不敢相信我們是同校的校友。

⓬ Let me introduce a friend to you. This is my fellow classmate, John.　John, this is Peter, we are in the school orchestra together.
請容我介紹一個朋友給你認識，這位是我的同班同學約翰。約翰，這是彼得，我和他都在學校的交響樂團演奏。

必背單字片語

☑ **in common**　ph. 共同

Even though we are brothers, we have nothing in common.

雖然我們是兄弟，但我們一點都不同。

- -

☑ **Text** [tɛkst]　vt.【口】傳簡訊（send a text message 的簡易口語）

Could you please text the registration details to me again? I didn't receive anything last week.

請你將註冊的細節用簡訊再傳一次給我好嗎？我上星期並沒有收到任何通知。

- -

☑ **Bite** [baɪt]　n.【口】便餐

I am starving.　Let's grab a quick bite before starting the project.

我餓昏了。開始做作業前讓我們先吃點東西吧。

- -

☑ **Recess** [rɪ`sɛs]　n. 休息；課間休息

Children loves running and screaming during recess.

孩子們喜愛在課間休息時間又跑又叫。

- -

☑ **Alumni** [ə`lʌmnaɪ]　n. 校友

Most of the alumni from this MBA program become important leaders in the corporate world.

這個企管碩士專班的校友多數變成重要的企業領導者。

- -

☑ **Orchestra** [`ɔrkɪstrə]　n. 管弦樂團

I love listening to the performance of the New York City symphony orchestra.

我喜歡聽紐約市立交響樂團的演奏。

① 日常交際

Unit 4 跟同事打招呼

這樣說英文

Ⓐ Hi. How was your weekend?
Ⓑ Not so good. I had a fender-bender and had to send my car in for repairs.
Ⓐ You too? I totaled my motorcycle but luckily I'm OK.

Ⓐ 嗨，週末過得如何？
Ⓑ 不太好。出了小車禍（擦撞意外），車子必須進廠送修。
Ⓐ 你也出車禍？我的摩托車撞毀了，但幸好我沒事。

....

Ⓐ You're back! How did the vacation go?
Ⓑ It was great. Look at the tan I got. You should have been there.
Ⓐ I wished I could go but I got a ton of work to get done.

Ⓐ 你回來了！假期過得如何？
Ⓑ 很棒呀！看我曬的古銅色，你應該去的。
Ⓐ 我也很想但是有一堆做不完的工作。

....

Ⓐ Hello, which department do you work in?
Ⓑ Audit. I make sure everyone stays within company regulations. What about you?
Ⓐ Sales. Hmm, I am late for an appointment. See you around.

Ⓐ 哈囉，你是哪個部門的？
Ⓑ 審計部。我的職責是確認每位員工遵守公司規定，那你呢？
Ⓐ 我在業務部。有個約我遲到了，回頭見了。

....

Vocabulary

Fender-bender [`fɛndɚ`bɛndɚ] n. 【口】小車禍；擦撞
Total [`totl] vi. 【俚】使完全毀壞

Tan [tæn] n. 曬成的棕褐膚色
Audit [`ɔdɪt] n. 審計
Regulation [ˌrɛgjəˈleʃən] n. 規章；規定

這樣用句型

011

Hi. How _____ **?**

· did your honeymoon go　嗨，你的蜜月旅行過得如何？
· was the company trip　嗨，員工旅遊玩得如何？
· was the customer visit　嗨，客戶來訪順利嗎？
· did you do on the exam　嗨，你考得如何？
· do you like your new apartment　嗨，你喜歡你的新公寓嗎？

I wished _____ **but** _____ .

· I could take off ... my boss wouldn't let me
我希望能離開，但老闆卻不准（假）。

· he would leave me alone ... he just wouldn't
我希望他不要來煩我，但他卻一直煩我。

· the customer would buy my product ... he didn't have any money
我希望客戶會買我的產品，但他卻沒錢買。

· I could work longer hours ... I got furloughed instead
我希望能工作長一點工時，但是卻被要求放無薪假。

· I could get a raise after the annual review...it never happened
我希望年度檢討後能加薪，但卻始終沒發生。

句型！ **I wish...but...** 這個句型主要是在表達無法實踐的願望及其緣由或與其相違的事件。因為是期望，有點假設語氣的意思，故所承接的子句必須用 would、could 或是過去式來呈現。

I am _____. See you around.

· running late for a meeting　我開會快遲到了，回頭見。
· falling asleep as we speak　當我們說話時，我快要睡著了，回頭見。
· having lunch with clients　我要去跟客戶吃午飯了，回頭見。
· hosting a meeting in 5 minutes　五分鐘後我要主持一個會議，回頭見。
· leaving for the HSR station now　我現在要出發去高鐵站了，回頭見。

句型！ 現在進行式不只是表達現在「正在做」的事情，也可以表達未來的計劃，如第四句。

用這句話更厲害！

012

❶ Morning! Are you ready for the week?
早安！準備迎戰新的一週了嗎？

❷ Hi. Are you psyched up for the weekend?
嗨，你對即將到來的週末感到興奮嗎？

❸ Hi. Had a nice break?
嗨，休假愉快嗎？

❹ Hello! How was your day off?
哈囉，休假過得如何？

❺ Hey. Are you ready for work?
嗨，準備好要工作了嗎？

❻ You're back! Now get to work.
你回來了！趕快上工。

❼ Welcome back to hell.
歡迎回到地獄。（語帶諷刺）

❽ Hi, want some caffeine?　嗨，需要來杯咖啡提神嗎？

❾ Hi, the boss wants to see you.　嗨，老闆找你。

❿ Hey, please go take care of that customer.
嘿，請你去處理那個客戶（的問題）。

⑪ There you are. Your phone has been ringing off the hook.
原來你在這。你的電話一直響個不停。

⑫ You're late. Some annoyed customer has been waiting for you.
你遲到了。那個很不爽的客戶在等著你。

必背單字片語

☑ **Psyche up** ph. 使興奮
John is so psyched up for his newborn boy.
約翰對他的剛出生的兒子感到很興奮。

- -

☑ **Break** [brek] n. 休息; 逃離
I really need a break from all the phone calls and paperwork.
我真的需要逃離所有的電話和文件。

- -

☑ **Day off** ph. 休假日
I cannot wait until my next day off!
我等不及下個休假日！

- -

☑ **Caffeine** [`kæfiɪn] n. 咖啡因
Caffeine keeps one awake at night.
咖啡因使人晚上睡不著。

- -

☑ **Annoyed** [ə`nɔɪd] adj. 惱怒的
I feel quite annoyed with his childish behavior.
我對他幼稚的行為感到相當不爽。

Unit 5 自我介紹

這樣說英文

013

Ⓐ Hello there. My name is Paul Woodhouse.
Ⓑ Good evening sir. My name is Scott Willington.
Ⓐ Delighted! Would you join me for some refreshments?

Ⓐ 哈囉，我名叫保羅・沃豪斯。
Ⓑ 晚上好，先生，我是史考特・威靈頓。
Ⓐ 很高興認識你！您要和我去喝點飲料嗎？

Ⓐ What's a girl like you doing in a place like this? Allow me to introduce myself.
Ⓑ I know you. Aren't you that guy who dumped my sister?
Ⓐ Uh...Excuse me. I have an appointment I need to go to. Goodbye!

Ⓐ 像你這樣的女孩在這種地方做什麼？容我自我介紹。
Ⓑ 我知道你是誰。你不就是拋棄我姐姐的那個男人嗎？
Ⓐ 嗯，恕我失陪，我需要赴個約。再見！

Ⓐ Can everyone give a brief self-introduction? We'll start from the front row.
Ⓑ Hi everyone. I'm John and I'm a recovering alcoholic. I've stayed dry for a month now.
Ⓐ Welcome John, to Alcoholics Anonymous.

Ⓐ 大家可以簡短自我介紹嗎？我們從最前排開始。
Ⓑ 哈囉各位。我叫約翰，正在戒酒。我已經一個月沒碰酒了。
Ⓐ 約翰，歡迎你來到匿名戒酒協會。

Vocabulary

Delighted [dɪˋlaɪtɪd]　adj. 高興的
Refreshment [rɪˋfrɛʃmənt]　n. 飲料；點心
Dump [dʌmp]　vt. 拋棄

Appointment　[əˋpɔɪntmənt]　n. 約會；會面的約定
Alcoholics Anonymous　ph. 匿名戒酒協會

這樣用句型

014

> **Would you join me** _____?

· for a walk in the park 　你想跟我去公園散步嗎？

· for dinner at this restaurant 　你想跟我去這家餐廳吃晚餐嗎？

· on a trip to the Bahamas 　你想跟我去巴哈馬群島渡假嗎？

· tonight 　你今晚想跟我在一起嗎？

· and my friends for coffee 　你想跟我和我朋友喝杯咖啡嗎？

> **I know you. Aren't you** _____?

· Mick Jagger 　我認識你。你不就是米克‧傑格？

· my ex-husband 　我認識你。你不就是我的前夫？

· high school teacher 　我知道你是誰。你不就是我高中老師？

· that lady who tried to run me down
　我知道你是誰。你不就是那個試著把我撞倒的女士？

· the famous chef from TV
　我認識你。你不就是那個在電視上有名的廚師？

註 Mike Jagger 是個有名的英國搖滾歌手，並且是滾石樂團（Rolling Stone）的創團者兼主唱。

> **I am** _____ **and I am** _____.

· Sandra... a mother of three intolerable kids
　我叫珊卓，是位有 3 個令人無法忍受的孩子的媽媽

· Michael... a fireman 　我是麥可，是一名消防員。

1 日常交際

- a five-year-old kid... a genius　我是名五歲天才。
- Clark Kent... a superhero　我是克拉克‧肯特，是名超級英雄。

註 電影《超人》中男主角戲中的英文名字就是 Clark Kent。

- your drill sergeant ... your worst nightmare
我是你們的操練官，也是你們最糟的惡夢。

用這句話更厲害！

015

❶ Hello, my name is John.
哈囉，我名叫約翰。

❷ My profession is a law enforcement officer.
我的職業是位執法人員。

❸ I'm new here.
我是新來的。

❹ You may have seen me on TV before.
你可能曾在電視上看過我。

❺ You may have heard of me before.
你可能曾聽說過我。

❻ Allow me to introduce myself.
容我自我介紹一下。

❼ Don't you know who I am?
你難道不認識我？

❽ I'm here on vacation. What about you?
我來這裡渡假，你呢？

❾ Hello. Here's my business card.
哈囉，這是我的名片。

❿ May I have your card, please?
請你給我你的名片。

⓫ How can I contact you?
我要怎麼跟你聯絡？

⑫ What line of work **are you in?**
你是做什麼的？

必背單字片語

☑ **Profession** [prə`fɛʃən]　n. 職業
She wants to devote her life in teaching profession.
她想要終生投入於教育事業。

- -

☑ **Law enforcement officer**　ph. 執法人員
Law enforcement officers who break the law are severely punished.
違法的執法人員會被嚴厲懲處。

- -

☑ **Hear of**　ph. 聽說過
She may be famous here but nobody has heard of her outside of Taiwan.
她也許在台灣有名，但是台灣以外的地方沒有人聽說過她。

- -

☑ **Introduce** [ˌɪntrə`djus]　vt. 介紹；引見
Let me introduce you to a charming young man who happens to look like a Korean pop star.
讓我為你介紹一位看起來很像韓國流行明星的年輕人。

- -

☑ **Business card**　ph. 名片
I ran out of business card so I have to get a new batch printed.
我的名片用完了，所以需要印一批新的。

- -

☑ **Line of work**　ph. 行業
In my line of work, you don't get to go home until late at night.
做我這一行的都要很晚才能回家。

❶ 日常交際

Unit 6 國籍

這樣說英文

 016

Ⓐ You don't look like you're from here.
Ⓑ That's right. I'm actually from England. Are you from Taiwan?
Ⓐ I'm from England too! My parents migrated there decades ago.

Ⓐ 你看起來不像這裡的人。
Ⓑ 對呀，事實上我是英國人。你是從台灣來的嗎？
Ⓐ 我也是英國來的。我父母很久之前移民到那裡。

Ⓐ This community is truly a melting pot.
Ⓑ Why? Is that because there are so many restaurants here?
Ⓐ No! That means there are many nationalities living together here.

Ⓐ 這個社區真是個文化熔爐。
Ⓑ 甚麼意思？是因為這裡有很多餐廳嗎？
Ⓐ 不是啦！意思是說這裡有許多國家的人住在這裡。

Ⓐ Guess what? His girlfriend is French, while he is Zimbabwean.
Ⓑ Wow. I heard his dad hails from Morocco and his mom from Spain!
Ⓐ That's bizarre. Then how is he Zimbabwean?

Ⓐ 你知道嗎？他的女友是法國人，而他是辛巴威人。
Ⓑ 真假？我聽說他父親來自摩洛哥，而她母親來自西班牙！
Ⓑ 真是怪了。那他怎麼會是辛巴威人？

Vocabulary

Migrate [`maɪˌgret]　vi. 移居
Melting Pot　ph. 文化熔爐；人種混雜的國家（場所）
Nationality [ˌnæʃə`nælətɪ]　n. 國籍

Hail from　ph.【口】來自；後面可接國家或城市。
Bizarre [bɪ`zɑr]　adj. 異乎尋常的

這樣用句型

> ### You look like _____.

- you are local　你看起來像本地人。
- you stick out like a sore thumb　你看起來很突兀。
- a Eurasian　你看似歐亞混血兒。
- you are lost　你看似迷路了。
- me　你看起來很像我。

> ### This _____ is truly _____.

- car... astonishing　這部車非常驚人。
- day... unforgettable　這一天實在令人難忘。
- ocean... full of lives　海洋中確實充滿了生機。
- country... at war　這個國家正在戰亂。
- honeymoon... what we had wished for　這次蜜月正如我們所期盼的。

😊 句型! **truly** 和 **really** 的小小差別在於，truly 有「毫無疑問」的意思。really 可以想成 very 來看。

> ### His girlfriend _____ while he _____.

- is rich... is poor　他女友很多金，而他卻很窮。
- eats.... sleeps　他女友在他睡覺時吃飯。
- sweeps... vacuums　他女友在掃地，當他在用吸塵器時。
- works... stays at home　他女友去工作，而他卻留在家裡。

· graduated... flunked school　他女友畢業了，而他卻死當。

句型!　... while... 如果兩個動詞或子句為相反的（例如：多金 vs. 沒錢），那中文的意思就是「A...，而 B 卻…」；如果兩個動詞或子句互不相干，而是描述同時間發生的事情，中文的意思就是「當 B...，A...」。

用這句話更厲害！

018

❶ His wife is an aboriginal.
他老婆是個原住民。

❷ He is of English heritage.
他有英國血統。

❸ I am the direct descendant of Genghis Khan.
我是成吉思汗的直系後裔。

❹ He is a naturalized citizen.　他是歸化的公民。

❺ There are many Asian Americans in California.
在美國加州有許多亞裔美國人。

❻ There are Chinatowns worldwide.
中國城遍及世界各地。

❼ What do you call a person who is born in Antarctica?
你會怎麼稱呼在南極出生的人？

❽ What is your mother tongue?　你的母語是甚麼？

❾ I'm Canadian living in France but I don't speak French.
我是住在法國的加拿大人，但是我不說法語。

❿ Do you need a visa to travel to Thailand?
你到泰國去旅行需要簽證嗎？

⓫ Labor laws prohibit discrimination against people of foreign origins.　勞工法禁止對外國人的歧視。

⓬ It is not right to refer to Filipino maids as "Maria".
將菲律賓來的女傭歸類為「瑪麗亞」是不好的。

必背單字片語

☑ **Descendant** [dɪ`sɛndənt]　n. 後裔；子孫
I am my grandfather's descendant.　我是我祖父的子孫。

☑ **Naturalized** [`nætʃərəlaɪzd]　adj. 歸化的；入籍的
Matt is a naturalized citizen of the United States.
馬特是歸化美國的公民。

☑ **Worldwide** [`wɜld͵waɪd]　adj./adv. 遍及全球的；在世界各地
There is a worldwide flu epidemic going on.
流感正在世界各地流行。

☑ **Mother tongue**　ph. 母語
My mother tongue is Mandarin but I speak English well
too.　我的母語是中文，但是我英文也講得很好。

☑ **Prohibit** [prə`hɪbɪt]　vt. 禁止；阻止
We are prohibited from bringing weapons into the plane.
我們被禁止帶武器上飛機。

☑ **Discrimination** [dɪ͵skrɪmə`neʃən]　n. 區別；歧視
There are laws against racial discrimination but they are
not enforced.　雖有法律禁止種族歧視卻沒有被強制執行。

1 日常交際

Unit 7 職業

這樣說英文

 019

Ⓐ I got fired from my last job. My boss accused me of being forgetful. I don't think that's true, though.

Ⓑ That's tough. How long did you work there?

Ⓐ I forgot.

Ⓐ 我被解雇了，老闆指責我健忘，不過我不這麼認為。

Ⓑ 真慘。你在那裡工作多久？

Ⓐ 我忘了。

Ⓐ I heard that his new girlfriend is a brain surgeon.

Ⓑ She must be not very smart then.

Ⓐ I agree. Whoever is going out with him can't be that bright.

Ⓐ 我聽說他的新女友是個腦外科醫師。

Ⓑ 她一定沒有很聰明。

Ⓐ 我有同感。會想跟他約會的人都不會太聰明。

Ⓐ Hello. What is your profession?

Ⓑ I used to be a flight attendant. But, I have decided to be a kindergarten teacher because I discovered I was afraid to fly.

Ⓐ Let's see if you will be afraid of little, uncontrollable brats.

Ⓐ 哈囉。你是做哪一行的？

Ⓑ 我曾經是空服員，但是因為我發現我害怕飛行，我已決定改當幼稚園老師。

Ⓐ 那我們就看看你是否會害怕無法管束的小搗蛋。

Vocabulary

Fire [faɪr]　vt.【口】解僱；開除
Accuse [əˋkjuz]　vt. 指控；指責
Forgetful [fəˋgɛtfəl]　adj. 健忘的

Surgeon [ˋsɝdʒən]　n. 外科醫師
Uncontrollable [ˏʌnkənˋtroləbl]　adj. 失控的；無法管束的

這樣用句型

020

_____ accused me of _____.

· My girlfriend... cheating　我的女友指控我劈腿。
· The students... cheating　學生們指控我作弊。
· The bank... fraud　銀行指控我詐欺。
· Her mother... stealing her necklace　她母親指控我偷她的項鍊。
· My father... being reckless　我父親指責我不顧事情的後果。

I heard that _____.

· she's married　我聽說她結婚了。
· there will be a sale　我聽說有個特賣會。
· it wasn't true　我聽說那不是真的。
· from her　我從她那裡聽說的。
· they are untrustworthy　我聽說他們不能被信任。

I used to _____, but I have decided to_____.

· smoke... quit　我曾經抽菸，但我已決定戒掉。
· drive fast... slow down　我曾經開快車，但我已決定放慢速度。
· exercise daily... take it easy　我曾經每天運動，但我已決定要放輕鬆。
· be fat... slim down　我曾經很胖，但我已決定要瘦下來。
· drink a lot... stay away from alcohol　我曾經酗酒，但我已決定不碰酒。

 句型! **used to+動詞原型** 表示曾經常常做什麼但現在幾乎不再這麼做。

35

①
日常交際

021

❶ What's your line of work?
你是做哪一行的？

❷ How do you make a living?
你做什麼維生？

❸ I'm sick of the daily 9 to 5 grind.
我對每天單調的朝九晚五感到厭倦。

❹ He commutes 2 hours to work every day.
他每天通勤兩小時。

❺ She is a dental specialist.
她是牙科專業醫師。

❻ I have an interview with that new company today.
我今天要去新公司面試。

❼ Unemployment is a social problem in this country.
失業是這個國家的社會問題。

❽ Have your resume ready for the interview.
面試時請準備好你的履歷。

❾ Do you qualify for the job?
你能勝任這個工作嗎？

❿ His father is retiring next year.
她父親明年退休。

⓫ Job hopping is becoming the norm.
換工作已變成常態。

⓬ Do you want to be somebody's employee or an entrepreneur?
你想當員工還是自己創業？

必背單字片語

☑ Grind [graɪnd]　n. 苦差事 vt. 磨（碎）；碾（碎）
I need to grind up some peppers for this recipe.
這道食譜我需要磨碎一些胡椒來做。

- -

☑ Commute [kə`mjut]　n.【口】通勤
Long commutes can really be a waste of time.
長途通勤真的是浪費時間。

- -

☑ Interview [`ɪntəˌvju]　n. 面試
I have had thirty interviews but no offers.
我面試了三十次卻沒有任何結果。

- -

☑ Retire [rɪ`taɪr]　vi. 退休
I am going to retire young and travel the world.
我要年輕時就退休，然後去環遊世界。

- -

☑ Norm [nɔrm]　n. 基準；規範
Short skirts and jeans are the norm among teenagers today.
短裙和牛仔褲是當今年輕人的穿著基準。

- -

☑ Entrepreneur [ˌɑntrəprə`nɝ]　n. 企業家；創業者
It is not easy being an entrepreneur but the rewards can be huge.
創業並不容易但是報酬可以很大。

❶ 日常交際

Unit 8 年紀

這樣說英文

022

Ⓐ How old are you?
Ⓑ Excuse me. Do you know it's rude to ask a girl her age?
Ⓐ Likewise, do you know it's uncouth to ask me how much I make?

Ⓐ 你今年貴庚？
Ⓑ 你知道問女孩子的年齡是很無禮的嗎？
Ⓐ 那你知道問我年薪多少是很沒教養的嗎？

Ⓐ That person is very, very old.
Ⓑ He's still riding a bicycle. How old do you think he is?
Ⓐ I think he's approaching 100. I'm astonished he's not in a wheelchair.

Ⓐ 那個人非常老了。
Ⓑ 他還騎腳踏車耶。你想他幾歲？
Ⓐ 我想他大概近百歲了。我很訝異他不是坐在輪椅上。

Ⓐ Age is just a number. We should not let it bother us.
Ⓑ You're not that young. Is it bothering you?
Ⓐ No, it doesn't. But it bothers the girls I'm trying to date.

Ⓐ 年齡只是個數字。我們不應該被它煩擾。
Ⓑ 你已沒那麼年輕。年齡困擾著你嗎？
Ⓐ 沒有，但它困擾到跟我約會的女孩們。

Vocabulary

Uncouth [ʌn`kuθ] adj. 無教養的；不文明的

Astonished [ə`stɑnɪʃt] adj. 驚訝的

Bother [`bɑðɚ] vt. 煩擾；使困惑
Date [det] vi./vt. 【口】約會；和…約會

這樣用句型

023

> **Do you know** _____?

- the time　你知道現在幾點嗎？
- where the bus is going　你知道這班公車要去哪裡嗎？
- yourself　你認識你自己嗎？
- my husband　你認識我先生嗎？
- what you are doing　你知道自己在做什麼嗎？

> **I'm astonished** _____.

- at the news　我對這個消息很訝異。
- that you are dating him　我很驚訝你在跟他約會。
- by his performance　他的表現令我很驚訝。
- to learn about her affair　對她的婚外情感到訝異。
- rather than horrified　我不是嚇到而是驚訝。

> _____ **is just a** _____.

- Jill... little girl　吉兒只是個黃毛丫頭。
- That dog... nuisance　那隻狗是個麻煩。
- My cat... glutton　我的貓是個貪吃鬼。
- Christmas... excuse to get fat　耶誕節只是個發福的藉口。
- Life... journey　人生只是一趟旅程。

1
日常交際

用這句話更厲害！

1 Creaking knees is a sign of aging.
發出嘎嘎聲的膝關節是老化的一個徵兆。

2 Age gracefully like wine.
像酒一樣優雅的老去。

3 He's depressed because he's over the hill.
他因為不再年輕而沮喪。

4 You're not getting any younger.
你也不再年輕。

5 She's younger than me. I'm older than he. And, he's older than she.
她比我年輕，我比他年長，那他又比她年長。

6 He wants to live forever.
他想要長生不老。

7 Plastic surgery can take care of wrinkles but it won't reverse your age.
整形手術可以去除皺紋，但無法使你變年輕。

8 The 90-year-old man married the 18 year old girl.
這位 90 歲老翁跟年僅 18 歲的女孩結婚。

9 Who's the youngest in the room?
這裡誰最年輕？

10 What's the legal drinking age in this country?
這個國家的合法飲酒年齡是幾歲？

11 You need to be 18 to be admitted.
你需要滿 18 歲才能入場。

12 Infants are older than newborns, while toddlers are older than infants.
嬰兒比新生兒大，而學步兒比嬰兒大。

必背單字片語

☑ **Gracefully** [`gresfəlɪ]　adv. 雅緻地；溫文地
It is difficult to talk gracefully when you are annoyed.
當你被惹惱時，要優雅地說話是很困難的。

☑ **Over the hill**　ph.【口】人老珠黃；過了巔峰期
He's only 20 but he acts like he's over the hill.
他雖然才 20 歲但他表現得似乎不再年輕。

☑ **Plastic surgery**　ph. 整形手術
Plastic surgery makes all the girls look like Korean celebrities.
整形手術使所有的女孩們看起來像韓國明星。

☑ **Wrinkle** [`rɪŋkḷ]　n. 皺紋
This cream can reduce wrinkles. 這瓶乳霜可以減少皺紋。

☑ **Admit** [əd`mɪt]　vt. 准許進入
He slammed his foot against the door and was admitted to the hospital.
他的腳被門猛力撞到而入院。

☑ **Toddler** [`tɑdlɚ]　n. 學步的小孩
Is there anything more annoying than a crying, kicking and screaming toddler?
有什麼是比又哭又鬧的學步兒更令人無法忍受嗎？

① 日常交際

41

Unit 9 外表

這樣說英文

025

Ⓐ Hello Cassie, you look marvelous! I love your new hair!
Ⓑ Why thank you, Laura! You're looking good yourself. I love your new bag!
Ⓐ Lovely isn't it? It cost my boyfriend's last paycheck.

Ⓐ 哈囉，凱西，你看起來好極了！我喜歡你的新髮型！
Ⓑ 謝了，蘿拉。妳看起來也很棒。我喜歡你的新包包！
Ⓐ 很棒吧，這可是花掉我男友上個月的薪水買的。

Ⓐ Did you see Jack's new girlfriend? She dresses funny.
Ⓑ Yes, I know. She was wearing a translucent blouse and a red bra. Isn't that tacky?
Ⓐ Sure, and she does selfies on Facebook all the time!

Ⓐ 你看過傑克的新女友嗎？她的穿著好奇特。
Ⓑ 對呀。她上次居然穿大紅色胸罩和透明的上衣。會不會太俗氣了點？
Ⓐ 就是說，而且她還一直把自己的自拍放在臉書上！

Ⓐ That girl is drop-dead gorgeous! Who's she?
Ⓑ That's Stephanie, but she's mine. Keep your hands off her.
Ⓐ Wait until she meets me. She'll forget you in no time.

Ⓐ 那女孩真是美若天仙！她是誰？
Ⓑ 那是史蒂芬妮，但是她是我女友，不准你碰她。
Ⓐ 等到她認識我之後，她就會立刻把你給忘了。

Vocabulary

Marvelous [`mɑrvələs]　adj. 妙極了
Paycheck [`pe͵tʃɛk]　n. 薪津
Translucent [træns`lusnt]　adj. 半透明的

Selfie　n. 自拍照
Gorgeous [`gɔrdʒəs]　adj. 極為漂亮的

這樣用句型

026

> **I love** _____.

- how your color contacts make your eyes look beautiful
  我喜歡角膜變色片使你的眼睛看起來很美。
- how your diet makes you look younger
  我喜歡你減肥後看起來更年輕的樣子。
- your new tan　我喜歡你新曬出來的膚色。
- what you did with your hair　我喜歡你的新髮型。
- the new you　我喜歡改變後全新的你。

> _____ **Jack's new girlfriend?**

- Have you seen　你曾看過傑克的新女友嗎？
- How do you like　你覺得傑克的新女友如何？
- What happened to　傑克的新女友怎麼了？
- Does anybody know about　有誰知道有關傑克的新女友的事情？
- Just how old is　傑克的新女友到底幾歲？

> **That girl is** _____. **Who's she? That's** _____.

- scantily dressed... my sister　那女孩幾乎沒穿。她是誰？她是我姊。
- so blonde... your new teacher
  那女孩一頭金髮。她是誰？她是你的新老師。

- wearing a tutu... Lisa's ballet instructress
  那女孩穿著芭蕾短裙。她是誰？她是麗莎的芭蕾舞老師。
- way too tall... Miss Congeniality from last year's beauty pageant
  那女孩實在太高。她是誰？她是去年選美大賽中的最有人緣小姐。
- obese and stout... the president's new wife
  那女孩又矮又胖。她是誰？她是董事長的新老婆。

用這句話更厲害！

027

1 Rick has blonde hair and blue eyes.
瑞克是金髮藍眼睛。

2 Sandra's new hair is making her cry.
珊卓拉不喜歡自己的新髮型。

3 Sophie likes to dye her hair in strange neon colors.
蘇菲喜歡將自己的頭髮染成奇怪的螢光色。

4 He looks like something the cat dragged out of the trash can.
他看起來很髒亂（像是剛從垃圾桶被抓出來的貓）。

5 Young Stanley is trying to grow a goatee.
年輕的史丹利想要留山羊鬍。

6 His eyes are too close together.
他雙眼長得太靠近。

7 She just had a nose job, and now she looks like Michael Jackson.
她剛去做隆鼻手術，現在她看起來像麥可傑克森。

8 He shaved his head bald.
他剃了個大光頭。

9 Your friend looks hideously pale. He should get a tan!
你那朋友看起來太慘白了。他應該去曬成棕褐色！

10 John's beer gut is as big as mine.
約翰的啤酒肚跟我的一樣大。

⑪ Popeye's biceps are obviously not real.
卜派的二頭肌很明顯不是真的

⑫ She has facial hair.
她臉上有細毛。

必背單字片語

☑ **Dye** [daɪ]　v. 用染料染色
Humans are the only animals who dye their food.
人類是動物界中唯一將食物染色的群種。

☑ **Drag** [dræg]　vt. 拖著行進；拉
Mom dragged me kicking and screaming to the dentist.
媽媽不管我的反抗，硬是把我帶去看牙醫。

☑ **Goatee** [goˋti]　n. 山羊鬍子
How would your grandfather look like with a goatee?
她祖父留山羊鬍子會是甚麼樣子？

☑ **Nose job**　ph. 鼻子整形手術
Some celebrities had more than nose jobs.
一些明星不只做過隆鼻手術。

☑ **Hideous** [ˋhɪdɪəs]　adj. 可怕的；駭人聽聞的
There's a hideous monster lurking under your bed.
你床底下藏有一個可怕的怪獸。

☑ **Biceps** [ˋbaɪsɛps]　n. 二頭肌
Lifting weights helps develop your biceps.
舉重可幫助你鍛鍊二頭肌。

日常交際①

Unit 10 喜好

這樣說英文

Ⓐ My favorite pastime is to watch TV.
Ⓑ You seem to watch a lot of TV shows. Don't you do anything else, like exercise?
Ⓐ No, then I won't have time to watch my favorite programs!

Ⓐ 我喜歡看電視打發時間。
Ⓑ 你好像看很多電視。你難道不做其他像運動之類的事嗎？
Ⓐ 沒有，因為那樣我就沒時間看我喜歡的節目了！

....

Ⓐ I like men who are fit, handsome, smart and friendly.
Ⓑ Is that why you have so many boyfriends?
Ⓐ Such men are hard to find so I'm just increasing my chances of meeting someone I like.

Ⓐ 我喜歡結實、帥氣又友善的男人。
Ⓑ 是因為這樣你有很多個男友嗎？
Ⓐ 這樣的男人很難找，所以我只是增加我遇到喜歡的人的機會。

....

Ⓐ I love spicy food. Let's go have curry.
Ⓑ No way! Last time I went with you I had diarrhea. Let's go light.
Ⓐ No way. Last time I went with you we had food that tasted like cardboard.

Ⓐ 我愛吃辣。我們去吃咖哩吧。
Ⓑ 才不要！上次我跟你去吃，我拉肚子。吃清淡點的吧
Ⓐ 才不要！上次我跟你去吃，那個東西嚐起來像厚紙板一般（無味）。

....

Vocabulary

Favorite [`fevərɪt]　n/adj. 喜愛（的）
Program [`progræm]　n. 節目；節目表
Chance [tʃæns]　n. 運氣；機會

Diarrhea [ˌdaɪə`rɪə]　n. 腹瀉
Cardboard [`kɑrd͵bord]　n. 厚紙板

這樣用句型 029

> **You seem to** _____.

· sleep all day　你似乎睡整天。

· be hungry　你似乎餓了。

· know everything　你似乎無所不知。

· get fatter every day　你似乎每天越來越胖。

· adore kittens　你似乎很喜歡貓。

> **I like** _____ **are,** _____ **and** _____.

· women who ... beautiful, intelligent ... confident
　我喜歡美麗、聰明又有自信的女人。

· dogs that ... small, furry ... obedient
　我喜歡又小又毛茸茸並且聽話的狗。

· foods that ... spicy, pungent ... sour
　我喜歡又辣又重口味又酸的食物。

· cars that ... fast, expensive and red
　我喜歡又昂貴、能飆速的紅色車子。

· to wear clothes that ... colorful, fashionable ... made of cotton
　我喜歡穿鮮豔、時尚的棉製衣物。

　句型!　看到中文部分的形容詞這麼的長，不要懷疑，這是形容詞子句。

> **The last time** _____.

- we came here, the food was good

  上一次我們來這裡吃時，食物很好吃。

- a hurricane hit this place was last year

  這個地方上次遭受颶風襲擊是去年。

- was also the first time　上一次也是第一次。

- she cried because her cat died　上次她哭是因為她的貓去世。

- Steve Jobs gave a presentation he was already sick

  史帝芬・賈伯斯最後一次發表產品時他已經病了。

用這句話更厲害！

❶ He loves fried food.

他喜歡油炸的食物。

❷ She fancies luxurious vacations.

她喜愛豪華式度假。

❸ I prefer vegetarian food to big juicy steak.

相較於又大又多汁的牛排，我更喜歡吃素食。

😊 句型! **prefer A to B** 喜歡 A 勝過 B

❹ I like her more than she likes me.

我喜歡她多過她喜歡我。

❺ I love dogs more than cats.　比起貓我更喜歡狗。

😊 句型! **love/like A more than** B 喜歡 A 勝過 B

❻ I like this brand over that brand.

我喜歡這個品牌勝過那個品牌。

😊 句型! **like A over B** 喜歡 A 勝過 B

❼ She likes vanilla the best.　她最喜歡香草口味的。

❽ I cannot get enough of Dim sum.　我很喜歡港式點心。

❾ He could not get enough of it.　這個他永遠嫌不夠。

⑩ Hands down, this is the best.　這是最棒的。

註 hands down 這個片語是來自以前賽馬時，當那匹馬贏定了或是贏得非常輕鬆簡單，馬夫就能
　　將手放鬆垂下，不需強拉著繮繩。後來這個片語被拿來比喻最好的。

⑪ I must have my coffee every day.　我每天一定要喝咖啡。

⑫ I am biased towards dark chocolates.　我偏愛黑巧克力。

必背單字片語

☑ **Vegetarian** [ˌvɛdʒəˋtɛrɪən]　n./adj. 素食（者）；素食的
They serve vegetarian meals on board.　飛機上有素食餐。

- -

☑ **Luxurious** [lʌgˋʒʊrɪəs]　adj. 奢侈的；豪華的
He could afford a luxurious home.　他買得起豪宅。

- -

☑ **Brand** [brænd]　n. 品牌；商標
My sister is very brand conscious. She doesn't use things without a brand.
我姐姐很重視品牌。她絕不用沒有品牌的東西。

註 brand conscious 的意思是很重視有品牌的東西。

- -

☑ **Hands down**　ph.【口】輕易大勝；垂手贏得
The team won the game hands down.
這個隊伍輕易地贏得這場球賽的勝利。

- -

☑ **Biased** [ˋbaɪəst]　adj. 存有偏見的
I am biased toward cheap Chinese products.
我對便宜的中國製商品有偏見。

Unit 11 討厭

這樣說英文

Ⓐ I cannot stand his new wife. She is just so annoying.
Ⓑ Calm down. You two just had a divorce. Give it some time.
Ⓐ But, that was just a week ago!

Ⓐ 我無法忍受他的新老婆。她真的讓我很不爽。
Ⓑ 冷靜點。你們兩個才剛離婚。給它一些時間。
Ⓐ 但是,那才一個星期前!

....

Ⓐ I hate how the weatherman lies to you.
Ⓑ Uh oh! What did the weatherman say?
Ⓐ He said there would be a downpour. Look at the sky. Where are the clouds?

Ⓐ 我真討厭不準的天氣預報。
Ⓑ 喔喔!這次預報員是怎麼說的?
Ⓐ 他說今天會下大雨。你看看天空,哪裡有雲?

....

Ⓐ I don't like the food. I don't like the décor.
Ⓑ But it's your own cooking, and it's your own kitchen.
Ⓐ I don't like how you remind me it's my cooking, either.

Ⓐ 我不喜歡這個食物,我不喜歡這裡的裝潢。
Ⓑ 但是這是你的廚房和你自己煮的菜。
Ⓐ 我也不喜歡你提醒我這是我煮的。

Vocabulary

Annoying [ə`nɔɪɪŋ]　adj. 討厭的;惱人的
Calm down　ph. 鎮定下來;平靜下來
Downpour [`daʊn,por]　n. 傾盆大雨

Décor [de`kor]　n. 裝飾;室內裝潢
Remind [rɪ`maɪnd]　vt. 提醒;使想起

這樣用句型

032

I cannot stand _____.

· this weather 　我無法忍受這種天氣。

· looking at his face 　我無法忍受看到他的臉。

· the way people drive around here 　我無法忍受這裡的人開車的方式。

· how my mother nags me 　我無法忍受我媽碎念我的方式。

· properly 　我無法好好站著。

 cannot stand 意思是無法站立，但是 cannot stand sth. 是指無法忍受的意思。

Look at _____. **Where** _____?

· her face...are the scars 　看看她的臉。疤痕在哪裡？

· the store... are all the customers 　這家店的顧客都到哪去了？

· how she dresses... is her decency 　看看她的穿著哪裡得體？

· the mess you have made ... do you think you're going
　看你弄得那麼亂，你還想去哪？

· Tom... do you think he's from 　你看湯姆是從哪裡來的？

I don't like _____.

· to work 　我不喜歡工作。

· his lazy attitude 　我不喜歡他懶惰的態度。

· hanging out with boring people 　我不喜歡跟無趣的人交往。

- myself　我不喜歡我自己。
- it but I don't hate it either　我不喜歡但也不討厭這個。

用這句話更厲害！

❶ Get me away from here.
讓我離開這裡。

❷ I despise mean people.
我鄙視刻薄的人。

❸ Are you kidding me?
開甚麼玩笑？

❹ I've had enough of this.
我受夠了。

❺ I can't stand rainy weather.
我無法忍受下雨天。

❻ She cannot bear spicy food.
她不能吃辣。

❼ I will not tolerate your behavior!
我不會容忍你的行為！

❽ She will not put up with you.
她不會忍受你。

❾ This is simply unacceptable!
這根本無法接受！

❿ He cannot stomach her lame excuses anymore.
他再也無法承受她無說服力的藉口。

⓫ I will not take this much more.
我無法再這樣下去。

⓬ I won't forget this.
我不會忘記的。

必背單字片語

☑ **Despise** [dɪ`spaɪz]　vt. 鄙視；看不起
I despise those who despise me. 我鄙視那些瞧不起我的人。

☑ **Bear** [bɛr]　vt. 承受
I cannot bear this breakup.　我無法承受這次的分手。

☑ **Tolerate** [`tɑləˌret]　vt. 忍受；容忍
She had to tolerate her husband's snoring.
她必須忍受她先生的打呼聲。

☑ **Excuse** [ɪk`skjuz]　n. 辯解
The kid kept making up excuses for skipping class.
這小孩一直找藉口翹課。

☑ **Unacceptable** [ˌʌnək`sɛptəbl̩]　adj. 不令人滿意的；不能接受的
Your offer is unacceptable.
我對你的出價不滿意。

☑ **Stomach** [`stʌmək]　vt. 承受；忍受（常用於否定句）
He cannot stomach failure.
他無法容忍失敗。

1 日常交際

Unit 12 婚姻

這樣說英文

034

Ⓐ Will you marry me?

Ⓑ That depends. Do you have a car? Do you have a job? What about a house? Do you want kids? How about my parents moving in with us?

Ⓐ I'm sorry I asked.

Ⓐ 妳願意嫁給我嗎？

Ⓑ 那要看情況。你有車嗎？有工作嗎？有房嗎？要小孩嗎？那我父母搬來跟我們住如何？

Ⓐ 算我沒問。

......

Ⓐ I'm having my third divorce.

Ⓑ I had mine two years ago. Now I'm on my fourth marriage and it's not looking good.

Ⓐ Isn't your third wife suing you for alimony?

Ⓐ 我正經歷第三次離婚。

Ⓑ 我兩年前就經歷過了。現在是梅開四度，但是似乎不是很順利。

Ⓐ 你的第三任老婆不是在跟你打贍養費官司嗎？

......

Ⓐ Tomorrow's our anniversary and I hope he has something to surprise me.

Ⓑ Oh, he's got something planned alright. He never ceases to surprise.

Ⓐ Thanks. Now you've lowered my expectations.

Ⓐ 明天是我們的結婚紀念日，真希望我老公給我驚喜。

Ⓑ 喔，他一定會計劃的。他一向都充滿驚喜。

Ⓐ 謝啦，你降低了我的期待。

Vocabulary

Divorce [də`vors]   n. 離婚

Alimony [`ælə͵monɪ]   n. 贍養費

Anniversary [͵ænə`vɝsərɪ]   n. 週年紀念

Expectation [͵ɛkspɛk`teʃən]   n. 期待

這樣用句型

035

> **How about** _____?

· the kids going away for the weekend　孩子們到別處去度週末？

· this? What about that　這個如何？那個怎樣？

· me? You never ask me out　那我呢？你從沒約我出去過！

· that? That's amazing　那真是驚人！那太好了！

· walking home instead　那走路回家如何？

註 How about that? 是一個慣用語，用來強調某事很驚人的意思。

> **Now I'm** _____ **and it's** _____.

· angry... going to be ugly　我現在很生氣，而且會鬧得很難看。

· on a diet... killing me　我現在的減肥計畫快把我搞死了。

· wasted... only eight in the morning　才上午八點我就喝得爛醉。

· broke... not funny　我破產了並不有趣。

· getting a divorce... going to be expensive　我這次離婚將會很昂貴。

> **He never ceases** _____.

· to infuriate me　他一直觸怒我。

· to annoy everyone around him　他一直煩他周遭的人。

· to learn　他從不停止學習。

· to care for you　他一直很關心你。

日常交際①

· complaining　他從未停止抱怨。

用這句話更厲害！ 036

❶ Marriage is like a fairy tale where you don't live happily ever after.
婚姻就像是不會從此過著幸福快樂生活的童話故事。

❷ Marriages that fall apart may be a blessing in disguise.
破碎的婚姻可能是一種偽裝的祝福。

❸ Forced marriages seldom work out.
強迫的婚姻很少會幸福美滿。

❹ Arranged marriages are still common in Asia.
長輩安排婚姻在亞洲還相當常見。

❺ She wouldn't have married him if she didn't get pregnant.
如果她沒懷孕的話不會嫁給他的。

❻ I am married to a mother of three kids and have become their stepfather.
我娶了有三個小孩的媽媽，變成了他們的繼父。

❼ Marriage is all about sacrificing your convertible for a family van.
婚姻就是為了買家庭式休旅車而犧牲你的敞篷車。

❽ This couple is now engaged.
這對情侶訂婚了。

❾ The wedding ceremony will be held tomorrow at the church.
婚禮明天將在教堂舉行。

❿ What should we give them as a wedding gift?
我們應該給什麼結婚禮物呢？

⓫ He was broke so he only got her a cubic zirconia ring but she didn't mind.
因為男方破產，但女方不介意男方只給她仿鑽戒指。

⓬ The wedding limousine had a flat.

結婚禮車的輪胎沒氣了。

必背單字片語

☑ **Fairy tale** [ˋfɛrɪˌtel]　n. 童話故事
She was like a princess in a fairy tale.
她就像童話故事裡的公主。

- -

☑ **Fall apart**　ph. 破裂；散開
His old jalopy is falling apart.
他的老爺車快解體了。

- -

☑ **Sacrifice** [ˋsækrəˌfaɪs]　n./vt. 犧牲
He sacrificed everything to keep his business afloat.
他犧牲一切使他的生意免於負債。

- -

☑ **Engage** [ɪnˋgedʒ]　vt. 交戰；訂婚
They are engaged in a war. 他們正在交戰。

- -

☑ **Ceremony** [ˋsɛrəˌmonɪ]　n. 儀式；典禮
His drunk uncle crashed their wedding ceremony.
他那酒鬼叔叔破壞了他們的婚禮。

- -

☑ **Flat** [flæt]　n. 洩了氣的輪胎
He had four flats at the same time.
他車子四個輪胎同時都洩了氣。

❶ 日常交際

57

Unit 13 子女

這樣說英文

037

Ⓐ How many kids do you have?
Ⓑ I have eight kids. I have seven daughters and a son. My son is the youngest.
Ⓐ You come from a very traditional family, don't you?

Ⓐ 你有幾個小孩？
Ⓑ 八個，共有七個女兒和一個最小的兒子。
Ⓐ 你的家人很傳統，對吧？

Ⓐ Do you have any children?
Ⓑ No, I don't. I want to have children but my husband doesn't. What about you?
Ⓐ I prefer not to have children but my husband prefers otherwise.

Ⓐ 你有小孩嗎？
Ⓑ 沒有。我想要小孩但我先生不要。你呢？
Ⓐ 我不想要小孩但我先生想要。

Ⓐ How did the physical exam go?
Ⓑ The doctor said I can't have children so I'm planning to adopt.
Ⓐ I have two adopted children and they are just adorable.

Ⓐ 你的檢查結果如何？
Ⓑ 醫生說我不能生育，所以我打算領養。
Ⓐ 我領養了兩個小孩，他們都很可愛。

Vocabulary

Traditional [trə`dɪʃənl̩]　adj. 傳統的
Prefer [prɪ`fɝ]　vt. 寧可；更喜歡
Otherwise [`ʌðəˌwaɪz]　adv. 不同樣地

Adopt [ə`dɑpt]　vt. 過繼；收養
Adorable [ə`dorəbl̩]　adj. 可愛的

這樣用句型 038

> ### I have _____ daughters _____ sons.

- five... and three 　我有五個女兒和三個兒子。
- more... than I have 　我的女兒比兒子多。
- beautiful... and handsome 　我有美麗的女兒和英俊的兒子。
- taught my... better than my 　我教出來的女兒比兒子好。
- spoiled my... but disciplined my 　我寵壞我的女兒卻嚴訓我的兒子。

> ### I want to _____ but my husband doesn't.

- go on a vacation 　我想去渡假，我先生卻不肯。
- have a dog 　我想養狗，但我先生不想。
- live with my parents 　我想跟我的父母親住在一起，我先生卻不肯。
- cuddle 　我想抱抱，但我先生不要。
- live in a big house 　我想住在大房子，我先生卻不肯。

> ### I have _____ and they are just _____.

- two dogs...lovable 　我有兩隻狗，牠們可愛極了。
- interfering parents... intolerable 　我有喜歡干涉的父母，簡直無法忍受。
- many girlfriends... crazy about me
  我有很多女朋友，他們都為我瘋狂。
- two houses... not big enough 　我有兩棟房子，但他們還是不夠大。
- met her children...so naughty 　我見過她的小孩，他們實在很調皮。

❶ 日常交際

❶ Do you have kids?
你有小孩嗎？

❷ Don't you want kids?
你不想要小孩嗎？

❸ Is she adopted?
她是領養的嗎？

❹ Are you her biological mother?
你是她親生母親嗎？

❺ Do you desire to have children?
你想要小孩嗎？

❻ I desperately want to have children.
我極度地想要小孩。

❼ I long for having children.
我渴望有小孩。

❽ How many daughters and sons do you have?
你有幾個女兒和兒子？

❾ Which one is your eldest?
哪個孩子是最年長的？

❿ She was an accident.
她是意外生出來的

⓫ I'm planning to have more little ones.
我正在計畫再生一些小孩。

⓬ Two is plenty.
兩個就夠了。

必背單字片語

Biological mother　ph. 親生母親
She has never met her biological mother.
她從未見過親生的母親。

- -

Desperately [ˋdɛspərɪtlɪ]　adv.【口】極度地
He desperately needs this job to make ends meet.
他極度需要這份工作來維持生活。

- -

Long for　ph. 渴望
Tom has longed for this overdue vacation.
湯姆一直渴望著這遲來的假期。

- -

Eldest [ˋɛldɪst]　adj. 最年長的（old 的最高級）
Lisa is the eldest daughter in her family.
麗莎是家中最年長的女兒。

- -

Accident [ˋæksədənt]　n. 意外；機遇
He was involved in a major car accident. 他出了嚴重的車禍。

- -

Plenty [ˋplɛntɪ]　adj./adv./n.【口】足夠的；很多的; 大量
I already have plenty of work to do this week.
這星期我已經有很多工作要做。

❶ 日常交際

Unit 14 邀請約會

這樣說英文

040

- Ⓐ Can I ask you for a date?
- Ⓑ I thought you'd never ask. I guess I was wrong!
- Ⓐ I'll pick you up on Saturday night at 7 sharp. I'll see you then.

- Ⓐ 我可以約你出去嗎？
- Ⓑ 我還以為你不想約我呢！我想我猜錯了！
- Ⓐ 星期六晚上七點我會準時去接妳，到時候見。

- Ⓐ How come he never asks me out?
- Ⓑ First of all, he doesn't know you! You have been stalking him forever! Go introduce yourself.
- Ⓐ How come he doesn't introduce himself to me?

- Ⓐ 為什麼他從不約我出去？
- Ⓑ 首先，他不認識妳！妳已經跟蹤他太久了！去跟他自我介紹吧。
- Ⓐ 那他為何不來跟我自我介紹？

- Ⓐ I get to see this girl on Saturday. We're going to the art gallery.
- Ⓑ Hang on a minute. Didn't you just invite the other girl to a movie?
- Ⓐ Oh no. I just remember I was supposed to meet another for dinner.

- Ⓐ 星期六我要跟這女孩出去。我們要去參觀藝廊。
- Ⓑ 等等，你不是才約另一個女孩去看電影？
- Ⓐ 糟糕，我剛想到我應該要跟另一個去吃晚餐。

Vocabulary

Pick up	ph. 用汽車搭載某人或接某人	Art gallery ph. 畫廊；美術館
Ask out	ph. 約出去（泛指約會）	Be supposed to ph. 認為應該
Stalk [stɔk]	vt. 偷偷靠近；追蹤	

這樣用句型

041

> ### I thought _____. I guess I was wrong.

- he was a mean person　我誤以為他是個卑鄙的人。我想我猜錯了。
- the train had left　我誤以為火車開走了。我想我猜錯了。
- she didn't want to meet me　我誤以為她不想見我。我想我猜錯了。
- he already had a date　我誤以為他已經有約會對象。我想我猜錯了。
- they were together　我誤以為他們在一起。我想我猜錯了。

> ### Oh no. I've just remember _____.

- I have work to do later that day　糟了，我剛想起我那天晚點還有工作。
- he is still married　糟了，我剛想起他還是已婚。
- I have an appointment with my dentist today
  糟了，我剛想起今天我還有牙科約診。
- I'm short of money　糟了，我剛想起我錢不夠。
- he's dead　糟了，我剛想起他已經去世了。

> ### How come he never _____?

- sleeps early　為何他從不早睡？
- shaves　為何他從不刮鬍子？
- asks any girl out　為何他從不約女孩子出去？
- talks softly　為何他從不輕聲說話？
- admits his mistakes　為何他從不承認他的錯誤？

1 日常交際

用這句話更厲害！

❶ Would you go out with me?
你願意跟我出去約會嗎？

❷ Are you free for coffee?
你有空一起喝杯咖啡嗎？

❸ Are you available?
你有空嗎？

❹ How about a date?
要跟我約會嗎？

❺ I was wondering if you are free.
我不知道你是否有空。

❻ I wouldn't mind your company.
我不介意你的陪伴。

❼ Can you come with me to the movies?
你可以跟我去看場電影嗎？

❽ Maybe we should go together. What do you think?
也許我們可以一起去，你覺得呢？

❾ I have a spare ticket. Want to join me?
我有多一張票，想跟我一起去嗎？

❿ Please go with me to the concert.
請跟我一起去聽音樂會。

⓫ I would be happy if you'd accompany me.
如果你陪我去我會很高興。

⓬ Do you want to escort me to the party?
你想陪我出席這場派對嗎？

必背單字片語

☑ **Available** [əˋveləb!]　adj. 有空的
There is no table available for tonight at this popular restaurant.
這家受歡迎的餐廳今晚沒有位子。

☑ **Wonder** [ˋwʌndɚ]　vt. 想知道；對⋯感到懷疑
She is wondering if Tom is interested in her.
她不知道湯姆對她有沒有興趣。

☑ **Company** [ˋkʌmpənɪ]　n. 陪伴；朋友
We really enjoy your company.
我們真的很喜歡跟你在一起。

☑ **Spare** [spɛr]　adj. 空閒的；多餘的
I love to read novels during my spare time.
我喜歡在空閒時間讀小說。

☑ **Accompany** [əˋkʌmpənɪ]　vt. 陪同；伴隨
My mother accompanies me to the doctor.
我媽陪我去看醫生。

☑ **Escort** [ˋɛskɔrt]　vt. 陪同；護衛；護送
The police escorts the armored car.
警察護送著運鈔車。

❶ 日常交際

這樣說英文

043

- Ⓐ It's been a pleasure to work with you for the last twenty years sir.
- Ⓑ The pleasure is all mine. I can't believe I won't see this place again.
- Ⓐ I can't believe I won't see you again, sir.

- Ⓐ 在過去 20 年間能與您在一起工作很愉快。
- Ⓑ 榮幸之至。真不敢相信我再也不會看到這個地方。
- Ⓐ 真不敢相信我再也見不到您了。

....

- Ⓐ Goodbye dear. I hope you have a good trip.
- Ⓑ Oh stop moping. I'll only be gone for a month and not forever. I will be back in no time.
- Ⓐ Goodbye is always the hardest word.

- Ⓐ 再見，親愛的，祝你旅途愉快。
- Ⓑ 好了，別悶悶不樂的。我只是去一個月，又不是永遠。我很快就回來了。
- Ⓐ 再見永遠是最難說出口的字。

....

- Ⓐ I hate farewells. It always brings tears to my eyes.
- Ⓑ How long have you known each other?
- Ⓐ I've known her ever since we were in grade school. I will miss her very much.

- Ⓐ 我最討厭道別，總是使我想哭。
- Ⓑ 妳們認識多久了？
- Ⓐ 從小學就認識了，我會非常想念她的。

Vocabulary

Pleasure [ˋplɛʒɚ]　n. 高興；愉快
The pleasure is all mine　ph. 榮幸之至
Mope [mop]　vi. 憂鬱；意氣消沉

Farewell [ˋfɛrˋwɛl]　n. 告別；送別
Grade school　ph. 【美】小學

這樣用句型 044

> ### I can't believe _____.

- I won the lottery　真不敢相信我中了樂透。
- he's gone　我無法相信他已經走了。
- my luck　我不相信自己的運氣。
- what I am seeing　我不敢相信自己的眼睛。
- what he is telling me　我無法相信他正在告訴我的。

> ### I will only be _____ and not _____.

- five next year... six　我明年只有五歲，不是六歲。
- having the appetizer ... the main course
  我只要吃前菜就好，不用主餐。
- a sophomore next year... a senior　我明年只是大二生，並非大四生。
- pulling in a million NT a year ... two　我年賺百萬，並非兩百萬。
- walking one mile... two　我只要走一英哩的路，而不是兩英哩。

> ### I've _____ ever since _____.

- been angry ... he tricked me　自從他騙了我之後我就一直生他的氣。
- been sleeping... she left an hour ago
  從她一小時前離開到現在我都在睡覺。
- looked everywhere ... I lost my dog yesterday
  從昨天我的狗走失至今我一直到處找。

・been home... the game ended　球賽結束後我一直在家。

・had no energy... I got sick　從我生病以來我都沒有元氣。

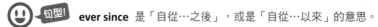 **ever since** 是「自從…之後」，或是「自從…以來」的意思。

用這句話更厲害！

❶ I won't be seeing you again.
我不會再見到你了。

❷ This is where we part.
這是我們告別的地方。

❸ Have a good trip.
祝旅途愉快。

❹ It's time to bid farewell.
是道別的時候了。

❺ I'll see you around.
回頭見。

❻ Later!
等會兒見！

❼ I won't forget you.
我不會忘記你的。

❽ I will remember you always.
我會永遠記得你的。

❾ We went our separate ways.
我們已分道揚鑣。

❿ I will be thinking of you.
我會想念你的。

⓫ Bon Voyage!
旅途愉快！

⓬ Good riddance.
走得好。

必背單字片語

☑ **Part** [pɑrt] vi./vt. 告別；分開
I cannot part from chocolate for too long.
我不能太久不吃巧克力。

☑ **Bid farewell** ph. 道別
He bids his parents farewell as he leaves for another country.
他遠赴另一個國度前與父母道別。

☑ **Later** [`letɚ] adv. 之後；以後
I will finish my pie later. 我等一下再把派吃完。

☑ **Separate** [`sɛpəˌret] vt. 使分離；分割
She cannot separate from her favorite doll.
她離不開她最愛的娃娃。

☑ **Bon voyage** ph. 旅途愉快
Bon voyage! Don't forget to send us postcards!
旅途愉快！別忘了寄明信片給我們！

☑ **Good riddance** ph. 可喜的分離（用在與不好或是不喜歡的人事物分開時）
She bids good riddance to her broken bicycle.
她將壞掉的腳踏車丟掉。

1 日常交際

Unit 16 閒聊

這樣說英文

 046

Ⓐ Have you been dating anyone? Do you want to talk about it?
Ⓑ Not really. Let's chat about something else.
Ⓐ OK, then let me tell you about my dating adventures.

Ⓐ 你最近有跟誰約會嗎？要聊聊嗎？
Ⓑ 沒有耶。聊點別的吧。
Ⓐ 好，那不然讓我告訴你關於我的約會歷險吧。

....

Ⓐ Those two old ladies have been doing nothing but gossiping the whole day.
Ⓑ Aren't we doing the same? We have been talking about others too.
Ⓐ Yes, but we're not old ladies.

Ⓐ 那兩個老女人整天無所事事就只會八卦。
Ⓑ 我們不也一樣？我們也一直都在談論其他人。
Ⓐ 也是，但我們不是老女人。

....

Ⓐ This is a casual talk show that talks about mundane topics.
Ⓑ We are sitting here talking about a casual talk show that talks about nothing?
Ⓐ I guess we have too much idle time, huh?

Ⓐ 這是個討論俗氣話題的閒聊性談話節目。
Ⓑ 而我們正坐在這裡談論這個沒重點的閒聊性談話節目？
Ⓐ 也許我們太閒了。

Vocabulary

Chat [tʃæt] vt. 閒談；搭訕
Adventure [ədˋvɛntʃɚ] n. 歷險；冒險
Gossip [ˋgɑsəp] vi. 閒聊；傳播流言蜚語

Casual [ˋkæʒʊəl] adj. 隨意的
Idle [ˋaɪdl̩] adj. 閒置的；空閒的

這樣用句型

047

> ### Do you want to talk about _____?

- her　你想談談她嗎？
- politics　你想討論政治嗎？
- why she left him　你想談談她為何離開他嗎？
- what to do for summer　你想談談暑假要做什麼嗎？
- what they were talking about　你想談談他們剛剛談的話題嗎？

> ### Yes, but _____.

- not me　好啊，可是我不要。
- let's not　可以，但是最好不要。
- maybe later　可以，但是也許要晚一點。
- you are wrong　也是，但是你錯了。
- I'm still not convinced　是這樣，但我還沒被說服。

> ### I guess we _____, huh?

- were wrong after all　我猜我們究竟還是錯了，對吧？
- nailed it　我猜我們搞定了，對吧？
- botched it up　我猜我們馬虎了事，對吧？
- are even　我猜我們扯平了，對吧？
- came a long way　我猜我們大有進步，對吧？

1
日常交際

71

用這句話更厲害！

❶ So, what do you think of global warming?
所以你對地球暖化有甚麼看法？

❷ Tell me what you have been up to.
告訴我你近來都做些甚麼？

❸ Haven't you heard already?
你還沒聽說嗎？

❹ Let me keep you abreast.
讓我來告訴你最新近況。

❺ I heard it through the grapevine.
我從小道消息聽說。

❻ We are used to the incoherent babbling coming out of grandma and her friend.
我們已經習慣祖母和她朋友之間無條理的嘮叨。

❼ The old men are rambling about politics again.
這老頭又在漫談政治了。

❽ We are having another long-winded and pointless conversation.
我們正在進行一個冗長卻沒有重點的談話。

❾ Guess what the employees do standing around the coffee maker?
猜猜看員工們圍繞著辦公室裡的咖啡機做什麼？

❿ Talking too much and doing too little is a form of procrastination.
說太多話和做太少事情是一種拖延。

⓫ What do you want to talk about?
你想談些什麼？

⓬ Can we switch gears and talk about something else?
我們能換個話題嗎？

必背單字片語

☑ **Global warming** ph. 地球暖化
Nobody seems to care about global warming.
似乎沒人理會地球暖化的議題。

☑ **Abreast** [əˋbrɛst] adv. 並排；並肩
It is important to keep abreast of the times.
跟上時代很重要。

☑ **Through the grapevine** ph. 消息途徑；秘密來源
She heard about her boyfriend's affair through the grapevine.
她從小道消息得知她男友劈腿的事。

☑ **Incoherent** [ˏɪnkoˋhɪrənt] adj. 無條理的；不一貫的
I tend to ignore that financial analyst's incoherent analysis.
我傾向忽略財務分析師無條理的分析。

☑ **Ramble** [ˋræmbḷ] vt. 漫談
She kept rambling on about her ex-husband.
她一直談論她的前夫。

☑ **Long-winded** [ˋlɔŋˋwɪndɪd] adj. 冗長的
The long-winded speech made everyone in the room sleepy.
冗長的演講使全場的人想睡覺。

❶ 日常交際

Unit 17 求助

這樣說英文

049

A Could you please show me the way home?

B Hello little girl. Why are you out here all alone?

A I ran away from home. But, I'm hungry and I want to go home now.

A 請問你能告訴我回家的路嗎？

B 哈囉，小女孩，你為何獨自一人在這？

A 我離家出走，但是我現在好餓，所以想回家。

A Somebody call for help! My house is on fire!

B I'll call for help immediately. Wait, aren't you my neighbor?

A Is that you John? I think your house is on fire too.

A 誰幫我打電話報案！我家失火啦！

B 我立刻幫你打…等等，你不是我的鄰居嗎？

A 是你嗎，約翰？我想你家也失火了。

A My car broke down. Can you give me a lift to the next gas station?

B Sure, get in. I'll give you a ride.

A You don't look too pleasant. I'll ask somebody else. Thanks.

A 我的車故障了。你可以載我到附近的加油站嗎？

B 沒問題，上車吧，我載你去。

A 你看起來不太友善，我還是來問別人吧。謝謝。

Vocabulary

Ran away　ph. run away 的過去式；逃走、逃避

On Fire　ph. 著火；失火`

Broke down　ph. break down 的過去式；故障

Give me a lift　ph. 載我一程；幫我一把

Pleasant [`plɛz(ə)nt]　adj. 友善的；令人愉快的

74

這樣用句型 050

> **Can somebody** _____?

- · show me the way　有誰可以教我？
- · get that for me　有誰可以幫我得到那個？
- · help me carry that box　有誰可以幫我搬那個箱子？
- · marry my daughter　有誰可以娶我的女兒？
- · clean up this mess　有誰可以善後？

> **I'll call** _____ **immediately.**

- · for assistance　我立刻尋求協助。
- · the tow truck　我立刻打電話給拖車公司。
- · your mother　我馬上打給你媽。
- · 110　我立刻打給 110。
- · the cops　我馬上報警。

> **My car** _____. **Can you** _____?

- · caught fire... help to put it out　我的車著火了，你能幫我滅火嗎？
- · has a flat... call a tow truck
  我的車輪胎漏氣了。你能幫我打電話叫拖車嗎？
- · wouldn't start... get a mechanic
  我的車拋錨了。你能幫我打給維修技師嗎？

1 日常交際

75

· was repossessed... lend me yours
我的車被收回（查封）了。你能借我你的車嗎？

· got towed... give me a lift to the impound
我的車被拖吊了。你能載我到保管場嗎？

用這句話更厲害！

① Can someone please help me?
拜託誰能幫我嗎？

② Would you come and lend a hand?
你願意過來幫忙嗎？

③ I need your help.
我需要你的幫忙。

④ Someone save me!
誰來救救我！

⑤ Does anybody here know CPR?
誰會做心肺復甦術？

⑥ Do we have a doctor on board?
艙內有醫生嗎？

⑦ Get me a doctor, now!
立刻幫我找醫生！

⑧ Somebody call an ambulance.
幫我叫部救護車。

⑨ Someone's robbing me! Help!
我被搶了！幫幫我！

⑩ I beg you to babysit my kids.
我求你幫我照顧小孩。

⑪ I implore you. You have to lend me the money!
我懇求您，借我一點錢！

⑫ I'm trapped. Please rescue me.
我陷入困境了，請救救我。

必背單字片語

☑ **Lend a hand**　　ph. 幫忙
You should lend a hand to those in desperate needs.
你應該對那些極需幫助的人伸出援手。

- -

☑ **CPR（Cardiopulmonary Resuscitation）**　　abbr. 心肺復甦
術的縮寫
Life guards are required to learn how to perform CPR.
救生員需要學習心肺復甦術。

- -

☑ **On board**　　ph. 在（火車、飛機、船）船上
There will be meal services on board. 在飛機上有供餐。

- -

☑ **Babysit** [`bebɪ,sɪt]　　vt. 臨時受雇來照料小孩
I earned my allowance by babysitting my nephews during college.
讀大學時我靠照顧我的外甥來賺零用錢。

- -

☑ **Implore** [ɪm`plor]　　vi./vt. 懇求；乞求
I implore you to leave me alone.
我懇求你不要來煩我。

- -

☑ **Trapped** [træpt]　　adj. 陷入困境
The family felt trapped by the sudden death of the husband.
這個家庭因為先生驟然離世而陷入困境。

❶ 日常交際

Unit 18　商量

這樣說英文

052

Ⓐ Let's talk about what we want to do for this summer.
Ⓑ Ok. Is there anywhere you want to go?
Ⓐ Excursions? No. I was thinking if we could just stay home and do some home improvement.

Ⓐ 我們來談談暑假要做什麼。
Ⓑ 好啊。你想去哪裡？
Ⓐ 出門旅行？不。我是想說是否就待在家中做點修繕裝修什麼的。

⋯⋯⋯⋯⋯⋯⋯⋯⋯⋯⋯⋯⋯⋯⋯⋯⋯⋯⋯⋯⋯⋯⋯⋯⋯⋯⋯⋯⋯⋯⋯

Ⓐ Shall we discuss business or something mundane?
Ⓑ Are we having a discussion on what we should be discussing?
Ⓐ That seems rather pointless. Let's just talk business.

Ⓐ 我們是否應該談論一些生意或是世俗的東西？
Ⓑ 我們在商量我們該談論什麼嗎？
Ⓐ 好像沒什麼意義。我們就來談生意好了。

⋯⋯⋯⋯⋯⋯⋯⋯⋯⋯⋯⋯⋯⋯⋯⋯⋯⋯⋯⋯⋯⋯⋯⋯⋯⋯⋯⋯⋯⋯⋯

Ⓐ Let's split the profit 50-50 down the line.
Ⓑ No, that is unreasonable. I do most of the work while you just hang around all day.
Ⓐ Without me, we wouldn't have landed this contract. I think I should get more than half.

Ⓐ 我們將獲利對半分。
Ⓑ 這樣不合理。我做大部分的事，而你只是整天閒晃。
Ⓐ 可是沒有我，我們就不會拿到這個案子。我想我應該拿比一半還要多。

Vocabulary

Excursion [ɪkˋskɝˏʒən]　n. 短期旅行；遠足
Mundane [ˋmʌnden]　adj. 世俗的
Split the profit　ph.【口】分享所得
Unreasonable [ʌnˋriznəbḷ]　adj. 不合理的
Land a contract　ph. 拿到合約

這樣用句型

> **I was thinking if _____.**

- you could spare me some change　我是想說你是否可以給我一些零錢。
- you would go out with me　我想說你是否願意跟我約會。
- you had the time　我是想說你知不知道時間。
- they were asleep　我在想他們是否睡著了。
- I could come along　我是在想說我可以自己來。

> **Shall we _____ or _____.**

- come... go　我們應該來還是去？
- proceed... wait　我們應該繼續還是等待？
- peddle forward... make a u-turn　我們應該繼續直行還是迴轉？
- hide... run　我們應該藏起來還是逃跑？
- sleep now... later　我們應該現在睡還是等會兒再睡？

> **I _____ while you _____.**

- sleep... work　我在你工作時睡覺。
- look at you... look at me　我倆互看。
- was crying... were laughing at me　我在你笑我的時候哭。
- zig...zag　我倆背道而馳。

· sped ahead... were stopped by the cops
當你被警察攔下時，我加速向前。

用這句話更厲害！

054

❶ Let's have a dialogue to understand this.
讓我們為了瞭解這個來對話。

❷ They debated what the best course of action was.
他們爭辯最好的行動方案。

❸ We talked about our plan.
我們討論過我們的計畫。

❹ Let's plot our escape.
讓我們計畫後路吧。

❺ She deliberated with the jury in length.
她跟陪審團商議很久。

😊 句型! **deliberate with+對象** 是指與那個對象商議
deliberate about+事件 是指對那個事件仔細考慮

❻ The boys chatted for hours about their strategy.
男孩們花了數小時討論他們的策略。

❼ They bounced ideas off each other.
他們徵求彼此的看法。

❽ They exchanged opinions on the subject.
他們彼此交換意見。

❾ Mother and sister are having a tête-à-tête conversation about her future.
母女倆正在討論女兒的未來。

❿ Let's explore the possibilities.
讓我們來探索可能性。

⓫ They argued about what to do.
他們為了該做甚麼而爭吵。

⑫ Let nobody speak about this matter again!
任何人都不准再討論這件事了！

必背單字片語

☑ **Dialogue** [`daɪəˌlɔg]　n. 對話；意見交換
Why don't you have a dialogue with them instead of fighting?
你為何不跟他們對話來取代打架？

☑ **Course of action**　ph. 行動方針
After the long discussion, do we have a course of action now?
經過冗長的商榷後，我們知道現在該怎麼做了嗎？

☑ **Deliberate** [dɪ`lɪbərɪt]　vi./adj. 商議；故意的
Her absence from the meeting was deliberate.
她故意缺席這個會議。

☑ **Chat** [tʃæt]　vt.【口】與…搭訕；閒聊
She likes to chat with cute boys. 她喜歡跟帥哥搭訕。

☑ **Bounced ideas off**　ph. 交換意見
During their time off, the researchers like to bounce ideas off each other.
研究人員在休息時間喜歡彼此交換意見。

☑ **Tête-à-tête**　ph.【法】私底下
I think somebody is eavesdropping on our tête-à-tête.
我覺得有人在偷聽我們的私下交談。

1 日常交際

Unit 19 解釋想法

這樣說英文

Ⓐ Why do you think that she is making a big mistake?
Ⓑ She barely knows him, yet she is moving in with him.
Ⓐ Well, let's just wait and see.

Ⓐ 為什麼你覺得她正在犯很大的錯誤？
Ⓑ 她幾乎不認識他，卻要跟他同居。
Ⓐ 那我們就拭目以待吧。

- -

Ⓐ I don't think I should be drinking this.
Ⓑ Why not? It's widely sold in supermarkets.
Ⓐ If you look closely, you'll see all the artificial ingredients.

Ⓐ 我不認為我應該喝這個。
Ⓑ 為何？這每個超市都有賣。
Ⓐ 如果你仔細看標籤，就會發現都是人工添加劑製成的。

- -

Ⓐ I think he will fail his exam miserably.
Ⓑ Why do you think so? Is it because he is not smart?
Ⓐ No, it's because he has been spending all his time online chatting with girls.

Ⓐ 我認為他這次考試會被當得很慘。
Ⓑ 你為何這麼認為？是因為他不聰明嗎？
Ⓐ 不是，是因為他把所有的時間花在網路上跟女孩子閒聊。

Vocabulary

Barely [`bɛrlɪ]   adv. 僅僅；幾乎沒有
Artificial [ˌɑrtəˋfɪʃəl]   adj. 人工的；人造的
Ingredient [ɪnˋgridɪənt]   n. 原料；要素

Miserably [`mɪzərəblɪ]   adv. 糟糕地；痛苦地
Online [`ɑnˌlaɪn]   adj. 連線作業的；在網路上的

這樣用句型

 056

> She _____, yet she _____.

- is a glutton for work... doesn't admit it
  她是個工作狂，但她並不承認。
- says she will do it... hesitates　她說她會去做，但卻猶豫不決。
- walks slowly... stumbles　她走很慢，卻跌倒了。
- is broke... is a spendthrift　她沒錢了，但卻還是過度揮霍。
- likes him... rejects him　她喜歡他，卻又拒絕他。

> If you _____, you'll _____.

- die... go to heaven　如果你死了，你將會去天堂。
- listen to me... be rich　如果你聽我的，你會很有錢。
- work hard... be rewarded　如果你勤奮工作，你將會得到該有的回報。
- ignore me... regret it　如果你不理我，你將會後悔。
- chase too many girls... be known as a Casanova.
  如果你追太多女孩，你將會被視為大眾情人。

註 Casanova [ˌkæzəˋnovə] 大眾情人

> Why do you think so? Is it cause _____?

- you are not sure　為何你會這麼想？是因為你不確定嗎？
- he is lazy　為何你會這麼想？是因為他很懶惰嗎？
- your boss is an idiot　為何你會這麼想？是因為你的老闆是白癡嗎？

① 日常交際

· she is tardy　為何你會這麼想？是因為她遲到了嗎？
· you're biased　為何你會這麼想？是因為你有偏見嗎？

用這句話更厲害！

057

1 He is prejudiced so he thinks like that.
他有成見，所以他的想法如此。

2 I can't explain why I feel this way.
我無法解釋為何有這種感受。

3 Since she hates him, she disagrees with him on everything.
因為對他懷恨，她到處跟他唱反調。

4 I think he is arrogant because he is ignorant.
我認為他的傲慢源於他的無知。

5 Her lack of empathy was the reason I despised her.
缺乏同情心是我鄙視她的原因。

6 I reckon she's smart because she is a straight-A student.
我猜想她很聰明因為她是個優秀的學生。

7 According to his estimates, the project would be delayed because there was a shortage of workers.
根據他的估算，這項計畫將因為勞工短缺而被延誤。

8 I am quite certain that your attitude made you fail.
我很確信你的態度使你失敗。

9 I cannot be sure if I agree with your arguments.
我不確定是否同意你的論點。

10 I believe he's the culprit due to the overwhelming evidence.
根據壓倒性的證據使我相信他是罪犯。

11 I thought so mainly because she convinced me so.
我之所以這麼想主要是因為她說服了我。

12 I considered all possibilities before I deemed it too risky.
在我評斷這件事太危險前已經考慮了所有可能性。

必背單字片語

☑ **Prejudiced** [`prɛdʒədɪst]   adj. 懷有偏見的；有成見的
I refuse to converse with a prejudiced person like her.
我拒絕跟像她一樣懷有成見的人說話。

- -

☑ **Arrogant** [`ærəgənt]   adj. 自大的；傲慢的
She dislikes arrogant men.
她不喜歡傲慢的男人。

- -

☑ **Ignorant** [`ɪgnərənt]   adj. 無知的
He dumped her because he thought she was ignorant and senseless.
他跟她分手因為他認為她既無知又愚蠢。

- -

☑ **Empathy** [`ɛmpəθɪ]   n. 移情；同情
He feels empathy and compassion for the orphans.
他對孤兒們感到同情和憐憫。

- -

☑ **Attitude** [`ætətjud]   n. 態度
What we don't need is somebody with an attitude problem.
我們不需要態度有問題的人。

- -

☑ **Overwhelming** [ˌovə`hwɛlmɪŋ]   adj. 壓倒性多數的；廣大的
The response from customers has been overwhelming.
顧客們有廣大迴響。

Unit 20 解釋原因

這樣說英文

 058

Ⓐ I'm sorry. I don't have my assignment because my dog ate it.
Ⓑ I find that dubious. Are you lying to me?
Ⓐ No, I swear I'm telling the truth. My dog was really hungry.

Ⓐ 抱歉，我沒有帶作業，因為我家的狗把它吃掉了。
Ⓑ 我認為有點可疑。你在騙我嗎？
Ⓐ 沒有，我發誓我說的是實話。我的狗真的很餓。

Ⓐ I'm leaving you because you are inconsiderate and bad-tempered.
Ⓑ But, that's because I'm just feeling confused and helpless.
Ⓐ There's the other reason. You never tell me what you're thinking.

Ⓐ 我要跟你分手因為你不體貼的，脾氣又很壞。
Ⓑ 但是，那是因為我感到困惑與無助。
Ⓐ 有另外一個原因，就是你從不告訴我你在想什麼。

Ⓐ Can you tell me why you were missing from work yesterday?
Ⓑ I'm sorry but I had to attend my grandma's funeral.
Ⓐ That would be the third time you have attended her funeral.

Ⓐ 你可以告訴我為何你昨天沒來上班？
Ⓑ 我很抱歉，不過我需要出席我奶奶的葬禮。
Ⓐ 那已經是第三次你要參加她的葬禮了。

Vocabulary

Assignment [ə`saɪnmənt]　n. 功課；工作
Dubious [`dubɪəs]　adj. 疑惑的；令人生疑的
Inconsiderate [ˌɪnkən`sɪdərɪt]　adj. 不顧他人的；不體貼的

Bad-tempered [`bæd`tɛmpəd]　adj. 脾氣不好的；易怒的
Funeral [`fjunərəl]　n. 葬禮

這樣用句型 059

> **I'm sorry.** _____ **because** _____ .

· I was late... my car wouldn't start
　真是抱歉。我因為車子無法發動而遲到了

· I failed my exams... I didn't pay attention in class
　真抱歉。我因為上課沒有專心而當掉考試。

· I can't eat this... I'm lactose intolerant
　真抱歉。我不能吃這個因為我有乳糖不耐症。

· she could not make it... she had another appointment
　真是抱歉。她不能來因為已經另外有約。

· he had to go... he didn't feel comfortable
　真抱歉。他因為不舒服必須先離開。

> **But, that's because** _____ .

· I didn't know what to do　但是，那是因為我不知道該做什麼。

· I am scared　但是，那是因為我很害怕。

· I had no choice　但是，那是因為我別無選擇。

· she was misled　但是，那是因為她被誤導了。

· he wasn't in the loop　但是，那是因為他沒有被告知。

> **Can you tell me why** _____ ?

· you're here　你可以告訴我你為何在這裡嗎？

· they're missing　你可以告訴我它們為何不見了嗎？

- and when this happened　你可以告訴我這是為何及何時發生的嗎？
- I'm talking to you　你可以告訴我為何我正在跟你說話嗎？
- they allow this nonsense　你可以告訴我他們為何允許這種無厘頭的事嗎？

用這句話更厲害！

060

❶ Please explain to me what happened here.
請跟我解釋這裡發生了什麼事。

❷ That's because I'm tired.
那是因為我很累。

❸ He lost everything due to his irresponsible behavior.
他因為不負責任的行為而失去一切。

❹ He said, "jump" so I did.
他說「跳」，我就跳了。

❺ Can you tell me the reasons why?
你可以告訴我原因為何嗎？

❻ She gave me an explanation.
她已解釋給我聽。

❼ Please, could somebody enlighten me?
拜託有誰能夠指點我一下嗎？

❽ So, what is your excuse this time?
所以你這次的藉口是什麼？

❾ What are their motives for doing this?
他們做這個的動機是什麼？

❿ No one could give me a clarification.
沒有人可以給我清楚的說明。

⓫ What spurred you to leave?
什麼激勵你離開？

⓬ Could you illuminate the differences between this and that?
你能夠闡明這兩者之間的差異嗎？

必背單字片語

☑ **Irresponsible** [ˌɪrɪˋspɑnsəbl̩]　adj. 不負責任的；無責任感的
How can you date such an irresponsible old coot?
你怎麼能跟個沒責任感的老頭約會？

☑ **Enlighten** [ɪnˋlaɪtn̩]　vt. 啟發；教導
I don't know the situation. Can you enlighten me?
我不知道情況，你可以告訴我嗎？

☑ **Motive** [ˋmotɪv]　n. 動機；目的
What are their motives for moving overseas?
他們搬到海外的動機是什麼？

☑ **Clarification** [ˌklærəfəˋkeʃən]　n. 澄清；說明
The victims' families are seeking further clarification from the authorities.
受害者家屬正在向主管當局尋求進一步的說明。

☑ **Spur** [spɝ]　v. 激勵；促進
His child spurred him into action.
他的孩子激勵他採取行動。

☑ **Illuminate** [ɪˋluməˌnet]　vt. 照亮；闡明
The glowing rocks illuminate the dark corners of the cave.
發亮的石頭照亮山洞裡的黑暗角落。

❶ 日常交際

Unit 21 建議別人

這樣說英文

 061

Ⓐ You look beat. Why don't you go to sleep?
Ⓑ I should and I would, but I want to finish this TV show.
Ⓐ You could find it on Youtube later.

Ⓐ 你看起來很累，何不去睡一覺？
Ⓑ 我應該也會去睡，但我想先看完這部電視劇。
Ⓐ 你以後在 Youtube 上就找得到了。

Ⓐ You should study hard and not play computer games when you are free.
Ⓑ I already study hard when I should. I want to have some time for leisure.
Ⓐ But, don't you want to excel in your exams?

Ⓐ 你有空時應該認真讀書，而不是玩電腦遊戲。
Ⓑ 我應該讀書的時候已經有讀書了。我想要有些悠閒的時間。
Ⓐ 但是，你不想在考試上勝過他人嗎？

Ⓐ You look dreadful. Put on some makeup please.
Ⓑ Speak for yourself! In fact, you look worse than a zombie. Maybe you should put on some makeup too.
Ⓐ Can I borrow your lipstick?

Ⓐ 你看起來糟透了。請你去化點妝。
Ⓑ 你說的是你自己吧！事實上，你看起來比個殭屍還糟。也許你也該去化妝。
Ⓐ 我可以借一下你的口紅嗎？

Vocabulary

Beat [bit] adj. 【口】筋疲力盡的；垂頭喪氣的
Leisure [`liʒɚ] adj. 空閒的
Excel [ɪk`sɛl] vi. 勝過他人
Dreadful [`drɛdfəl] adj. 【口】糟透的
Zombie [`zɑmbɪ] n. 殭屍

這樣用句型

 062

> ### You look _____. Why don't you _____?

- dead... sleep　你看起來精疲力盡的，為何不去睡一覺？
- famished ... eat　你看起來餓昏了，為何不去吃點東西？
- lost... ask for directions　你看起來迷路了，為何不去問路？
- ridiculous... pick another dress
  你看起來很滑稽，為何不選另外一件洋裝？
- like you haven't slept for weeks... go upstairs and lie down for a while
  你看起來像是好幾個星期沒睡了，為何不上樓去躺一下。

 句型！ 感官動詞的用法可以後面直接加形容詞（如第一到第四句）。其他感官動詞還有 taste（嚐起來）、smell（聞起來）等。

> ### You should _____ and not _____.

- chew slowly... devour it　你應該細嚼慢嚥，而不是狼吞虎嚥。
- walk carefully... skip around　你應該小心走路，不該蹦蹦跳跳。
- kiss me... her　你應該親我而不是親她。
- drive... he　你應該開車，不是他開。
- swallow ... spit　你應該吞下去，不該吐出來。

> ### In fact, _____.

- you're the crazy one　事實上，你是瘋狂的那個。
- you are the one who needs help　事實上，你才是需要幫助的人。

91

· you should listen to my suggestions　事實上，你應該聽我的建議。

· I am late for the meeting　事實上，我開會已經遲到了。

· he's the clueless one　事實上，他一無所知。

用這句話更厲害！

063

1 I suggest you go now.
我建議你現在去。

2 You may want to rethink this.
你也許想要再思考一下。

3 I advise you to stop.
我建議你停止。要重新考慮一下。

4 I recommend this and not that.
我推薦這個而不是那個。

5 She advocates this action.
她主張這項行動。

6 I want you to go home.
我要你回家。

7 Why not?
為何不？

8 I think you should go.
我認為你應該去。

9 I propose we stop here.
我建議我們就此打住。

10 She really must stop smoking.
她真的必須戒菸。

11 You date her, and not her!
你跟她約會，而不是跟她！

12 Hurry up and eat before the noodles turn cold.
在麵冷掉前趕快吃。

必背單字片語

☑ **Suggest** [sə`dʒɛst]　vt. 建議；提議
What do you suggest we do for today?
你建議我們今天做什麼？

- -

☑ **Recommend** [ˌrɛkə`mɛnd]　vt. 建議；推薦
I highly recommend this restaurant for your anniversary.
你們的結婚紀念日，我非常推薦這家餐廳。

- -

☑ **Advocate** [`ædvəket]　vt. 主張；提倡
The attorney advocates this course of action instead of that.
律師主張以這個方式代替那個。

- -

☑ **Advise** [əd`vaɪz]　v. 建議；勸告
I advise you to leave immediately if you value your life.
如果你珍重你的生命，我勸你立刻離開。

- -

☑ **Propose** [prə`poz]　vt. 建議；提議；求婚
He proposed to her but she threw the ring back at his face.
他向她求婚，但她將戒指丟回他的臉。

① 日常交際

Unit 22 祝賀別人

這樣說英文

 064

Ⓐ I hear you passed your exams with flying colors! Congratulations!
Ⓑ I think you got me mixed up with someone else. I flunk my exams. I hope you're not joking.
Ⓐ Who are you? I'm not talking to you. I'm talking to the person behind you.

Ⓐ 我聽說你成功地通過考試！恭喜你啦！
Ⓑ 我向你把我跟另一個人搞混了。我當掉了。希望你不是在開我的玩笑。
Ⓐ 你是誰？我又沒在跟你說話。我是在跟你後面那一位仁兄說話。

. . . .

Ⓐ Congratulations. So, he popped the question, huh?
Ⓑ It's about time! I was going to ditch him for making me wait so long.
Ⓐ What are you talking about? You guys have only been dating for a month!

Ⓐ 恭喜啊！所以他求婚了嗎？
Ⓑ 早該如此了！我本來打算因為等他太久而離開他。
Ⓐ 你在說甚麼？你們才一個月前開始約會耶！

. . . .

Ⓐ I must congratulate you on your success to rule the world, Dr. Evil.
Ⓑ Ha! My diabolical plan worked! You can watch me as I gloat over your defeat.
Ⓐ Not if I can help it. I'll get you once I get my hands untied!

Ⓐ 邪惡博士，我必須恭喜你成功統治了全世界。
Ⓑ 哈哈！我邪惡的計畫成功了。你可以看我因為你的失敗而幸災樂禍。
Ⓐ 我真的不願意這麼做。等我的手鬆綁後將會立即將你打敗！

Vocabulary

With flying colors　ph. 成功地
Mix up　ph. 搞混

Ditch [dɪtʃ]　vt.【俚】拋棄；丟棄
Diabolical [ˌdaɪə`bɑlɪkl]　adj. 邪惡的

這樣用句型

065

> ### I'm not _____. I'm _____.

- fat... just gravitationally challenged　我不胖，我只是被重力考驗的。
- lazy... just useless　我不懶惰，我只是有點沒用。
- crazy... just a little drunk　我沒瘋，我只是有點醉。
- going to school... going to sleep　我不去上學。我要去睡覺。
- anorexic... just extremely thin　我不是厭食，我只是極度的瘦。

> ### It's about time! _____

- I've waited for over an hour for you
  你早該來的！我已經等你超過一小時了。
- She finally got married after dating for 10 years
  她早該如此的！總算在愛情長跑十年後結婚了。
- It finally dawned on him that his wife was cheating on him
  該是時候了！他總算發現他老婆外遇了。
- The plane is finally backing away from the boarding gate
  飛機早該推離登機門的。
- Your mother is finally moving out　該是你媽搬出去的時候了。

> ### I must _____ you _____.

- praise... for your cooking　我必須讚美你的廚藝。
- scold... for your insolence　我必須責怪你的傲慢無禮。

- commend ... for your courage　我必須稱讚你的勇氣。
- slap... for your ostentatious behavior
  我必須因為你的炫富行為打你。
- search... for any hidden narcotics
  我必須對你進行搜身來找出任何藏身的毒品。

用這句話更厲害！

❶ Congratulations, you have survived the toughest level in the game.
恭喜你在遊戲最難的關卡存活下來。

❷ I must congratulate you for winning the tournament.
我必須恭喜你贏得這場錦標賽。

❸ She congratulated herself for being independent.
她為自己的獨立慶賀。

❹ Congratulations! This must be your fourth child, right?
恭喜了！第四胎了吧！

❺ This is really good food. My compliments to the chef!
這餐點真好吃，我向主廚致意！

❻ The lecturer left the student a congratulatory note for his excellent exam results.　講師給這次考試優異的學生一封祝賀信。

❼ The king praised the knight for rescuing his daughter from the dratted dragon.　國王讚揚這位騎士從惡龍那裏救出他的女兒。

❽ The hero failed to rescue the damsel in distress. Still, I applaud his valiant efforts.
這位勇士沒有成功救出落難少女，但我還是稱讚他英勇的努力。

❾ Everybody congratulated the old man for graduating from college at 80 years old.
每個人都為這位八十歲從大學畢業的老翁祝賀。

❿ Congrats, you are now officially divorced from the witch.
恭喜你正式跟那個壞女人離婚了。

⓫ I would like to make a congratulation toast to the man who made the company a resounding success.

我想要為讓公司如此成功的男人舉杯敬賀。

必背單字片語

☑ **Tournament** [ˋtɝnəmənt]　n. 比賽；錦標賽
The whiz kid won the world chess tournament.
這個聰明的小孩贏得世界圍棋大賽。

- -

☑ **Compliment** [ˋkɑmpləmənt]　vt. 祝賀；讚美
She compliments him on his expensive Italian suit.
她讚美他那套昂貴的義大利製西服。

- -

☑ **Drat** [dræt]　vt.【口】【婉】詛咒
I drat the day I have to visit the dentist.
我詛咒必須去看牙醫的那一天。

- -

☑ **Distress** [dɪˋstrɛs]　n. 危難
The sinking ship is sending out a distress signal.
這艘快沉的船正在傳出危難求救訊號。

- -

☑ **Toast** [tost]　n. 敬酒；祝酒
It is awkward to have your ex-husband propose a toast at your wedding.
在你的婚禮上由你的前夫提議為你的幸福而乾杯是很尷尬的。

日常交際 ➊

Unit 23 表達看法

這樣說英文

067

Ⓐ I think they should close this highway and make the repairs.
Ⓑ I think it should remain open though repairs are obviously needed.
Ⓐ There are potholes everywhere. It's just too hazardous to keep it open.

Ⓐ 我認為他們應該將高速公路封閉起來維修。
Ⓑ 我認為高速公路雖然顯然需要維修，但應該維持通車。
Ⓐ 路上到處是坑洞，維持通車太危險了。

....

Ⓐ She should just stick to short skirts. That long skirt doesn't look good on her.
Ⓑ Her mother told her to dress modestly.
Ⓐ But, it's making her look really old.

Ⓐ 她應該就穿短裙。那件長裙在她身上不好看。
Ⓑ 她媽媽要她穿得莊重一點。
Ⓐ 但是那使她看起來很老。

....

Ⓐ The way things are going, I think the economy will continue to sink.
Ⓑ I agree. It appears that the president is managing the country into the toilet.
Ⓐ I beg to differ. I feel that it is beyond his control.

Ⓐ 再這樣下去，我想經濟會繼續衰退。
Ⓑ 我同意。看來總統要帶領這個國家走向衰敗。
Ⓐ 我不認為。我覺得這不是他能掌控的情勢。

Vocabulary

Obviously [`ɑbvɪəslɪ]　adv. 明顯地；顯然地　　Sink [sɪŋk]　v. 下降；沉沒
Hazardous [`hæzɚdəs]　adj. 有危險的；冒險的　　Beg to differ　ph. 恕我不能同意
Modestly [`mɑdɪstlɪ]　adv. 謙虛地

這樣用句型

068

> **I think they should** _____.

- go　我覺得他們應該離開了。
- stop talking　我覺得他們應該閉嘴。
- enlist in the army　我覺得他們應該去當兵。
- be careful at all times　我覺得他們應該隨時小心。
- not eat so much　我覺得他們不應該吃這麼多。

> **She should stick to** _____ . _____ **does not** _____.

- her diet. Eating fried chicken... make her skinny
  她應該照著她的節食計畫。吃炸雞不會讓她變瘦。
- the route. Making turns randomly... take her home
  她應該留在這條路上。隨便轉彎並不能回到她家。
- her resolution. Procrastinating... produce results
  她應該忠於她的決心。拖延並不能有效果。
- her own profession. Changing jobs... suit her
  她應該忠於她的專業。換工作並不適合她。
- her husband. The other guy... respect her
  她應該忠於她先生。另一個男人並不尊重她。

> **The way things are going,** _____.

- he's toast　再這樣下去，他完蛋了。
- she's going to be very miserable　再這樣下去，她會變得很淒慘。

1 日常交際

- we won't be going on vacation anytime soon
  再這樣下去，我們短期內不能夠去度假。
- we're going to be millionaires in no time
  再這樣下去，我們馬上就會成為百萬富翁。
- I'll be broke soon and she'll need to find work
  再這樣下去，我會破產然後她就需要去找工作。

用這句話更厲害！

069

❶ I strongly feel that I should go.
　我真的覺得我應該去。

❷ I think not.
　我不認為。

❸ She opined that he was a bad person.
　她認為他是個壞人。

❹ From my point of view, this is the perfect situation.
　在我看來這是個完美的情況。

❺ It will be like I have described.
　事情會像我所描述的。

❻ I oppose what she just said.
　我反對她剛說的。

❼ He agrees with my choice.
　他同意我的選擇。

❽ She is being ambiguous about her relationship status.
　她對於感情狀態刻意含糊不清。

😊 句型！ 人 + be 動詞 + adj. 是指人的本質。You are silly 是「你真糊塗」。You are being + adj. 是指此時此刻的狀態，不見得是那個人的本質，有點刻意的意思。例如：You are being silly 是「你在裝傻」。

❾ They objected fiercely to his controversial statement.
　他們極度地反對他具有爭議的發言。

⑩ I would and I should. But, I can't so I won't.
我願意也應該，但是我不行，所以我不要。

⑪ What do you think about her? 你覺得她怎麼樣？

⑫ How do you feel about him? 你對他感覺如何？

必背單字片語

☑ **Opine** [o`paɪn] vi./vt. 表示意見；認為
She opines that the girls stop wearing short skirts.
她表達女孩們不穿短裙的意見。

- -

☑ **Situation** [ˌsɪtʃʊ`eʃən] n. 情況；局面
How do you get out of a nasty situation like this?
你會如何脫離這種險惡的情況？

- -

☑ **Describe** [dɪ`skraɪb] vt. 描述；形容
She described him as tall, strong and handsome.
她將他形容成高眺、強壯又帥氣。

- -

☑ **Ambiguous** [æm`bɪgjʊəs] adj. 含糊不清的
They kept making mistakes because the instructions they received were ambiguous at best.
他們一直犯錯因為他們得到的指示都含糊不清。

- -

☑ **Object** [`abdʒkt] vt. 反對
The radicals objected violently by firing into the crowd.
激進份子暴力地往群眾開槍來表達他們的反對。

- -

☑ **Controversial** [ˌkɑntrə`vɝʃəl] adj. 有爭議的
People like to talk about controversial issues like gay marriages.
人們喜歡談論像是同性結婚這種有爭議性的話題。

① 日常交際

Unit 24 表達感覺（視覺、聽覺、嗅覺）

這樣說英文

070

Ⓐ I can see many colors in the sky. It's gorgeous! It must be a rainbow.

Ⓑ I can see rain, smog and black smoke bellowing from factories in the distance too.

Ⓐ You don't always look at the bright side of things, do you?

Ⓐ 我能看到天空中有好多顏色。好漂亮！一定是彩虹。

Ⓑ 我也能看到雨、霾害、和從遠處工廠冒出的黑煙。

Ⓐ 你一直看不到事情的光明面嗎？

. . . .

Ⓐ Do you smell his cologne? It just titillates me. I think I'm in love!

Ⓑ That's coming from his brother who just walked by.

Ⓐ In that case, I'm in love with his brother.

Ⓐ 你有聞到他身上的古龍水嗎？好讓我愉悅的味道，我好像戀愛了。

Ⓑ 那是從他剛走過的哥哥身上散發出來的。

Ⓐ 這樣的話，我愛上的是他哥哥。

. . . .

Ⓐ Did you hear about that guy who had his left ear cut off?

Ⓑ Oh no! That's awful! What happened then?

Ⓐ His hearing is all right now.

Ⓐ 你有聽說過那個割下自己左耳的傢伙嗎？

Ⓑ 天呀，好恐怖！後來呢？

Ⓐ 他的聽力恢復了。

Vocabulary

Smog [smɑg]　n.（空氣污染的）煙霧
(smoke and fog)

Bellow [`bɛlo]　vi. 轟鳴；大聲發出

Distance [`dɪstəns]　n. 距離

Titillate [`tɪtḷ͵et]　vt. 使高興

Awful [`ɔfʊl]　adj. 可怕的；【口】極糟的

這樣用句型

> **You don't always** _____ **, do you?**

- tread carefully　你通常都不會小心走路的吧？
- pray before you sleep　你睡前都不祈禱的吧？
- look both sides before you cross
  你過馬路通常不會先看一下兩方來車的吧？
- talk down to your peers
  你不會總是以高高在上的態度對你的同事說話的吧？
- flatter yourself　你不常誇耀自己的吧？

> **In that case,** _____ **.**

- I have no reason to stay　若是如此，我沒有理由留下來。
- I don't buy it　這樣的話我就不買。
- I should run away　這樣的話我應該逃走。
- let's do this another time　這樣的話我們下次再做。
- we will go on strike　這樣的話我們就罷工。

> **Did you hear about** _____ **?**

- her new boyfriend　你聽說過她的新男友嗎？
- how he crashed his car　你聽說過他如何撞毀他的車嗎？
- what happened to her dog　你聽說過她的狗發生什麼事了嗎？
- their divorce　你聽說他們離婚了嗎？

①日常交際

103

用這句話更厲害！

❶ I smelled her cooking and fainted.
我聞了她煮的東西後就昏倒了。

❷ I caught a whiff of the fish.
我聞到魚腥味。

❸ She sniffed and immediately sneezed.
她嗅了一下就打噴嚏。

❹ He listened intently but couldn't get what she said.
雖然他專心地聽她講話卻還是聽不懂。

❺ He heard the train approaching.
他聽到火車接近的聲音。

❻ I examined every detail of her work.
我細查她工作的每一細項。

❼ I witnessed the crime.
我親眼目擊犯罪活動。

❽ She inspected it and then gave it her stamp of approval.
她審查後蓋章認可。

❾ He eavesdropped on their conversation.
他偷聽她們的對話。

❿ She watched the instruction video before attempting the sewing project.
她在嘗試縫紉工作前先觀看示範影片。

⓫ They like listening to gossip.
他們喜歡聽八卦消息。

⓬ She threw out the trash before it stunk the room up.
她在房間充滿臭氣之前把垃圾丟掉。

必背單字片語

☑ **Faint** [fent]　vi. 暈倒；昏厥
She fainted after she looked at his handsome face.
她看到他英俊的臉龐後就昏倒了。

☑ **Whiff** [hwɪf]　n. 一陣氣味；一點點
A whiff of this whiskey can knock you out.
這瓶威士忌的一點點就能將你醉倒。

☑ **Examine** [ɪg`zæmɪn]　vt. 檢查；細查
I examined myself and found a needle stuck to my foot.
我檢查了一下我自己，然後發現有根針卡在我的腳上。

☑ **Inspect** [ɪn`spɛkt]　vt. 檢查
Care to inspect the merchandise?
想要檢查這項商品嗎？

☑ **Eavesdrop** [`ivz͵drɑp]　vi. 竊聽
It's rude to eavesdrop, but everybody does it.
偷聽人家的談話是無禮的，但是大家還是這麼做。

☑ **Stunk** [stʌŋk]　(Stink 的過去式)　vi. 發惡臭
She didn't bathe for days and she stunk but he didn't mind.
她好幾天沒洗澡而發出惡臭，但是他不在乎。

Unit 25 表達感覺（味覺、觸覺）

這樣說英文

Ⓐ Would you try a bit of my cooking?
Ⓑ Yuck! That's putrid! Are you trying to kill me?
Ⓐ Oh I'm sorry. This one is trash. My cooking is in another container.

Ⓐ 你想試試我煮的菜嗎？
Ⓑ 啐！那都腐敗了！你想把我毒死嗎？
Ⓐ 喔，對不起！這是廚餘。我煮的菜是裝在另外一個保鮮盒裡面。

......

Ⓐ Come and feel this blouse. It is so soft and cool.
Ⓑ This blouse is made of silk, I presume. And it is rather reasonably priced.
Ⓐ But it says here "100% polyester".

Ⓐ 來摸摸看這件上衣，好輕柔又涼爽。
Ⓑ 我推斷這件上衣是絲質的，而且價位合理。
Ⓐ 但是這裡寫著「100%聚酯纖維」。

......

Ⓐ My brother kicked me in the shin and I retaliated by boxing him on the chin.
Ⓑ You are all bruised up. You're in great pain, aren't you?
Ⓐ Yes, but not as much as he is.

Ⓐ 我哥哥踢我的小腿，我回報了他的下巴一拳反擊。
Ⓑ 你傷痕累累了，應該很痛吧？
Ⓐ 是呀，但沒有像我哥哥一樣痛。

Vocabulary

Putrid [`pjutrɪd]   adj. 腐臭的
Presume [prɪ`zum]   vt. 推測；認為
Polyester [ˌpɑlɪ`ɛstɚ]   n. 聚酯纖維

Retaliate [rɪ`tælɪˌet]   vi./vt. 報復；回敬
Bruise [bruz]   vi. 產生傷痕；瘀傷

這樣用句型

074

That's _____ ! Are you trying to _____ ?

· really good... impress me　那真的很好吃！你試著感動我嗎？
· crazy... get yourself killed　真是瘋狂！你試著自殺嗎？
· impossible... lie to me　那不可能！你試著騙我嗎？
· your problem...pull me in　那是你的問題！你試著把我拖下水嗎？
· nonsense... test my patience　廢話連篇！你在考驗我的耐心嗎？

Please stop _____, or else _____.

· gambling... I'm leaving you　請不要再賭博了，不然我將會離你而去。
· procrastinating... I'll have to fail you
請不要再拖延了，不然我就得把你當掉。
· eating so much... you'll get fat　請不要再吃那麼多了，不然你會變胖。
· the car... I'll stop it for you　請停車，不然我將幫你讓車停下來。
· looking at me... I'll run away　請不要再看著我，不然我將會逃走。

You are _____. That means _____.

· in trouble... I'm in trouble too　你惹上麻煩，意謂著我也惹上麻煩了。
· broke...you spent everything　你破產了，意謂著你散盡積蓄。
· crazy...I need to stay away from you
你瘋了，意謂著我需要離你遠一點。
· brokenhearted...he left you　你心碎了，意謂著他離開你了。

107

· not listening to me...you don't respect me
你不聽我的話，意謂著你不尊重我。

用這句話更厲害！

❶ I pinched her and she squealed.
我捏她，然後她尖叫。

❷ She tasted it and threw up.
她吃了之後就吐出來了。

❸ I sampled it and spit it out.
我淺嚐後吐出來。

❹ They devoured the entire meal and felt ill.
他們整頓飯狼吞虎嚥的吃而生病。

❺ She brushed me and smiled.
她帶著微笑輕撫而過。

❻ They felt the winter chill when the wind blew.
當風吹來時他們感到冬天的寒冷。

❼ The splinter in my finger is irritating me.
我手指上扎的刺使我很不舒服。

❽ She rubbed her skin with lotion.
她在肌膚上塗上乳液。

❾ This cloth has a smooth, silky touch.
這布料有滑順絲柔的觸感。

❿ This cheap roll of toilet paper felt like sandpaper.
便宜的衛生紙擦起來像砂紙。

⓫ I wondered why the football looked bigger and bigger and then it hit me.
我好奇為何足球看起來越來越大，然後就打到我。

⓬ I broke my finger. On the other hand, I was feeling ok.
雖然我的手指頭骨折。但就另一方面（雙開語：另一隻手），我感覺還好。

必背單字片語

☑ **Squeal** [skwil]　vi. 尖叫；【俚】告密
She squealed on her friends and now they don't trust her anymore.
她告發了她的朋友，所以她們再也不信任她。

☑ **Sample** [`sæmpl]　vt. 品嚐
I sampled a variety of snacks at the food exhibition.
我在食物展裡品嚐多種零食。

☑ **Brush** [brʌʃ]　vi./vt. 輕觸；刷
She brushed her teeth with my toothbrush.
她用我的牙刷刷牙。

☑ **Splinter** [`splɪntɚ]　n. 尖片；碎片
He ran his hand over the rough surface and got painful splinters all over.
他將手劃過粗糙的表面，結果手上到處扎了疼痛的刺。

☑ **Irritate** [`ɪrəˌtet]　vt. 使惱怒；使難受
Apply some cream to the irritated skin.
在過敏的皮膚上塗些藥膏。

☑ **Sandpaper** [`sændˌpepɚ]　n. 砂紙
Carpenters use sandpaper to smooth the surface of the wood.
木匠利用砂紙將木頭表面磨平。

1 日常交際

Unit 26 談論興趣嗜好

這樣說英文

 076

Ⓐ You golf really well. I am quite impressed with that hole in one. You must have had a lot of practice to swing so well.

Ⓑ Thanks. I have accumulated a lot of experience since I was a teenager.

Ⓐ Maybe next time you can play with my dad. But don't forget to let him win.

Ⓐ 你高爾夫球打的不錯。我對那次的一桿進洞印象深刻。你必定練了很久才能打得這麼好。

Ⓑ 謝謝。我從青少年時期開始打球，累積了不少經驗。

Ⓐ 也許下次你可以跟我爸一起打球，但是別忘了讓他贏球喔。

Ⓐ I will be heading off to Europe this summer, and then I'll hop on a flight to South America before I head off to China for winter.

Ⓑ I love to travel too but I wish I had the money to go around like that.

Ⓐ Sweetheart, it helps to marry a rich husband. Meanwhile, I'll remember to send you postcards.

Ⓐ 今年暑假我將去歐洲，然後冬天去中國之前將搭飛機去南美洲一趟。

Ⓑ 我熱愛旅遊但我期盼有那麼多錢這樣旅行。

Ⓐ 親愛的，嫁個一個有錢的老公是很有幫助的。在這期間我會記得寄明信片給你。

Ⓐ My girlfriend loves to cook, and I love eating her cooking daily.

Ⓑ What glue are you sniffing? Isn't her cooking horrible? Besides, didn't she almost burn your kitchen down?

Ⓐ Her old hobby was shopping and spending every penny I had. Between that and cooking, I think I can tolerate some burnt food.

Ⓐ 我女朋友喜歡烹飪，而我也喜歡每天吃她煮的菜。

Ⓑ 你是哪根筋不對？她的菜不是很難吃嗎？再者，她不是曾經差點把廚房燒掉嗎？

Ⓐ 她的舊嗜好是去購物並把我的錢花光。兩者之間，我想我能忍受燒焦的食物。

Vocabulary

Hole in one　ph.【高爾夫球】一桿進洞
Accumulate [ə`kjumjə‚let]　vt. 累積；聚積
Hop [hɑp]　vi./vt.【口】坐飛機旅行

Sniff [snɪf]　v. 用鼻子吸入【有害藥物】
Tolerate [`tɑlə‚ret]　vt. 忍受；容許

這樣用句型

You must have ＿＿＿＿＿ to ＿＿＿＿＿.

· said something bad... anger him　你一定是說不好的事情惹他生氣。

· eaten something bad... have diarrhea
你一定吃了什麼不新鮮的東西才拉肚子。

· annoyed him... make him yell at you
你一定是惹惱他了才會對你大吼大叫。

· offended her... make her dislike you
你一定是做了什麼得罪她的事，她才不喜歡你。

句型！　**must have p.p.** 表示「當時一定是⋯」的意思。因為有助動詞 must，所以後面都是接原型動詞 have。

I love to ＿＿＿＿＿ but ＿＿＿＿＿.

· travel... I haven't got the time　我熱愛旅遊，但是我沒時間。

· eat... I'm too fat　我熱愛吃美食，但是我太胖了。

· sleep... I'm getting too lazy　我熱愛睡覺，但是我變得太懶散了。

· smoke... my boyfriend hates it
我喜歡抽菸，但是我男友非常討厭抽菸。

Between _____ and _____, I _____.

· now... then... will learn a new language
在這段期間我將學一個新的語言。

· here... there... will plant a flower　這裡和那裡之間我要種一朵花。

· five... six... will cook dinner　我在五、六點之間煮晚餐。

· Russian... English... find the former to be difficult
俄語和英語之間，我覺得前者很難。

用這句話更厲害！

❶ My hobbies are reading, traveling and watching movies.
我的嗜好是閱讀、旅遊和看電影。

❷ I have no hobbies and I am constantly bored.
我沒甚麼興趣，而且我一直感到無聊。

❸ She loves to collect bugs but her boyfriend has entomophobia.　她喜好收集昆蟲，但她的男友對昆蟲有恐懼症。

❹ Promoting his business is one of his most important interests.　宣傳他的生意是他其中一項最重要的興趣。

❺ There is a gathering of model airplane hobbyists at the convention center.　展覽館中聚集了一群模型飛機的愛好者。

❻ As a child, she has had an interest in all sorts of poetry.
她小時候喜歡各種詩詞。

❼ Are you interested in learning how to make exotic cuisines?
你有興趣學做異國料理嗎？

❽ Which convertible would you add to your collection?
你會想收藏哪一部敞篷跑車？

❾ Does your kid like music or painting as a hobby?
你家小孩喜歡的興趣是音樂還是畫畫？

⑩ He developed a hobby in football just by watching his friends play.　他只是從看朋友玩足球就對足球產生興趣。

⑪ Make sure your hobby doesn't turn into an obsession!
務必不要太過著迷於你的嗜好！

必背單字片語

☑ **Constantly** [ˋkɑnstəntlɪ]　adv. 不斷地；時常地
Why is he constantly harping on his wife to be thinner while he is as big as an elephant?
為何他一直嘮叨他老婆去減肥而自己卻胖得像隻大象？

- -

☑ **-phobia** [ˋfobɪə]　n. 恐懼；憎惡
I have acrophobia but they insist that I try bungee jumping.
我有懼高症，但他們仍堅持我該嘗試高空彈跳。

- -

☑ **Convention** [kənˋvɛnʃən]　n. 大會；會議
Couples-to-be on a budget should visit the wedding exhibition at the local convention hall for good wedding deals.
想省錢的準新人們應該去當地會議中心舉辦的婚紗展撿便宜。

- -

☑ **Convertible** [kənˋvɝtəbl̩]　n. 有活動摺篷的車
Driving a convertible with the top down in the middle of winter is pure lunacy.
在寒冬中開車頂打開的敞篷車純粹是愚蠢的行為。

- -

☑ **Develop** [dɪˋvɛləp]　vt. 開始有
He developed a fear of water ever since his brother threw him into the deep end of a swimming pool.
從他哥哥將他丟進游泳池的深水區後，他開始對水有恐懼。

Unit 27 談論流行話題

這樣說英文

Ⓐ There should be plenty of blockbuster movie releases in the summer.

Ⓑ I am so thrilled. What movies do you like? Do you want to watch a movie together?

Ⓐ Sorry, but I only watch movies with my boyfriend, and you can't come with us.

Ⓐ 這個暑假應該會不少賣座鉅片上映。

Ⓑ 我好開心。你喜歡哪一個電影？你想一起去看部電影嗎？

Ⓐ 抱歉，我只跟我男朋友一起看電影，而且你不能跟我們一起看。

Ⓐ I see you visiting the bookstore very often. Do you like reading?

Ⓑ Yes, I go there to browse new books and magazines. What about you?

Ⓐ I browse them on the Internet and read them on my tablet. It's a lot cheaper and I get to stay home in my pajamas.

Ⓐ 我看你很常去逛書店，你喜歡閱讀嗎？

Ⓑ 是啊，我去那裡翻閱新出版的書籍和雜誌。你呢？

Ⓐ 我在網路上瀏覽並在平板上閱讀。便宜多了，而且我能待在家中穿著睡衣。

Ⓐ You have at least three TV sets at home. Why do you need so many screens?

Ⓑ I have one in the living room, one in the bedroom and one in the bathroom. That way I won't miss my favorite flix.

Ⓐ It's no wonder that you have no time for anything else.

Ⓐ 你家中有至少三台電視。你為何需要如此多台呀？

Ⓑ 我放一台在客廳、一台在臥室、一台在浴室，這樣我才不會錯過最喜歡的影片呀！

Ⓐ 難怪你沒時間做其他的事。

Vocabulary

Blockbuster [`blɑk͵bʌstɚ] n.【口】耗費甚多，風靡一時的電影巨片

Thrilled [θrɪld] adj. 高興的；興奮的

Browse [braʊz] vt. 瀏覽；翻閱

Pajamas [pə`dʒæməs] n. 睡衣褲

Flix (flicks) [flɪks] n.【俚】電影

這樣用句型

080

> **There should be _____ in the _____.**

· plenty of food... refrigerator　冰箱裡應該有充足的食物。

· no food or drinks ... museum　在博物館裡不應該飲食。

· no cockroaches ... kitchen　廚房裡不應該有蟑螂。

· people... auditorium　禮堂裡應該有人。

> **I see you _____. Do you like _____?**

· staring at her... her　我看到你正在盯著她看。你喜歡她嗎？

· buying a crate of cola... fizzy drinks
我看你要買整箱可樂，你喜歡喝汽水嗎？

· crying your eyes out at the cinema... tearjerker movies
我看你在戲院裡哭的死去活來的，你喜歡賺人熱淚的電影嗎？

· making a black forest cake ... baking
我看你正在做黑森林蛋糕，你喜歡烘焙嗎？

> **You have _____. Why do you _____?**

❶ 日常交際

· much to do... procrastinate　你有很多事要做，為何要拖延？

· no money... spend so much　你沒有錢，為何要花這麼多？

· five credit cards... need more　你有五張信用卡了，為何需要更多？

· a wonderful girlfriend... treat her like dirt
你有個很棒的女友，為何把她看的一文不值？

用這句話更厲害！

081

❶ What genres do you like best: comedy, horror or science fiction?
你最喜歡哪一類型的電影：喜劇、恐怖片還是科幻片？

❷ I like going to the concession stand at the movies.
我看電影時喜歡買零食吃。

❸ The company policy does not prohibit employees from wearing jeans and sneakers to work.
公司並沒有規定員工不能穿牛仔褲和布鞋來上班。

❹ I love watching Sci-Fi movies on a big screen with 3D effects and surround sounds.
我喜歡在有 3D 特效和立體環繞音效的大螢幕上面看科幻片。

❺ I bought a big screen OLED TV so I can enjoy my Star Wars trilogy movies.
為了觀賞星際大戰三部曲，我買了台大螢幕的 OLED 電視。

❻ She is in a pensive mood after reading a book about slavery.
讀了有關奴隸的書之後她陷入了哀思的情緒中。

❼ I am reading a book about how to read a book properly.
我正在讀一本如何正確閱讀的書。

❽ This is a purported best-seller but I didn't think it was worth reading.　這本書是傳說中的暢銷書，但我並不認為它值得我閱讀。

❾ I subscribe to cable TV and I have over a hundred channels of junk.　我申辦訂購了有線電視，然後得到了一百多個頻道的垃圾節目。

⑩ I won't change the channel not because there's something interesting on TV but because the remote is broken.

我不換台並非因為現在的節目很有趣,而是遙控器壞掉了。

⑪ Infomercials convinced me to buy things I never knew I needed. 購物頻道的廣告說服我購買我從不認為需要的東西。

必背單字片語

☑ **Genre** [`ʒɑnrə] n.【法】文藝作品的類型
She absolutely loathes this genre of music.
她極為厭惡這種音樂。

- -

☑ **Concession stand** ph. 賣零食的攤位
I bought a giant bag of popcorn and a supersize soda at the concession stand.
我在零食攤位買了一包巨大的爆米花和一杯重量杯的汽水。

- -

☑ **Prohibit** [prə`hɪbɪt] vt. 禁止
Unauthorized personnel are prohibited from entering this area.
未經許可的人員禁止進入這一區。

- -

☑ **Pensive** [`pɛnsɪv] adj. 沉思的;哀愁的
The girl sat by the balcony and looked pensively at the sunset as if she had lost her love.
這女孩坐在陽台上哀傷地望著夕陽,彷彿失去了她的愛人。

- -

☑ **Purport** [`pɝport] vt. 聲(號)稱;意圖
This imposter is not the person he purports to be!
這個冒牌貨不是他所號稱的那個人!

①
日常交際

Unit 28 談論健康話題

這樣說英文

 082

Ⓐ Don't drink so many sugary drinks unless you want to gain weight or risk getting diabetes.

Ⓑ If that's true then I'll switch to diet soda. That should do the trick.

Ⓐ Diet soda has artificial sweeteners that are detrimental to your health. Can't you drink water?

Ⓐ 不要喝太多加糖的飲料，除非你想變胖或是增加罹患糖尿病的機率。

Ⓑ 如果是這樣，那我就改喝無糖汽水就不會了。

Ⓐ 無糖汽水中有對健康有害的人工糖精。你難道就不能喝水就好嗎？

....

Ⓐ Why are you stuffing yourself at the buffet table like a hungry wolf?

Ⓑ I just went to the gym for a workout and I'm starving. Besides, I can eat because I exercised, right?

Ⓐ No wonder you couldn't slim down. You eat more than you burn.

Ⓐ 你為何像餓狼般吃自助餐把自己撐死？

Ⓑ 我剛從健身房運動回來所以很餓。再加上，因為我有運動所以就可以吃，對吧？

Ⓐ 難怪你瘦不下來，你吃的比你燃燒得更多。

....

Ⓐ Smoking is really bad for you. You should consider quitting before it kills you.

Ⓑ Listen, not everyone who smokes will get sick. Besides, I could get hit by a bus instead and die.

Ⓐ In that case, light up and puff away. Maybe bus drivers will think you're a chimney and avoid running into you.

Ⓐ 抽菸對你真的不好。在它害死你之前你應該考慮戒菸。

Ⓑ 聽著，不是每個吸菸的人都會生病。另外，我也可能被公車撞死。

Ⓐ 如果是這樣，趕快抽吧，也許公車司機會誤以為你是個煙囪而不去撞你。

Vocabulary

Artificial [ˌɑrtəˈfɪʃəl]　adj. 人造的；人為的
Detrimental [dɛtrəˈmɛntl]　adj. 有害的
Workout [ˈwɝkˌaʊt]　n. 【口】訓練；測驗

Slim [slɪm]　vi. 減輕體重
Chimney [ˈtʃɪmnɪ]　n. 煙囪

這樣用句型

 083

> **Don't** _____ **unless** _____.

· make any noise... you want a tight slap across the face
　除非你想被賞巴掌，不然就不要出聲。

· run away... you want those Rottweiler dogs chasing you
　除非你想被那些羅威那犬追，不然就不要逃跑。

· jaywalk ... you want a fine　如果你不想被罰款就不要擅自穿越馬路。

· kiss her... you really like her　如果你沒有真正喜歡她就別親她。

> **Why are you** _____ **like a** _____?

· drinking... fish　你為何如此牛飲？

· driving your car recklessly... maniac
　你為何要開車如此魯莽，像是個瘋子一樣？

· yelling at your workers... person gone insane
　你為何如此發瘋似的對你的員工大吼大叫？

> **Not everyone who** _____ **will** _____.

① 日常交際

- studies diligently... pass the exam
  不是每個用功讀書的人都能通過考試。

- asks her out... get a date　不是每個人都能約她出去。

- robs a bank... get away with it
  不是每個搶銀行的人都能夠僥倖逃脫。

- throws a shoe at the minister... be pardoned
  不是每個向部長丟鞋的人都會得到原諒。

用這句話更厲害！

❶ According to the food pyramid, you're eating all the wrong foods.　根據食物金字塔，你吃的食物都是錯的。

❷ Proper exercise and diet should help you maintain a good figure.　適當的運動和飲食可以幫助你維持好身材。

❸ I could tell that you are a coffee drinker just by looking at your teeth.　我從看你的牙齒就知道你喝很多咖啡。

❹ She never goes for health checkups and insists she never gets sick.　她從不去健康檢查，並堅決認為她從來不生病。

❺ Do you think medical insurance is worth buying?
你認為醫療保險值得買嗎？

❻ She went to the optometrist and got herself prescription glasses.　她去找驗光師配眼鏡。

❼ He had acute renal failure and subsequently needed dialysis treatment.　他罹患了急性腎臟衰竭，隨後需要洗腎治療。

❽ Mental health is just as crucial as physical wellness.
精神上的健康和身體上的健康一樣重要。

❾ One in three Americans are obese because of sugar overconsumption.
三個美國人中就有一位是因為吃太多糖而病態肥胖。

❿ Excessive drinking can damage your liver and brain.
過度酗酒會損害你的肝跟大腦。

⓫ Instead of dieting, he is going through liposuction to remove excess fat.　他去做抽脂手術取代節食來除去多餘的脂肪。

必背單字片語

☑ **Figure** [`fɪgjɚ]　n. 形體；體態
She watches her figure by eating only nutritious fruits and vegetables.
她只吃營養的蔬果來保持身材。

- -

☑ **Checkup** [`tʃɛkˌʌp]　n. 檢查
Everyone should go for an annual checkup to determine his or her health condition.
每個人必須做年度健康檢查來確認自己的健康狀況。

- -

☑ **Prescription** [prɪ`skrɪpʃən]　n. 處方；藥方
This medicine is only available with a doctor's prescription.
這種藥需要醫師處方。

- -

☑ **Acute** [ə`kjut]　adj. 嚴重的
The acute housing shortage problem is prompting the government to take swift actions.
嚴重的房屋不足使政府必須立即採取行動。

- -

☑ **Crucial** [`kruʃəl]　adj. 決定性的；重要的
This is a crucial moment for him as he tries to save his company from bankruptcy.
當他試著防止公司倒閉時，對他來說是個重要的時刻。

- -

☑ **Consumption** [kən`sʌmpʃən]　n. 消耗；消費
This sports car runs very fast but its fuel consumption is horrendous.
跑車雖然跑得很快，但它的油耗量是可怕的。

① 日常交際

Unit 29 談論新聞話題

這樣說英文

085

Ⓐ Did you hear about that celebrity's husband? He cheated on her again!
Ⓑ Where did you hear all this gossip? Did you get it off some tabloid?
Ⓐ It was on the 8 o'clock news. If it's TV news then it should be important, right?

Ⓐ 你有聽說那位明星的老公嗎？他又劈腿了！
Ⓑ 你是從哪裡聽到這些傳聞的？你又是從小報裡讀到的嗎？
Ⓐ 在八點的晚間新聞聽到的。如果上了電視新聞，應該就是重要的，對吧？

. . . .

Ⓐ I find 24-hour news channels redundant and absurd.
Ⓑ I hear you. The same news keeps repeating over and over it's like a broken record.
Ⓐ Everything on it is breaking news but I think it's more like "broken news".

Ⓐ 我覺得 24 小時的新聞台有點重複和可笑。
Ⓑ 我懂。一樣的新聞一直重複播報，像是跳針的唱片。
Ⓐ 每則新聞都是最新消息，但是在我看來更像是 "跳針消息"。

註 broken record 跳針的黑膠唱片，指的是會一直重複一段歌詞。

. . . .

Ⓐ In the weather news, Tom our weatherman will bring you the latest on Taipei's weather. Tom, how's the weather in Taipei?
Ⓑ Same old same old, wet and miserable, back to you.
Ⓐ And there you have it, ladies and gentlemen: weather is so depressing our weatherman thinks it's pointless to elaborate.

Ⓐ 關於氣象，我們請氣象主播湯姆來告訴大家台北最新的天氣狀況。湯姆，現在台北的天氣如何？
Ⓑ 老樣子，又濕又慘，把時間交還給主播。
Ⓐ 各位先生女士，情況就是這樣，天氣狀況令人沮喪到連氣象主播都懶得說明。

Vocabulary

Gossip [ˋgɑsəp] n. 報刊上有關個人隱私的社會新聞或小道傳聞

Tabloid [ˋtæblɔɪd] n.（以轟動性報導為特點的）小報

Redundant [rɪˋdʌndənt] adj. 多餘的；累贅的

Absurd [əbˋsɝd] adj. 愚蠢可笑的

Elaborate [ɪˋlæbəˌret] vt. 詳細說明

這樣用句型

086

Where did you _____? Did you _____?

· get that dress... buy it at the discount store
你是在那裡買這件洋裝的？在暢貨中心買的嗎？

· lose your passport... leave it in the hotel
你是在哪裡遺失你的護照的？你有把它遺留在旅館嗎？

· learn how to speak Mandarin... have a Chinese girlfriend
你是在那裡學說中文的？你有中國女友嗎？

I find _____ and _____.

· your boyfriend handsome... irresistible
我覺得妳的男友既英俊又令人無法抗拒。

· this skirt too short... too tasteless
我覺得這件裙子既太短也太不雅觀。

· her books informative... humorous
我覺得她的書既內容豐富也很幽默。

The ___ is so ___ that our ___ thinks ___.

- journey... time-consuming... tour guide... we should set off early
  這趟旅程如此耗時，以至於導遊覺得我們應該早點出發。

- restaurant... expensive... guest... it's a rip-off
  這家餐廳如此昂貴，以至於我們的客人都覺得被敲竹槓。

- TV picture... clear... cat... the fish on TV is real
  這電視的畫質如此清晰，以至於我們家的貓都以為電視上的魚是真的。

用這句話更厲害！

 087

❶ The ten o'clock news with the attractive anchorman will be on in a minute. 　有英俊主播的晚間十點新聞就要開始了。

❷ The network likes to get men with soothing baritone voices to say the introduction to news programs.
新聞台喜歡用有悅耳的男中音的男人來為新聞節目開場。

❸ Are men listening to the news or are they just staring at the anchorwomen? 　男人到底是在聽新聞還是只是盯著女主播看？

❹ Can you read all the words that are scrolling around in all directions on the TV screen? Are you dizzy?
你可以看完所有在電視螢幕上所有跑馬燈的字嗎？你會頭暈嗎？

❺ The same news is told differently according to whom the editor is and who the sponsors are.
同樣的新聞會因為不同的編輯和不同的贊助商而以不同方式報導。

❻ School does not teach you this: there is no such thing as unbiased news. 　學校不會教你的是：沒有公正報導的新聞這件事。

❼ Newspaper circulation has been dropping drastically ever since people started reading news off the internet.
自從人們開始上網閱讀新聞後，報紙發行量就大大的減少。

❽ In some countries where freedom of the press is stifled, the TV becomes a propaganda machine.
在一些媒體自由被限制的國家，電視成為了宣傳的機器。

❾ Somebody messed up the teleprompter and the anchor read the wrong script to the audience.

有人把電子提詞機弄壞了，所以主播把錯誤的稿子唸給觀眾聽。

❿ Reporters are shoving microphones up against the celebrity and asking him inappropriate questions.

記者們紛紛將麥克風向著明星推擠並問他不恰當的問題。

必背單字片語

☑ **Anchorman** [`æŋkə‚mæn]　n. 男新聞主播
The station changed their news anchorman and now their ratings are through the roof.
這個新聞台更換了他們的男新聞主播，現在他們的收視率節節攀升。

☑ **Baritone** [`bærə‚ton]　n. 男中音（歌手）；上低音
I mistook that woman with a baritone voice for a man.
我把有上低音聲音的女人誤當成男人。

☑ **Stifle** [`staɪfl̩]　vi./vt. 悶住；窒息；受阻止
The prime minister let off a fart and the dignitaries had to stifle their giggles.
首相放了個屁，那些貴賓必須抑制他們的笑聲。

☑ **Propaganda** [prɑpə`gændə]　n. 宣傳活動；傳教總會
During World War 2, many young people were brainwashed with the propaganda of hate.
在二次世界大戰期間，許多年輕人被充滿仇恨的宣傳所洗腦。

☑ **Inappropriate** [‚ɪnə`proprɪɪt]　adj. 不恰當的
I think it's inappropriate for you to wear flip-flops to weddings.
我覺得穿夾腳拖鞋去參加婚禮是不適當的。

❶ 日常交際

Chapter **2**
喜怒哀樂

Unit 1

喜歡

這樣說英文

088

Ⓐ Oh I really like this guy. He has captivating blue eyes.
Ⓑ I can't believe it! You just said that about another guy a minute ago.
Ⓐ Can't I like every one of them?

Ⓐ 我真的很喜歡那個男孩。他有一雙迷人的藍眼睛。
Ⓑ 我真不敢相信！你剛剛在談關於另一個男孩時才說的是同樣的話。
Ⓐ 我難道不能喜歡他們每一個嗎？

....

Ⓐ I adore this cat! Look, it is purring and rubbing up against me.
Ⓑ It's up for adoption. Would you be interested?
Ⓐ No, thank you. I already have five cats at home.

Ⓐ 我好愛這隻貓！看，牠正在呼嚕並且在我身上磨蹭。
Ⓑ 牠正等著被領養。你有興趣嗎？
Ⓐ 不用，謝了，我家裡已經有 5 隻貓了。

....

Ⓐ I admire this quilt. Whoever made it is an artistic genius!
Ⓑ Do you want to buy it? It is only NT$5,000.
Ⓐ Maybe I don't like it that much after all.

Ⓐ 我真欣賞這件拼布被。做出這件作品的人真是個藝術天才！
Ⓑ 你想把它買下來嗎？只要新台幣 5,000 元。
Ⓐ 也許我沒那麼喜歡它。

Vocabulary

Captivating [`kæptə͵vetɪŋ]　adj. 極為迷人的
Purr [pɝ]　vi. 貓滿足時發出的嗚嗚聲
Adoption [ə`dɑpʃən]　n. 收養

Quilt [kwɪlt]　n./vt. 被子／拼布
Genius [`dʒinjəs]　n. 天才

這樣用句型

089

> ### I can't believe it! _____ !

· He ate everything!　我真不敢相信！他把全部的東西吃光了！

· She spent all her money!　我真不敢相信！她花光了全部積蓄！

· It failed for the third time!　我真不敢相信！這個故障三次了！

· I got straight A's on my exam!　真不敢相信！我考試全部拿到 90 分以上！

· He actually asked me out!　我真不敢相信！他真的來約我出去！

> ### No, thank you. _____ .

· I prefer to walk　不，謝了，我寧可走路。

· I don't smoke　不，謝了，我不抽菸。

· I have had enough to drink　不，謝了，這些夠我喝了。

· I should be going home now　不，謝了，我現在該回家了。

· I am lactose intolerant　不，謝了，我有乳糖不耐症。

> ### Do you want _____ ? It is only _____ .

· to go in... NT 100 per person　你想進去嗎？一人只要新台幣 100 元。

· to sleep... six o'clock in the evening　你想睡了嗎？現在才晚上 6 點。

· to walk there... a mile away　你要走路去那裡嗎？只有 1 英哩遠。

· me to help... fair that I do　你要我幫忙嗎？我有幫忙才公平。

· her to leave... a misunderstanding　你要她離開嗎？只是誤會一場。

用這句話更厲害！

❶ I like this, not that.
我喜歡這個，不是那個。

❷ It's just my preference, nothing more.
這僅僅只是我的偏好。

❸ She felt attracted to him.
她喜歡他。

❹ I am mesmerized by her charm and beauty.
我為她的嫵媚和美麗而著迷。

❺ She is impressed by his achievements.
他的成就給她留下深刻印象。

❻ This flavor of ice cream is what draws the crowd.
這個口味的冰淇淋是吸引顧客的原因。

❼ I can't seem to get her out of my mind!
我似乎不能將她忘懷！

❽ She is leaning towards him as a favorable candidate.
她偏向選擇他為喜歡的參選者。

❾ I don't mind going out with her at all.
我完全不介意跟她約會。

❿ She needs what she wants.
她需要她所想要的。

⓫ I like her but I don't love her.
我喜歡她，但不愛她。

⓬ She fancies blueberry pancakes for breakfast.
她喜愛把藍莓鬆餅當早餐。

必背單字片語

☑ **Preference** [`prɛfərəns]　n. 偏好
What is your preference when it comes to women?
你對女人有甚麼偏好？

☑ **Mesmerize** [`mɛsmə͵raɪz]　vt. 著迷；迷惑
She is easily mesmerized by sweet talk.
她很容易被甜言蜜語所迷惑。

☑ **Be impressed by**　ph. 給…深刻印象
Some girls are impressed by sports cars.
有些女孩對跑車留下深刻印象。

☑ **Candidate** [`kændədet]　n. 候選人
These are the candidates for mayor.
這些是選市長的候選人。

☑ **Don't mind**　ph. 不介意
I don't mind cooking tonight.
我不介意今晚煮飯。

 don't mind 的後面一定要接 V-ing，不能夠接其他動詞型態。

☑ **Fancy** [`fænsɪ]　vt.【口】喜愛；想要
What kind of dessert do you fancy?
你想要吃哪一種甜點？

2 喜怒哀樂

Unit 2 快樂

這樣說英文

 091

Ⓐ The client just placed a huge order. I am ecstatic!

Ⓑ I'm not surprised at all because I always knew you were a good salesman.

Ⓐ Good? I'm the best! Watch and learn, young grasshopper.

Ⓐ 這個客戶下了一張很大的訂單。我欣喜若狂！

Ⓑ 我一點也不訝異，因為我一直認為你是個好的推銷員。

Ⓐ 好的推銷員？我是最好的！看著我學吧，菜鳥。

Ⓐ She's overjoyed because her son scored straight A's.

Ⓑ I don't think her son is so thrilled, however. He didn't have much of a social life.

Ⓐ It's a sacrifice he must make, unfortunately.

Ⓐ 她因為兒子成績優異而萬分高興。

Ⓑ 但是我不認為她兒子有那麼高興。他根本沒有社交生活。

Ⓐ 很遺憾，這就是他必須做的犧牲。

Ⓐ He proposed to me! I'm so happy I could die!

Ⓑ Finally, after all these years! What compelled him to do that?

Ⓐ Well, I did threaten him I'll leave him for another man.

Ⓐ 他跟我求婚了！我高興得要死！

Ⓑ 這麼多年後總算求婚了。是什麼迫使他這麼做的？

Ⓐ 這個嘛，我有威脅他，要跟他分手去跟另外一個男人在一起。

Vocabulary

Ecstatic [ɛkˋstætɪk]　adj. 狂喜的；著迷的
Thrilled [θrɪld]　adj. 非常激動的；高興的
（這個形容詞不用於名詞前）
Sacrifice [ˋsækrəˌfaɪs]　n. 犧牲

Compel [kəmˋpɛl]　vt. 強迫；使不得不
Leave...for...　拋棄某人（某事）而追求他人
（他事）

這樣用句型

> I'm not _____ at all because _____.

- hungry... I had a huge lunch　因為我午餐吃很多,所以我一點都不餓。
- going to consider the trip... I loathe traveling overseas
  因為我厭惡到海外旅行,所以我完全不考慮參加這個旅行。
- talking to him... he is a louse
  因為他是個卑鄙小人,所以我完全不想理他。
- taking any breaks... I need to get it done
  因為我需要將這個完成,所以我一點都不能休息。
- bothered... it doesn't concern me
  因為這不關我的事,所以我一點都不煩惱。

> It's a _____, unfortunately.

- scam　不幸地,這是場騙局。
- dream and not reality　令人遺憾地,這是場夢而不是現實。
- fake dollar bill　令人遺憾地,這是張偽鈔。
- malignant tumor　不幸地,這是個惡性腫瘤。
- rejection letter　令人遺憾地,這是封回絕函。

> He _____! I'm so _____!

- called... happy　他打電話來!我好開心!
- disappeared... scared　他失蹤了!我好害怕!

2 喜怒哀樂

- didn't show up... disappointed　他失約了！我好失望！
- found out... done for　他發現了！我完蛋了！
- got fired... pleased　他被解雇了！我很滿意！

用這句話更厲害！

1 I'm so glad he asked me out.
他邀我出去約會我很開心。

2 Either be contented with what you have, or be angry about what you don't have.
知足你所擁有的，或是為你所沒有的而憤怒。

3 His father is pleased with his obedience.
他父親對他的順從感到滿意。

4 I'm delighted with her performance.
我為她的表現感到高興。

5 She can't be happier with the 10-carat ring.
她對十克拉鑽戒感到萬分滿意。

6 They were joyful for finally discovering their true selves.
他們因為終於發現真實自我而感到喜悅。

7 Be jubilant, for the time has come to reap the rewards of thy labor.
歡呼吧！此時是你們收穫辛苦工作所得到的報酬。

8 I have no relish for cigars.
我對雪茄沒興趣。

9 She takes pleasure in seeing others suffer.
她喜歡看到別人受苦。

10 He saved my son from disaster. I am simply overjoyed!
他在災難中救了我兒子。我真是太高興了！

11 I'm absolutely elated that my team won.
我的團隊獲勝使我非常得意。

⑫ He's **in high spirits** after winning the lottery.
他贏得樂透後很愉快。

必背單字片語

☑ **Contented** [kən`tɛntɪd]　adj. 滿足的；滿意的
I'm not contented with what I have. That's why I lost everything eventually.
我不滿足我所擁有的，所以我最後失去全部。

- -

☑ **Pleased with**　ph. 感到滿意
She is pleased with the meeting outcome.
她對此會議結果感到滿意。

- -

☑ **Relish** [`rɛlɪʃ]　n. 喜歡；享受；調味品
I put mustard, ketchup and relish on my hotdog.
我在熱狗堡上加了芥末、番茄醬和調味品。

- -

☑ **Jubilant** [`dʒublənt]　adj. 喜氣洋洋的；歡騰雀躍的
The team is jubilant over their championship.
這支隊伍因為得到冠軍而雀躍不已。

- -

☑ **Elated** [ɪ`letɪd]　adj. 得意洋洋的；興高采烈的
She is elated for the new promotion.
她對新的升遷感到得意。

- -

☑ **In high spirits**　ph. 很愉快
After a few shots of spirits, he eventually got into high spirits.
在幾杯烈酒下肚後，他漸漸感到愉悅。

2 喜怒哀樂

Unit 3 確定

這樣說英文

094

Ⓐ Are you sure the project's going to be canceled?
Ⓑ I'm absolutely positive. I got it straight from the horse's mouth.
Ⓐ I'm not so sure, so I am going to have to ask you to confirm the cancellation again.

Ⓐ 你確定這個案子將被取消嗎？
Ⓑ 我非常確定。我是從可靠消息來源得知的。
Ⓐ 我不是那麼確定，所以我必須請你再去確認這個取消的消息。

......

Ⓐ Hands down, she has got to be one of the worst drama queens I've ever met.
Ⓑ What made you say that?
Ⓐ She threatened to slit her wrist if her boyfriend did not want to marry her.

Ⓐ 她真的是我遇過最糟糕的演員。
Ⓑ 你為何這麼說？
Ⓐ 如果她男友不娶她的話，她恐嚇要鬧自殺。

......

Ⓐ I'm quite certain the company will lay off some employees although the management denies it.
Ⓑ I'm convinced they would, too. I wonder who would be made redundant.
Ⓐ I heard you're one of them.

Ⓐ 雖然管理階層否認，但我非常確定公司即將解僱一些員工。
Ⓑ 我也確信他們會這麼做。我想知道誰會被解僱。
Ⓐ 我聽說你是其中之一耶。

Vocabulary

Horse's mouth　ph. 從可靠消息來源
Slit [slɪt]　vt. 縱向切開

Lay off　ph. 解僱
Redundant [rɪ`dʌndənt]　adj. 被解僱的

這樣用句型

I'm not so sure, so _____.

- I have to check again　我並不是那麼確定，所以我必須再次確認。
- I'm asking her for confirmation
  我並不是那麼確定，所以我會再跟她確認。
- she will ask someone else instead
  我並不是那麼確定，所以她會去問其他的人。
- proceed with caution　我並不是那麼確定，所以請小心進行。
- I'll have to get back to you later
  我並不是那麼確定，所以我必須以後再回答你。

Hands down, _____.

- she's the fastest typist　她絕對是我看過最快的打字員。
- he's the best-looking guy in the office　他絕對是在公司裡最帥的男人。
- that's the tastiest cake ever　這絕對是我吃過最好吃的蛋糕。
- this is the costliest project we've done
  這絕對是我做過最昂貴的案子。
- he's the nastiest boss I've encountered
  他絕對是我遇過最討厭的老闆。

I'm quite certain _____ **although** _____.

- she's the culprit... everyone else isn't
  我很確定她是主嫌，雖然其他人不這麼想。

- I'm going to win... my opponent doesn't think so
  我很確定我會贏，雖然我的對手不這麼認為。
- he's going to die... he is still holding on to hope
  雖然他還抱著希望，但我很確定他即將死亡。
- we'll win the project... we have the most expensive bid
  我很確定能拿下這個案子，雖然我們的出價最高。
- it's a duck... it doesn't quack like one
  我很確定這是隻鴨子，雖然牠的叫聲不像。

用這句話更厲害！

096

❶ Are you sure?
你確定嗎？

❷ How confident are you?
你有多少把握？

❸ I stand firm on my beliefs.
我堅持我的想法。

❹ His defeat is inevitable.
他一定會失敗。

❺ My theory is watertight.
我的理論無懈可擊。.

❻ Without a doubt, I am the winner.
我確實是優勝者。

註 without a doubt 無疑地；確實地

❼ He would bet the farm on it.
他相當確定（賭上他的一切般確定）。

❽ She is, without question, the most obnoxious person here.
無庸置疑的，她是這裡最令人討厭的人。

❾ He hesitated, so he lost.
他遲疑了，所以他輸了。

⑩ The end is undeniably near.
終點確實很近了。

⑪ It is evident that he's the perpetrator.
他很明顯就是犯案者。

⑫ I will stake my reputation on it.
我將為此賭上我的名聲。

必背單字片語

☑ **Confident** [ˋkɑnfədənt]　adj. 有信心的；確信的
How confident are you in winning? 你多有信心會贏？

☑ **Inevitable** [ɪnˋɛvətəbl̩]　adj. 不可避免的
War would be inevitable if the enemy invaded our country.
如果敵軍入侵我們的國土戰爭將會是無法避免的。

☑ **Obnoxious** [əbˋnɑkʃəs]　adj. 令人不快的；討厭的
I can't believe he dated such an obnoxious person.
我真不敢相信他居然跟那麼討人厭的人約會。

☑ **Hesitate** [ˋhɛzəˏtet]　vi. 躊躇；猶豫
Why did you hesitate? I thought you knew what you were doing.
你為何猶豫？我以為你知道自己在做什麼。

☑ **Undeniable** [ˏʌndɪˋnaɪəbl̩]　adj. 不可否認的；公認優秀的
He is a man of undeniable character. 他是個公認優秀的人。

☑ **Reputation** [ˏrɛpjəˋteʃən]　n. 名聲
Your reputation precedes you. 久仰大名。

Unit 4 同意與反對

這樣說英文

Ⓐ Do you agree to take a 20% haircut on your paycheck?
Ⓑ I don't have to agree to that! Why should I?
Ⓐ Because if you don't, you'll have to agree to leave.

Ⓐ 你同意降薪兩成嗎？
Ⓑ 我不需要同意吧。我為何應該同意？
Ⓐ 因為你若是反對，你就必須同意離職。

. . . .

Ⓐ You're going to clean the dishes, sweep the floor, do the laundry and mow my lawn for free. Do you concur?
Ⓑ I concur. I shall adhere to everything you say.
Ⓐ Good, I like your subordination. Now snap to it!

Ⓐ 你要免費幫我洗碗、掃地、洗衣服和割草。你同意嗎？
Ⓑ 我同意。我會遵從您的一切指示。
Ⓐ 很好，我喜歡你的服從。那就趕快開始吧。

. . . .

Ⓐ Did you say "yes"? Or, did you say "no"?
Ⓑ Neither. I said "maybe". We haven't agreed to any deal yet.
Ⓐ The only thing we can agree on is how slow you make decisions.

Ⓐ 你是說「好」還是說「不好」？
Ⓑ 都不是。我是說「也許」。我們還沒達成共識。
Ⓐ 我們唯一有共識的事情是你作決定的速度很慢。

Vocabulary

Haircut [ˋhɛrˌkʌt]　理髮；【口】折扣
Adhere [ədˋhɪr]　vi. 遵守；黏附
Subordination [səbˌɔrdnˋeʃən]　n. 附屬；
【語】主從關係

Snap to it　ph. 快開始
Deal [dil]　n. 協議；【口】成交（願意做某事）

這樣用句型

> ### Do you agree to _____?

· my request　你同意我的要求嗎？

· stop harassing her　你同意不再騷擾她嗎？

· work harder　你同意更加勤奮工作嗎？

· marry her　你同意娶她嗎？

· disagree　你同意投反對票嗎？

 句型! **agree to do sth.** 即是同意某件事情。也可以用 agree on sth. 或者agree that+子
句。

> ### You are going to _____. Do you concur?

· work for free　你同意無償工作嗎？

· give me all your cash　你同意給我所有身上的現金嗎？

· stop procrastinating　你同意不再拖延嗎？

· throw in the towel　你同意放棄嗎？

· ignore everyone else but me　你同意除了我之外忽視其他人嗎？

> ### Did you _____? Or, did you _____?

· propose to her... run away　你有向她求婚嗎？還是逃走了？

· walk... run　你走路嗎？還是跑步？

· agree with John... agree with Lisa　你跟約翰還是跟麗莎達成共識？

・sing... choke　你唱歌嗎？還是唱不出來？

・prosper... falter　你成功了嗎？還是衰敗了？

用這句話更厲害！

❶ Are you OK with that?
那樣你同意嗎？

❷ Don't disagree with him.
不要跟他唱反調。

❸ She's fine with it.
她認為這樣很好。

❹ They countered me with colorful language.
他們用華麗的言語來反駁我。

❺ She is all right with your decision.
她對你的決定沒意見。

❻ I oppose your suggestion.
我反對你的建議。

❼ She deliberately went against him.
她故意反對他。

❽ He is deviating from what we agreed on.
他偏離了我們的協定。

❾ I can't agree with him more.
我非常同意他的意見。

❿ I'm going along with his recommendation.
我要依照他的建議進行。

⓫ My stomach doesn't agree with your cooking.
我吃了你煮的菜後胃腸不適。

⓬ Agreeing to disagree is an oxymoron.
同意保留反對意見是相互矛盾的。

必背單字片語

☑ **Counter** [`kaʊntɚ]　vt. 反對；反駁
She countered his criticism with witty remarks.
她以機智的評論來反駁他的批評。

☑ **Oppose** [ə`poz]　vt. 反對
Why do you oppose everything I say?
你為何要反對我所說的一切？

☑ **Deliberately** [dɪ`lɪbərɪtlɪ]　adv. 故意地
He deliberately pushed her over the edge.
他故意將她逼瘋。

☑ **Deviate** [`dɪvɪˌet]　vt./vi. 脫離；脫軌
Deviate from the path and you will get lost.
脫離這個路徑你就會迷路。

☑ **Recommendation** [ˌrɛkəmɛn`deʃən]　n. 推薦；建議
What recommendation do you have for our anniversary dinner?
你建議我們結婚紀念日的晚餐吃什麼？

☑ **Oxymoron** [ˌɑksɪ`mɔrɑn]　n. 矛盾修辭法
Cruel kindness is another example of an oxymoron.
殘忍的慈悲是另外一種逆喻。

> **註** oxymoron 是將兩個互相矛盾的字放在一起後來獲得特殊效果的一種修辭法。
> 殘忍和慈悲、同意和不同意都是相反的詞，放在一起以獲得另一個意思。

② 喜怒哀樂

Unit 5 相信與不相信

這樣說英文

Ⓐ I don't see any convincing evidence. I believe he is innocent.
Ⓑ Well, I believe he is guilty. After all, he is a convicted felon.
Ⓐ He may be a felon, but it doesn't mean he is guilty this time.

Ⓐ 我看不到任何可信的證據。我相信他是無辜的。
Ⓑ 可是，我相信他是有罪的。他畢竟是個被判刑的罪犯。
Ⓐ 他也許是個罪犯，但是那不代表他這次是有罪的。

Ⓐ He dumped me! Can you imagine that?
Ⓑ No way! I can't believe it. How can he do something so despicable?
Ⓐ And, he did that by sending me an email!

Ⓐ 他拋棄我！你能想像嗎？
Ⓑ 怎麼可能？！我不相信。他怎麼可以做出這麼卑鄙的事情？
Ⓐ 而且他還用電子郵件來告知我！

Ⓐ Do I really have to go through this operation?
Ⓑ I deem it necessary. I think it's imperative that you do so.
Ⓐ Ok, I trust your judgment.

Ⓐ 我真的需要動這個手術嗎？
Ⓑ 我覺得需要，我認為這個手術是必要的。
Ⓐ 好吧，我相信你的判斷。

Vocabulary

Convincing [kən`vɪnsɪŋ]　adj. 有說服力的
Felon [`fɛlən]　n. 重罪犯
Despicable [`dɛspɪkəbl]　adj. 可鄙的；卑劣的

Imperative [ɪm`pɛrətɪv]　adj. 必要的；極重要的
Judgment [`dʒʌdʒmənt]　n. 判斷；審判；認真思考過後的意見

這樣用句型

> Well, _____. After all, _____.

- we should just sleep... it's late　我們該睡了，現在畢竟很晚了。
- let's go... she's never going to show up
  那我們走吧。她最終還是不會來。
- don't be sad... it's only money　不要傷心，那畢竟只是錢而已。
- keep looking... we have to find it
  那繼續找吧。我們終究還是要找到它。
- forget about it... you can try again
  忘了它吧，你還是可以再試一次。

> He _____! Can you imagine that?

- stood me up　他居然放我鴿子！你能想像嗎？
- ate a scorpion　他居然吃了一隻蠍子！你能想像嗎？
- has five girlfriends　他居然有五個女友！你能想像嗎？
- finished the job in time　他居然在期限內完成工作！你能想像嗎？
- skipped town　他居然跑路！你能想像嗎？

> Do I really have to _____?

- listen to this nonsense　我真的必須聽這些沒營養的東西嗎？
- walk that far　我真的必須走那麼遠嗎？
- kiss her　我真的必須親她嗎？

②
喜怒哀樂

- work today　我今天真的必須上班嗎？
- wake up now　我現在真的必須起床了嗎？

用這句話更厲害！

1 The results are just unbelievable.
結果真是令人無法置信。

2 I believe that prices will fall.
我相信價格會調降。

3 I suppose what she's telling me is true, then.
那麼我認為她告訴我的是事實。

4 He blindly believed the lies she told him.
他盲目相信她所撒的謊。

5 You cannot believe everything you see.
你不能相信你所看到的每件事。

6 I trust that you find this suit exquisite.
我相信你會覺得這件西裝很精緻。

7 Nothing can shake his faith in superheroes.
他對超級英雄的信仰是無可動搖的。

8 I believe in exercise and proper nutrition.
我相信運動和均衡飲食的效用。

9 The plane is believed to have crashed.
人們認為這架飛機已經墜毀。

10 Do you believe in me? If not, I shall curse you!
你相信我嗎？如果不信的話，我應該詛咒你！

11 She is a believer but I am a skeptic.
她是個有信仰的人，而我卻是個多疑者。

12 Believe it or not!
信不信由你！

必背單字片語

☑ **Unbelievable** [ˌʌnbɪˋlivəbl̩] adj. 無法置信的；（由於太好或太糟而）令人難以置信

The view from here is unbelievable!

從這裡看出去的景色真是令人驚豔！

- -

☑ **Blindly** [ˋblaɪndlɪ] adv. 盲目地

How can you blindly follow his instructions?

你怎能盲目地遵從指令？

- -

☑ **Exquisite** [ɪkˋskwɪzɪt] adj. 精緻的；細緻的

This wine is exquisite. No wonder it costs a bomb.

這酒很香醇，難怪這麼貴。

- -

☑ **Faith** [feθ] n. 信念；信仰

Have faith! We shall survive the fight!

要有信心！我們可以在這場紛爭中倖存！

- -

☑ **Nutrition** [njuˋtrɪʃən] n. 營養

She doesn't care about proper nutrition so she often gets sick.

她不在乎均衡營養，所以常生病。

- -

☑ **Skeptic** [ˋskɛptɪk] n. 疑慮極深的人；懷疑論者

Sometimes it is healthy to be a little skeptical.

有時有點疑慮是好的。

2

喜怒哀樂

Unit 6 堅持

這樣說英文

Ⓐ She insists that I go out with her.
Ⓑ Boy! She's an aggressive girl! What are you going to do?
Ⓐ I'm going to ignore her and go out with her sister instead.

Ⓐ 她堅持要我跟她約會。
Ⓑ 哇！那麼強勢的女孩！那你要怎麼做呢？
Ⓐ 我不理她，並要跟她妹妹約會。

Ⓐ Let me have the check, please.
Ⓑ No, no. We haven't met for a long time. Let me get this instead.
Ⓐ Ok, if you insist!

Ⓐ 請幫我買單。
Ⓑ 不行，我們這麼久沒見面了，這攤我來付。
Ⓐ 好吧，如果你堅持！

Ⓐ He thinks that being persistent is the key to success.
Ⓑ He is just being stubborn as he resists change.
Ⓐ You are right. He shouldn't hesitate to change.

Ⓐ 他認為堅持到底是成功的關鍵。
Ⓑ 他只是固執因為他抗拒改變。
Ⓐ 說的沒錯。他不該不願意改變。

Vocabulary

Aggressive [ə`grɛsɪv] adj. 侵略的；好鬥的；強勢的

Insist [ɪn`sɪst] vt. 堅持；強調

Persistent [pə`sɪstənt] adj. 堅持不懈的

Resist [rɪ`zɪst] v. 反抗；抗拒

Hesitate [`hɛzə͵tet] vi. 猶豫；躊躇 vt. 有疑慮；不願意

這樣用句型

> **She insists** _____.

- on procrastinating　她堅持要拖延。
- that everyone agrees with her　她一定要全部的人都同意她的意見。
- upon my going with her to the party　她堅持要我跟她一起出席派對。
- that we accept her gifts　她一定要我們收下她的禮物。
- that he cheated on her　她堅決認為他劈腿。

2 喜怒哀樂

> **We haven't** _____. **Let** _____ **instead.**

- even started yet... us stop dillydallying and get to it
  我們根本還沒開始。讓我們不要再三心二意並趕快行動吧。
- been paying attention... us focus　我們一直沒在專心。讓我們專注。
- showered yet... us go home and clean up
  我們還沒洗澡,趕快回家清理一下。
- gotten a nose job and we don't want one... them go get one
  我們還沒隆鼻,也不想去。讓他們去做吧。
- eaten for days... us stop fake politeness and eat
  我們好幾天沒吃飯了,讓我們停止假裝並趕快吃吧。

用這句話更厲害！

1 She insists that she is always right.
她堅持她一直是對的。

2 I insist that I go in place of him.
我堅持要代替他去。

3 Why do you insist on opting for her?
你為何堅持要選擇她？

4 He insists on putting out superior quality products.
他堅持要做出最高品質的商品。

5 His insistence is starting to aggravate me.
他的固執開始惹惱我。

6 She insists that she saw him do it.
她一口咬定看到是他做的。

7 Insist on getting a receipt!
一定要記得拿發票！

8 The priest insists that you must resist temptation.
牧師堅持你一定要抵抗誘惑。

9 They insist that they are happily married.
他們堅持他們的婚姻是美滿的。

10 I insist on getting a ticket right this moment!
我堅持立馬要拿到票！

11 The more you insist, the more I resist!
你越是堅持，我越是反抗！

12 Insist all you want but I still wouldn't sanction it!
你可以繼續堅持，但我不會認同！

必背單字片語

☑ **Opt** [ɑpt]　vi. 選擇
Do you opt for this? Or do you want that instead?
你選這個？或者你想要那個？

☑ **Superior** [sə`pɪrɪɚ]　adj. 優秀的；上等的
This outfit is made of superior materials.
這件服飾是以上等的材料縫製而成。

☑ **Aggravate** [`ægrə͵vet]　vt. 【非正式】惹怒；激怒
She got aggravated and started screaming at him.
她被激怒而開始對他叫罵。

☑ **Temptation** [tɛmp`teʃən]　n. 誘惑
I succumbed to temptation and ate all the candy.
我屈服於誘惑並吃了所有的糖果。

☑ **Right this moment**　ph. 立馬；在這當下
She cried out loud right this moment and startled everyone.
她在這當下放聲痛哭嚇壞所有的人。

☑ **Sanction** [`sæŋkʃən]　vt. 認可；批准　n. 國際制裁
The country was slapped with economic sanctions for developing nuclear weapons.
這個國家因為發展核武而被施予經濟制裁。

2

喜怒哀樂

Unit 7　鼓勵

這樣說英文

Ⓐ We encourage you to step up and take charge of your life.
Ⓑ I'm afraid, and I don't have the courage.
Ⓐ In that case, join our leadership seminar. It'll only cost you five thousand dollars.

Ⓐ 我們鼓勵你站出來為你的人生負責。
Ⓑ 我很害怕，沒有勇氣這麼做。
Ⓐ 這樣的話，請加入我們的領袖研討會。這只會花你五千元。

⋯⋯⋯⋯⋯⋯⋯⋯⋯⋯⋯⋯⋯⋯⋯⋯⋯⋯⋯⋯⋯⋯⋯⋯⋯⋯⋯⋯⋯

Ⓐ She received plenty of consolation and encouragement from her friends.
Ⓑ What happened? Did she fail her exams again?
Ⓐ No. Nobody wants to take her to the dance.

Ⓐ 她從朋友那裡得到不少安慰和鼓勵。
Ⓑ 發生了什麼事嗎？她又當掉了嗎？
Ⓐ 不是的，是沒人想要邀請她去舞會。

⋯⋯⋯⋯⋯⋯⋯⋯⋯⋯⋯⋯⋯⋯⋯⋯⋯⋯⋯⋯⋯⋯⋯⋯⋯⋯⋯⋯⋯

Ⓐ Ignore him. He is just trying to discourage you.
Ⓑ But, whatever he said made perfect sense. I'm just hopeless!
Ⓐ Ok, I'm through trying to encourage you. Go ahead and wallow in your self-pity.

Ⓐ 不要理他。他只是試著要使你灰心。
Ⓑ 但是，他講的都很有道理。我就是如此無能！
Ⓐ 好吧，我也不想再鼓勵你了，繼續自怨自哀吧。

Vocabulary

Take charge of　ph. 負責；管理
Seminar [`sɛmə͵nɑr]　n. 研討班；討論會
Consolation [͵kɑnsə`leʃən]　n. 安慰；慰藉

Hopeless [`hoplɪs]　adj. 無望的；【口】無能的
Wallow in self-pity　ph. 自怨自哀

這樣用句型

> **We encourage you to _____ and _____.**

· be happy... contented　我們鼓勵你快樂和滿足。

· try harder... not give up　我們鼓勵你更努力嘗試並且不要放棄。

· move on... love again　我們鼓勵你放下並且再去戀愛。

· run faster than everyone else... win the race
我們鼓勵你跑得比別人更快並且贏得賽跑。

· pick yourself up... start again　我們鼓勵你再次站起來並重新開始。

> **What happened? Did _____?**

· she run away　怎麼了？她逃跑了嗎？

· he die　怎麼了？他死了嗎？

· I startled you　怎麼了？我嚇到你了嗎？

· the market crashed　發生什麼事了？股市崩盤了嗎？

· the dog chew up your wires　發生甚麼事了？小狗把你的電線咬碎了嗎？

> **Ignore him. _____.**

· He's just trying to get your attention
別理他，他只是試著引起你的注意。

· He's just throwing a tantrum　別理他，他只是在發脾氣。

· He's not worth it　別理他，他不值得。

喜怒哀樂 ②

· He's just a crazy old man　別理他,他只是個老癲瘋。

· He's dangerous　別理他,他很危險。

用這句話更厲害!

108

① What encouragement can you give to the downtrodden?
你能如何激勵那些被欺壓的人?

② I encourage you to relinquish control.
我鼓勵你放棄掌控權。

③ Her constant nagging encourages her son to move out.
她不停地嘮叨促使她的兒子搬出去住。

④ He was discouraged by his exam results.
他對考試成績很灰心。

⑤ The coach cheered his team to victory.
這支隊伍在教練的鼓勵下獲勝。

⑥ She pushed on despite the tremendous odds.
雖然經歷巨大的困難,她還是繼續努力。

⑦ She motivated me to start a business.
她鼓勵我自己開業。

⑧ I persuaded her to stop crying.
我勸她別哭了。

⑨ The school discourages negative behavior like playing truant.
學校勸阻類似像曠課等負面行為。

⑩ There are government policies that discourage people from smoking, although the major tobacco companies are run by the government.
政府的政策勸阻人民吸菸,雖然主要的煙草公司是政府所擁有。

註 discourage sb from V+ing 勸阻/說服某人不要⋯

⑪ Don't be discouraged by trivial matters.
別因為一些小事而感到灰心。

12 Why encourage with words when you can motivate with money?

當你能用錢來激勵他人，何必以文字來鼓勵呢？

必背單字片語

☑ **Downtrodden** [`daʊn`trɑdn]　adj. 被權勢者踐踏的；受壓迫的
Please help the poor and the downtrodden.
請幫助窮苦的和受壓迫的人。

☑ **Relinquish** [rɪ`lɪŋkwɪʃ]　vt. 放棄；交出（權力或職位）
The king relinquished his throne for the sake of his people.
國王為了他的人民而放棄了他的王位。

☑ **Nagging** [`nægɪŋ]　adj. 嘮叨的；挑剔的
Can you stand a person who cannot stop nagging?
你能忍受無法停止嘮叨的人嗎？

☑ **Odds** [ɑdz]　n. 可能性；困難
The odds are stacked up against him.
他面臨著重重考驗。

☑ **Motivate** [`motə,vet]　vt. 激發；促動
What motivates you to get up in the morning?
早上激勵你起床的動力是什麼？

☑ **Persuade** [pɚ`swed]　vt. 說服；勸服
How did she persuade you to do her dishes?
她是如何說服你幫她洗碗的？

Unit 8 幫了大忙

這樣說英文

109

Ⓐ Say, I need a really big favor from you. Do you think you could help?
Ⓑ Sure, anything you need. How can I help you?
Ⓐ Could you let me use your sports car tonight?

Ⓐ 哎呀，我需要你幫一個很大的忙。你能幫我嗎？
Ⓑ 當然，不論你需要的是什麼。你要我怎麼幫你？
Ⓐ 今晚你能讓我開你的跑車嗎？

. . . .

Ⓐ I'm heading out to the shops. Do you want anything?
Ⓑ Yes, can you get me a rich, handsome boyfriend? I would like him to be a philanthropist as well.
Ⓐ I can do you favors, but even that is too much.

Ⓐ 我要出門買東西，你需要什麼嗎？
Ⓑ 有，你能幫我找一個多金又帥的男友嗎？希望他也是個慈善家。
Ⓐ 我可以幫你，但是那有點太超過了。

. . . .

Ⓐ Can you help me move the TV upstairs? Otherwise, I'll ask someone else.
Ⓑ I'll be glad to help! Do you need anything else?
Ⓐ Yes, the couch, table, refrigerator, king-sized bed and this ten ton safe as well. Much obliged!

Ⓐ 你能幫我把電視搬上樓嗎？要不然我還要去問別人。
Ⓑ 我很樂意幫忙！你還需要我幫其他的事嗎？
Ⓐ 是的，還有沙發、桌子、冰箱、加大的雙人床、以及這個十噸重的保險箱。謝啦！

Vocabulary

Favor [`fevɚ]　n. 幫助；恩惠；善意的行為
Head out　ph. 出門
Philanthropist [fɪ`lænθrəpɪst]　n. 慈善家

Safe [sef]　n. 保險箱
Much obliged　ph. 多謝

這樣用句型

110

> Say, _____. Do you think _____?

· I'm running short of cash... you can loan me some money
哎呀，我最近缺錢用，你想可以借我一點錢嗎？

· it's getting dark... I can spend the night at your place
哎呀，天色變暗了，你覺得可以讓我借住一宿嗎？

· she's lost... you could help her out
哎呀，她迷路了，你覺得你可以幫她嗎？

· the car is out of gas... you can pull over and fill her up
哎呀，車子沒油了，你覺得可以停下來加油嗎？

② 喜怒哀樂

> I can _____, but _____.

· do you a favor... could you do me one too
我能幫你，但是你也能幫我一次嗎？

· afford it... I don't think he can　我買得起，但是我不認為他買得起。

· skip class... I don't think it's a good idea
我能翹課，但我不認為那是個好主意。

· hardly see... that is because I am not wearing my glasses
我不太看的到我看不太到，但是那是因為我沒戴眼鏡。

> Can you _____? Otherwise _____.

· go away... I'm calling the cops　請你離開，不然我就要報警了。

· buy this... I'll throw a tantrum　你要不要買下來？不然我就要發脾氣了。

157

- hand me the robe... I'll be stark naked
  請你拿件浴袍給我，不然我將會光溜溜的。

- get a medic... I'll bleed to death
  請幫我尋求醫療人員，不然我會失血而死。

用這句話更厲害！

1 He's doing you a favor by lending you money.
他借你錢幫了你大忙。

2 She stuck her neck out for you by asking the boss to retrench somebody else.
她為了你冒險去要求老闆裁員時裁別人。

3 He pulled me out of the burning car right before it blew to smithereens.
他在火燒車快爆炸之前將我拖了出去。

4 He is just throwing me a bone.
他只是給我一點幫助。

5 The dehumidifier is a life-saver during the rainy season.
除濕機在雨季幫了大忙。

6 The Federal Reserve (FED) bailed out the banks with taxpayer money.
美國聯邦儲備局用納稅人的錢幫助銀行脫離財務危機。

7 Economic tailwinds favor employment opportunities.
經濟成長有利於就業市場。

8 You have been a great help.　你真是幫了我個大忙。

9 He saved my neck by fighting off the attacking guard dogs.
他幫我擊退攻擊我的看門狗，使我保住性命。

10 You scratch my back and I'll scratch yours.　我們互相幫忙。

註 字面上是說你抓我的背我就抓你的背，是一種互惠關係。這是用來形容人與人之間的互助。

11 Thanks. You saved my life！　謝謝，你救了我一命！

⑫ He saved us from another weekend of boredom by bringing us to a dance performance.

他帶我們去一場舞蹈表演，幫助我們度過無聊的週末。

必背單字片語

☑ **Retrench** [rɪˋtrɛntʃ]　vi. 緊縮；減少
He was retrenched and could not afford to pay his credit card bills.
他被裁員了，所以付不起他的信用卡帳單。

☑ **Throw a bone**　ph. 給甜頭或幫助；施捨
I need some help. Somebody throw me a bone, please?
我需要幫忙，拜託幫我一下好嗎？

☑ **Tailwind** [ˋtel͵wɪnd]　n. 順風
Tailwinds gave the plane a speed boost.
飛機順風時飛得比較快。

☑ **Smithereens** [͵smɪðəˋrinz]　n.【複】【非正式】把某物撞成碎片
The sergeant threw a grenade into the bunker and blew it to smithereens.
中士把手榴彈丟進地堡，將它炸成碎片。

☑ **Scratch** [skrætʃ]　vt. 抓；刮
She is livid because somebody had scratched up her new car with a key.
她非常生氣因為有人用鑰匙刮傷她的新車。

☑ **Performance** [pəˋfɔrməns]　n. 表演；執行；表現
The piano performance begins at 7 o'clock.
鋼琴表演在 7 點開始。

Unit 9 請放心

這樣說英文

112

Ⓐ What am I going to do? The pipe broke and now my apartment is flooded!

Ⓑ Not to worry. I know a plumber I can call who will take care of it.

Ⓐ Thank you! You are a savior!

Ⓐ 我該怎麼辦？水管破了，我家公寓整個大淹水！

Ⓑ 不用擔心，我可以請我認識的水電工幫妳處理。

Ⓐ 謝謝！你是個救星！

....

Ⓐ Every time my son gets into a fix I will sort it out.

Ⓑ Aren't you spoiling your kid by taking care of everything for him?

Ⓐ Don't worry, I also teach him how to fix the problem at the same time.

Ⓐ 每次我兒子遭遇困境，我都幫他解決。

Ⓑ 你這樣幫他不會把他寵壞嗎？

Ⓐ 不用擔心，我也同時教我兒子怎麼解決問題。

....

Ⓐ He is winning the confidence of the voters.

Ⓑ How is he achieving that?

Ⓐ Oh, he's assuring them that he will resolve all their problems. But, I'm doubtful of his promises.

Ⓐ 他正贏得選民們的支持。

Ⓑ 他是如何辦到的？

Ⓐ 喔，他向大家擔保會解決他們所有的問題。但是，我懷疑他的承諾。

Vocabulary

Flood [flʌd]　v. 淹水
Savior [`sevjɚ]　n. 救星
Fix [fɪks]　n.【口】困境

Achieve [ə`tʃiv]　vt. 完成；達到
Resolve [rɪ`zɑlv]　v. 解決

這樣用句型

> **Not to worry.** _____.

· I am here to help　不用擔心，我來幫你。

· It's really not that bad　不用擔心，情況並沒有那麼糟。

· You will have another chance　不用擔心，你會有另一個機會的。

· We can take the bus instead　不用擔心，我們可以改搭這班公車。

· There are other fish in the sea　不用擔心，還有很多選擇。

② 喜怒哀樂

> **Every time** _____ **I will** _____.

· I'm hungry... open the refrigerator　每次我餓了，我就會開冰箱。

· she calls... hang up　每次她來電，我就會掛斷。

· the boss approaches... pretend I am working
　每次老闆接近時，我就會假裝在工作。

· I go on a vacation... switch off my phone
　我每次度假時都會把電話關機。

· he joins us... leave　每次他參與我們，我就會離開。

> **Oh,** _____. **But** _____.

· it's expensive... it's worth every penny　這很貴，但值回票價。

· he's not so bright... his good looks shields it
　他沒那麼聰明，但他帥氣的臉龐掩飾了這一點。

· she's pretty... her temper is something to avoid.
　她很漂亮，但要避開她發脾氣的時候。

- the dog is cute... it'll tear up your furniture
  這隻狗很可愛，但是牠會破壞你的傢俱。
- the trip is going to be fun... it'll cost you a bomb
  這趟旅程會很好玩，但是會花你很多錢。

用這句話更厲害！

❶ Why worry? He will bail you out.
何必擔心？他會幫助你擺脫困境的。

❷ I knew I could count on you.
我就知道你靠得住。

❸ Fear not, for I am here!
不用怕，我在！

❹ She assures me that things will sort themselves out.
她向我保證事情會解決的。

❺ Stop fretting because the situation is not severe.
不要再煩憂了，因為情況並沒那麼糟。

❻ You have no need to be anxious.
你不需要焦慮。

❼ Stay calm and trust me. If you panic, all hell will break loose.
冷靜點並相信我。如果你恐慌的話，一切都完了。

❽ We guarantee you piece of mind.
我們保證你放心。

❾ Did he fulfill his promise to help?
他履行幫忙的承諾了嗎？

❿ Can you rely on him to take care of all your woes?
你能依賴他去處理你所有的困難嗎？

⓫ We should be wary when someone says he can solve all our problems.
當有人說他會解決我們所有問題時，我們應該小心一點。

⑫ You cannot take care of anyone if you cannot take care of yourself.

你若不能幫助你自己，你就沒有能力幫助任何人。

必背單字片語

☑ **Bail sb. out (Bail out sb.)**　ph. 保釋某人；救助某人脫離財務困境

The government had to bail out the banks with tax money.

政府用稅收來解決銀行的財務困境。

☑ **Fret** [frɛt]　vt./vi. 苦惱；煩憂

Why do you fret so much?

你為何如此苦惱？

☑ **Anxious** [`æŋkʃəs]　adj. 焦慮的；掛念的

She is always anxious about her future.

她總是為了未來而焦慮。

☑ **Panic** [`pænɪk]　n./vi. 恐慌

Don't panic. Just do as I say.

不要慌。照著我的話做就好了。

☑ **Fulfill** [ful͵fɪl]　vt. 履行；實踐

He promised his daughter that her birthday wishes will be fulfilled.

他對女兒承諾她的生日願望將會實現。

☑ **Woes** [wos]　n. 困難；災難；悲哀

A lucky person tends to turn his woes into opportunities.

幸運的人通常會將逆境變為轉機。

②
喜怒哀樂

Unit 10 安慰

這樣說英文

Ⓐ There, there! Don't weep. Tell me what's going on.
Ⓑ My house got blown away by a tornado!
Ⓐ Well, at least you don't have to pay your mortgage anymore.

Ⓐ 好了好了！不要再哭泣了。告訴我究竟是怎麼回事 。
Ⓑ 我的房子被龍捲風吹走了。
Ⓐ 喔，至少你再也不用付房貸了。

....

Ⓐ My girlfriend left me for another.
Ⓑ Didn't she rack up your credit cards? You should be happy she's spending someone else's money now.
Ⓐ Yeah, you have a point there. Thanks, I feel much better now.

Ⓐ 我的女友跟別人跑了。
Ⓑ 她不是把你的信用卡刷爆了嗎？你應該高興現在她花的是別人的錢。
Ⓐ 對喔，有道理。感謝你，我已經感到好多了。

....

Ⓐ Now that is one sweet ride! He just likes to drive luxurious sports cars, nothing less. I wish I had one someday.
Ⓑ The insurance for that car costs a bomb, and with gas prices heading north you'd be crying at the pumps with a guzzler like that. Besides, you'll be going nowhere fast in this traffic.
Ⓐ You are right. Taking public transportation beats driving a sports car any day, especially in this horrific jam.

Ⓐ 那真是個愉快的兜風！他只喜歡最高級的跑車。我希望有一天我有一輛。
Ⓑ 那部車的保險費很貴，然後加上汽油價格節節飆升，有這種油耗量高的車你會付油錢付到手軟。另外，這種交通狀況你也開不快。
Ⓐ 你說的對。任何時候搭乘大眾運輸系統勝過開超跑，尤其是碰上可怕的塞車。

註 price heading north 字面是價錢往北，形容價格節節上升或是飆升。guzzler 則是很耗油的車。

Vocabulary

Weep [wip]　vi. 哭泣；流淚
Mortgage [`mɔrgɪdʒ]　n. 抵押借款
Rack up　ph. 累計；傷害

Sweet [swit]　adj. 甜的；新鮮的；愉快的
Beat [bit]　vt. 打敗；勝過

這樣用句型

There, there! _____.

· Everything will be ok　好了，好了，一切都會沒事的。

· Don't feel bad　好了，好了，不要自責了。

· Things are not as bad as it seems　好了，好了，事情並沒有那麼糟。

· Stop worrying so much　好了，好了，不要再擔心那麼多了。

· She didn't mean to yell at you　好了，好了，她並不是故意要吼你的。

Didn't _____? You should _____.

· she scold you... stop being a jerk
她不是才剛罵你嗎？你的態度不應該再那麼惡劣。

· I tell you to quit... just listen to me
我不是才叫你停下來嗎？你應該要聽我的。

· you hear the music... start dancing
你剛沒聽到音樂嗎？你應該開始跳舞。

· they issue a warrant for you... turn yourself in
他們不是才開出你的拘捕令嗎？你應該去自首。

He likes _____, nothing less.

- extravagant parties　他只喜歡非常奢華的派對。
- silk covers　他只喜歡純絲質的被子。
- 5-star hotels　他只喜歡不亞於五星級的酒店。
- complete servitude　他只喜歡完全的奴役權。
- expensive Italian suits　他只喜歡昂貴的義大利製西服。

用這句話更厲害！

❶ Riding in a crammed subway car isn't very comfortable, but it gets you to your destination quickly during rush hour.
乘坐擁擠的地鐵並不很舒服，但是它能避開交通阻塞將你送到目的地。

❷ Count your blessings. There is still hope.
多往好處想，還是會有希望的。

❸ Tomorrow is another day. She will eventually forget about all these.　明天又是嶄新的一天，她會漸漸忘記這一切的。

❹ Look on the bright side! At least you are still alive and able.
樂觀一點！至少你還活著並且具有能力。

❺ She gave comfort to the grieving mother.
她安慰著悲傷的母親。

❻ Cheer up! We will figure out a way to solve this mess.
振作一點！我們會想辦法解決這個困境的。

❼ You have to believe in yourself. No pain no gain.
你要相信自己，沒有付出就沒有收穫。

❽ Cold comfort is when you tell a starving man he should get a job.　當你叫一個飢餓的人去找份工作是種冷漠的安慰。

❾ I find it comforting to know that he is in charge.
知道是他負責的便使我安心。

⑩ Fried chicken with beer is comfort food to me.

炸雞配啤酒是可為我帶來慰藉的食物。

⑪ You can't advance if you don't get out of your comfort zone.

如果你不離開你的舒適圈，你將無法突破。

⑫ I can always turn to her for comfort.

我通常能向她取暖（得到安慰）。

必背單字片語

☑ **Crammed** [kræmd]　adj. 擠滿的
She lives in a crammed one room apartment.
她住在擁擠的公寓套房中。

- -

☑ **Grieve** [griv]　vi. 悲傷；哀悼
He is going through a grieving period. 他正在哀悼。

- -

☑ **Cheer up**　ph. 使某人更高興起來
Lecturing is not an effective way to cheer someone up.
說教並不能有效的振奮人心。

- -

☑ **Starve** [stɑrv]　vt. 使挨餓；使餓死
She starved the animals to death.
她將動物們餓死。

- -

☑ **Advance** [əd`væns]　vi. 推進；進步；提升
How can you advance if you keep wasting time?
你如果一直浪費時間，要怎麼進步呢？

- -

☑ **Zone** [zon]　n. 地區；範圍
You need to get out of the danger zone.
你需要離開危險地帶。

Unit 11 感謝

這樣說英文

118

Ⓐ I am thankful for all the help you rendered.
Ⓑ I'm glad to help. Don't hesitate to ask me if you need anything else.
Ⓐ I'm hoping you would say that.

Ⓐ 我很感謝你所給予的所有幫助。
Ⓑ 我很樂意幫助。如果需要其他幫忙，請儘管告訴我。
Ⓐ 我就是希望聽你這麼說。

Ⓐ She really appreciates the money you loaned her.
Ⓑ And, I'm grateful for all the years she has looked after me.
Ⓐ Since we're on this subject, I was wondering if you could lend me some money too.

Ⓐ 她真的很感激你借她錢。
Ⓑ 我也很感恩這些年來她如此照顧我。
Ⓐ 既然我們已經談到這個話題，我在想你能否也借我點錢。

Ⓐ How gratuitous! There's a hundred dollar bill on the floor!
Ⓑ Someone must have dropped it. I think you should return it to...
Ⓐ What an unexpected stroke of luck! I am so grateful for the extra cash!

Ⓐ 真是天上掉下來的禮物，地上有 100 元的鈔票！
Ⓑ 一定是有人掉了。我認為你應該還回去⋯
Ⓐ 真是意外的好運，我很感恩有多出來的現金！

Vocabulary

Render [`rɛndɚ]　v. 提供服務；表達
Appreciate [əˋpriʃɪˌet]　v. 感激；欣賞
Grateful [ˋgretfəl]　adj. 感謝的；感激的

Gratuitous [grəˋtjuətəs]　adj. 免費的；無報酬的
Unexpected [ˌʌnɪkˋspɛktɪd]　adj. 意想不到的；突如其來的

這樣用句型

I am thankful _____.

- for all the birthday gifts　我很感謝收到這些生日禮物。
- to be alive　我很感謝還活著。
- although I don't have much　雖然我有的不多，我心存感激。
- because I am old and I am healthy　我很感謝因為我很老卻很健康。
- the hurricane is gone　我很感謝暴風雨已經平息。

Since we're on this subject, _____.

- can we talk about it　既然我們已經談到這個話題，我們能談談嗎？
- do you mind if we discuss it
  既然我們已經談到這個話題，我們討論一下你介意嗎？
- let's spend some time on it
  既然我們已經談到這個話題，讓我們花點時間在這上面。
- why don't you elaborate on it
  既然我們已經談到這個話題，為何你不詳細的說明一下？
- I was hoping you'd help me understand it better
  既然我們已經談到這個話題，我本來是希望你可以幫我更了解一點。

What _____! I am _____!

- luck... totally psyched　真幸運！令我欣喜若狂！
- a calamity... flabbergasted　真是場大災難！令我大吃一驚！

- a coincidence... speechless　真巧！令我目瞪口呆！
- a beauty... in awe　真美！令我大為驚嘆！
- a travesty... in shock　真是拙劣的模仿！令我錯愕！

用這句話更厲害！

❶ Give thanks for everything you have received.
對你所擁有的每件事心存感謝。

❷ You ingrate! I will never help you again!
忘恩負義的傢伙！我再也不幫你了！

❸ Gratitude is an attitude that is worth embracing.
感恩是值得接受的態度。

❹ There's a 5% gratuity tagged onto the bill.
這帳單上的金額附加 5% 的小費。

❺ I want to express my gratitude for your generosity.
我想為你的慷慨的行為表示感激。

❻ I cannot thank you enough for saving me.
非常感謝你救了我。

❼ How can you be so ungrateful towards your guardians?
你怎能對你的監護人如此忘恩負義？

❽ We value your participation in our program.
我們重視你對這個節目的參與。

❾ How would you show your appreciation?
你會如何表示你的感激？

❿ Thanks, but no, thanks.　謝謝你，但是我不用。

⓫ He looked her in the eye and immediately she knew he was grateful.
他看著她的眼睛，她立刻知道他心存感激。

⓬ Thanks so much. I knew I could count on you!
多謝，我就知道能指望你！

必背單字片語

☑ **Embrace** [ɪm`bres]　vt. 擁抱；包括；欣然接受
She wished she had given him a warm embrace that lasted an eternity.
她希望能給他一個永遠不分開的擁抱。

☑ **Tag** [tæg]　vt. 加標籤
The chicken is tagged with conflicting price labels.
這隻雞被標了不一樣的價標。

☑ **Express** [ɪk`sprɛs]　vt. 陳述；表達
He expresses his love for her with a hundred red roses.
他以 100 朵來表達對她的愛意。

☑ **Generosity** [ˌdʒɛnə`rɑsətɪ]　n. 慷慨大方的行為
The fund raisers are appealing to his generosity.
這些勸募者正在懇求他的慷慨行為。

☑ **Guardian** [`gɑrdɪən]　n. 監護人；保護者
She acts like my guardian angel and protects me from harm.
她就像我的守護天使般保護著我不讓我受害。

☑ **Participate** [pɑr`tɪsəˌpet]　vi. 參與
Do you want to participate in that competition?
你想參加這項競賽嗎？

Unit 12 讚嘆與欣賞

這樣說英文

Ⓐ She admires men who are adventurous, confident, humorous and generous.

Ⓑ That's too bad, because you're conservative, timid, boring and a scrooge.

Ⓐ It takes one to know one.

Ⓐ 她欣賞勇於冒險、有自信、具幽默感和大方的男性。

Ⓑ 那太慘了，因為你既保守、畏縮、無趣又是個吝嗇鬼。

Ⓐ 你我臭氣相投。

. . . .

Ⓐ I think she's admiring your garden.

Ⓑ Not just she, but everyone is admiring my garden too! Look at how colorful and lush it is.

Ⓐ I bet you spend all your time tending to it.

Ⓐ 我認為她很欣賞你的花園。

Ⓑ 不只是她而已，每個人也都欣賞我的花園！看看它是多麼的色彩繽紛和茂盛。

Ⓐ 我猜你花所有的時間照料這花園。

. . . .

Ⓐ I despise that man. Oh! I don't want to look at him.

Ⓑ Am I hearing things? Everyone admires him! He's a hero around here.

Ⓐ I think his speeches are disingenuous. Also, I find him highly pretentious.

Ⓐ 我看不起那個男人。喔！我不想看到他。

Ⓑ 我聽錯了嗎？每個人都很欣賞他，他是這裡的英雄。

Ⓐ 我認為他的演說很虛偽，而且我覺得他非常狂妄。

Vocabulary

Scrooge [skrudʒ] n. 吝嗇鬼
Lush [lʌʃ] adj. 蒼翠繁茂的
Tend [tɛnd] vt. 照料；管理

Disingenuous [ˌdɪsɪn`dʒɛnjʊəs] adj. 虛偽的
Pretentious [prɪ`tɛnʃəs] adj. 做作的；自命不凡的

這樣用句型

> **That's too bad, because _____.**

· she almost made it to the finish line　真糟糕，因為她就快要到終點了。
· he was going to ask you out　真糟糕，因為他本來要邀你去約會的。
· you just missed the last train　真糟糕，因為你剛剛錯過最後一班火車。
· that man just took the last concert tickets
　真糟糕，因為那個人剛買走最後的演唱會門票。

> **Not just _____ but _____ too.**

· her... him　不只是她，他也是。
· our money got stolen... theirs　不只是我們的錢被偷，他們的錢也被偷。
· today... tomorrow　不只有今天，明天也是。
· this car... that car got totaled　不只是這部車，另外一部車也全毀。

> **I think _____. Also, _____.**

· she's crazy... she's probably dangerous
　我認為她瘋了，而且她也許很危險。

2 喜怒哀樂

- I'm pregnant... I think my sister's pregnant as well
  我想我懷孕了，而且我覺得我姊姊也懷孕了。
- I'm done for the day... you should stop and rest too
  我想今天做這樣就好，另外，你也應該停下來休息。

用這句話更厲害！

1 I admire his brand new sports utility vehicle.
我稱讚他的全新休旅車。

2 He is basking in admiration of the swooning girls.
他沉浸於對他心醉神迷女孩的讚賞中。

3 She admires your courage.
她欽佩你的勇氣。

4 He despises her for no apparent reason.
他不因特別的理由而鄙視她。

5 I admire the view from your condo.
我讚嘆你公寓看出去的景觀。

6 I hold our country's leaders in high esteem.
我非常尊敬我們國家的領導者。

7 She respects people who walk the talk.
她尊重說到做到的人。

8 I loathe women who marry for money and then take everything but the kitchen sink when they divorce their spouses.
我厭惡那些為錢結婚然後離婚時把另一半的一切都拿走的女人。

9 They deserved admiration from the crowd. Instead, they got booed off the stage.
他們應該得到群眾們的讚嘆，但他們卻被噓聲趕下台。

10 I admire your work, but I admire her work even more.
我很欣賞你的作品，但我更欣賞她的。

⑪ This school is admired for the achievements of its students.

這所學校因為學生的成就而備受讚嘆。

⑫ Stop admiring yourself in the mirror.

不要對著鏡子自我欣賞了。

必背單字片語

☑ **Swoon** [swun]　vi. 昏倒；心醉神迷

She swooned right into the arms of a handsome young man.

她昏倒在一個英俊年少的男子懷裡。

- -

☑ **Courage** [ˏkɝ-ɪdʒ]　n. 勇氣；膽量

They lack the courage to venture into the darkness.

他們沒有進入黑暗裡探險的膽量。

- -

☑ **Apparent** [ə`pærənt]　adj. 明顯的；顯而易見的；表面的

Why did you perform such a shameless act? Have you no esteem?

你為何做出如此不恥的行為？你沒尊嚴嗎？

- -

☑ **Esteem** [ɪs`tim]　n. 尊重；價值

The fund raisers are appealing to his generosity.

這些勸募者正在懇求他的慷慨行為。

- -

☑ **Everything but the kitchen sink**　ph. 可以拿走的東西

The burglars took everything but the kitchen sink.

小偷將可拿走的東西都拿走了。

- -

☑ **Achievement** [ə`tʃivmənt]　n. 完成；成就

The company awarded us for our career achievements.

公司表揚我們的工作成就。

Unit 13 真有意思

這樣說英文

Ⓐ I heard that her husband ran away with another woman.
Ⓑ Now, that is interesting! Isn't that what happened to you too?
Ⓐ What happens to me is really none of your business.

Ⓐ 我聽說他老公跟另一個女人跑了。
Ⓑ 真有意思！那不是跟你的遭遇雷同嗎？
Ⓐ 我的遭遇實在是與你無關。

....

Ⓐ Do you know the world's largest living organism is a mushroom in Oregon?
Ⓑ Wow, I never knew that. I thought it was an elephant.
Ⓐ I thought it was a whale!

Ⓐ 你知道世界上最大的生物是在美國奧勒岡州的巨型蘑菇嗎？
Ⓑ 哇，我從不知道，我以為是大象呢。
Ⓐ 我曾以為是鯨魚！

....

Ⓐ I want to know how much money he made last year.
Ⓑ I think he raked in a million dollars just by operating an online store
Ⓐ That's intriguing. Can he teach me how to do that?

Ⓐ 我想知道他去年賺多少錢。
Ⓑ 我想他光靠網路店面就賺進百萬元。
Ⓐ 真是令人感興趣，他能教我怎麼做嗎？

Vocabulary

Run away　ph. 逃跑；逃避	Rake in　ph. 大量地斂集（錢財）
None of your business　ph. 不關你的事	Intriguing [ɪn`trɪgɪŋ]　adj. 引起好奇心的；
Organism [`ɔrgən͵ɪzəm]　n. 生物；有機體	令人感興趣的

這樣用句型

I heard that _____.

- you lost your job. Is that true　我聽說你失業了，是真的嗎？
- she won the competition　我聽說她比賽贏了。
- he travelled around the world　我聽說他環遊世界了。
- they went on strike　我聽說他們罷工了。
- she speaks five languages　我聽說她會說五種語言。

Do you know _____?

- who I am　你知道我是誰嗎？
- where she is going　你知道她要去哪嗎？
- how to make space cakes　你知道怎麼做「太空蛋糕」嗎？

註 「太空蛋糕」是一種在麵糊中加入大麻和烈酒所烘焙而成的蛋糕，吃了會使人飄飄欲仙，就彷彿身於太空中漂浮而得名。

- what is going on　你知道發生什麼事嗎？
- when the concert is starting　你知道演唱會何時開始嗎？

I want to know _____.

- how to get there by bike　我想知道騎腳踏車怎麼到那裡。
- if she will marry me　我想知道她是否會嫁給我。
- when my problems will disappear　我想知道我們問題何時會解決。

2
喜怒哀樂

- whether he would quit smoking　我想知道他是否會戒菸。
- what movies are showing at the cinema
  我想知道戲院裡正在上映哪些電影。

用這句話更厲害！

❶ How interesting! Tell me more!
真有趣！再告訴我多一點！

❷ I am literally bored to death.
我實在是無聊到掛。

❸ He has absolutely no interest in the news of her new baby.
他對她剛出生寶寶的訊息完全沒有興趣。

❹ She captivated audiences all over the country.
她使全國各地的觀眾著迷。

❺ Fairytales kept the little girl spellbound.
童話故事使小女孩入迷。

❻ Some people find gambling stimulating. I, on the other hand, find it boring.
有些人覺得賭博很刺激，我卻覺得很無趣。

❼ The new ride at the amusement park is attracting plenty of thrill-seekers.
遊樂園裡的新設施吸引了許多找尋刺激的人前來。

❽ Newspaper headlines make articles more interesting than they really are.
新聞頭條使文章聽起來更吸引人。

❾ She did not even bat an eyelid when she heard the news.
她聽到消息時面不改色。

❿ She exaggerated the facts just to make it sound interesting.
她誇大事實使它聽起來有趣。

⓫ He received the horrible news with his usual nonchalance.
他聽到噩耗時跟平時一般冷靜。

⓬ This book is a real page-turner.
這本書真的很有趣。

必背單字片語

☑ **Literally** [ˋlɪtərəlɪ]　adv. 實在地；照字面上地；逐字地
That man took the criticism literally and got mad.
那個人照字面聽取批評後變得很生氣。

- -

☑ **Captivate** [ˋkæptəˏvet]　vt. 使著迷
She has captivating blue eyes. 她有迷人的藍眼睛。

- -

☑ **Spellbound** [ˋspɛlˏbaʊnd]　adj. 入迷的
She was a seducer that held many men spellbound.
她勾引許多男人為她著迷。

- -

☑ **Not bat an eyelid** [nɑt bæt ənˋaɪˏlɪd]　ph. 面不改色；泰然處之
Jack hit the jackpot but he didn't even bat an eyelid.
傑克意外得到一筆大錢，但他泰然處之。

- -

☑ **Exaggerate** [ɪgˋzædʒəˏret]　vt. 誇大；對⋯言過其實
I didn't lie but merely exaggerated the facts a little.
我沒說謊，只是將事實誇大一點。

- -

☑ **Nonchalant** [ˋnɑnʃələnt]　adj. 冷靜的；漠不關心的
He faced his angry girlfriend with a nonchalant stare.
他冷漠地看著發飆的女友。

Unit 14 滿意

這樣說英文

Ⓐ I am so thirsty. Can somebody give me a drink?
Ⓑ There's some iced water there. Knock yourself out.
Ⓐ Ah! That feels so good! Much obliged! Now can I have some food?

Ⓐ 好渴喔，有飲料嗎？
Ⓑ 這裡有些冰水，請便。
Ⓐ 啊，真好喝！多謝多謝！那有東西吃嗎？

....

Ⓐ My boss fired me. What a bummer.
Ⓑ Really? Is that right? I heard your boss got the pink slip himself.
Ⓐ That news is strangely satisfying.

Ⓐ 我被老闆開除，真不爽。
Ⓑ 真的嗎？確定？我聽說你老闆自己也被解雇。
Ⓐ 這個消息很奇妙地大快人心。

....

Ⓐ The airline messed up and canceled my reservation so I couldn't get on the plane.
Ⓑ Oh no, that's aggravating. But, you don't look upset at all.
Ⓐ On the contrary, I am so delighted and speechless. To compensate, they rebooked me on another flight and upgraded me to first class for free!

Ⓐ 航空公司搞砸了，把我的訂位取消，所以我無法登機。
Ⓑ 哇，真是令人生氣。但是，你看起來一點都不生氣。
Ⓐ 相反的，我滿意到說不出話來。他們將我重新訂了另一個航班並免費升等到頭等艙作為補償！

Vocabulary

Knock yourself out　ph. 請便
Bummer [`bʌmɚ]　n. 令人失望或煩惱的情形

Satisfying [`sætɪsˏfaɪɪŋ]　adj. 滿意的
aggravating [`ægrəˏvetɪŋ]　adj. 可惱的

這樣用句型

128

> **I am _____. Can somebody _____?**

- so tired... give me a hand　我好累喔，有人能幫我嗎？
- so lonely... find me a girlfriend　我好孤單喔，誰能幫我找個女朋友嗎？
- very hungry... make me a sandwich　我好餓喔，誰能幫我做個三明治？
- overwhelmed... please come to my rescue
  我受不了了，拜託誰來救救我？
- confused... explain this question to me　我好困惑，誰能來幫我解惑？

> **Really? Is that right? _____?**

- He got into a fight with the law　真的嗎？確定？他觸犯法律嗎？
- She married him　真的嗎？確定？她嫁給了他？
- He got a tummytuck　真的嗎？確定？他去做腹部整型？
- They are planning a strike　真的嗎？確定？他們正在計畫罷工？
- He has become a millionaire　真的嗎？確定？他變成了百萬富翁？

> **I am so _____ I _____.**

- sleepy... can fall asleep now　我已經想睡到現在都能馬上睡著。
- hungry... can eat a horse　我已經餓到快昏過去了。

註 I can eat a horse　意思是餓到能吃下一匹馬，意味著快餓昏過去的意思。

- sick... can barely move　我已經病到不能動了。

- drunk... can't walk straight　我已經醉到不能走直線了。
- fat... can't see my feet　我已經胖到看不到自己的腳了。

用這句話更厲害！

❶ I'm so ecstatic I got all my assignments done in time.
我很開心能按時把所有作業完成。

❷ Curiosity killed the cat. Satisfaction brought it back.
好奇心殺死貓，但是只要好奇心被滿足就沒事。

❸ Ah! That was a fantastic meal.
啊！真是頓很棒的餐點。

❹ He is contented with his life.
他對自己的人生很滿足。

❺ I can't tell you how pleased I am with his work.
我對他的工作滿意到言語無法形容。

❻ Always be satisfied with what you have.
經常對所擁有的感到滿足。

❼ He is deliriously happy with his exam results.
他對自己考試成績極為滿意。

❽ She satisfied her contractual obligations.
她履行了合約上的義務。

❾ Find the variables that satisfy the equation.
找出解這個公式的變數。

❿ His lies failed to satisfy her inquisitiveness.
他的謊言無法消除她的好奇多問。

⓫ Satisfy your hunger with this feast.
吃大餐來消除飢餓。

⓬ You can satisfy a man through his stomach.
你能以抓住男人的胃來滿足他。

必背單字片語

☑ **Assignment** [ə`saɪnmənt]　n. 任務；工作；作業
Have you finished your assignments yet?
你功課寫完了嗎？

☑ **Curiosity** [ˌkjʊrɪ`asətɪ]　n. 好奇心
Children should nurture their scientific curiosity.
小孩子應該培養對科學的好奇心。

☑ **Contented** [kən`tɛntɪd]　adj. 滿足的；知足的
You can be contented with what you have, or angry about what you don't.
你能因為所擁有的而滿足，或是因為所沒有的而生氣。

☑ **Delirious** [dɪ`lɪrɪəs]　adj. 神智混亂的；特別高興地
The old, delirious man mumbled incomprehensibly.
這位神智混亂的老人口中含糊地說著聽不懂的話。

☑ **Obligation** [ˌɑblə`geʃən]　n. 義務；責任
I have an obligation to follow the rules to the letter.
我有義務要嚴謹地遵從規則。

☑ **Inquisitive** [ɪn`kwɪzətɪv]　adj. 好問的；過分好奇的；愛打聽的
Stop being so inquisitive! You are starting to get on my nerve.
不要問那麼多！很煩耶。

Unit 15　感動

這樣說英文

Ⓐ Why is he still holding on to this job? The hours are long and the pay pathetic.

Ⓑ His wife is terminally ill and his parents are bedridden. He has five kids to feed and he is up to his eyeballs in debt. Yet, he takes it all in stride and refuses to give up.

Ⓐ Where can you find tenacity like that?

Ⓐ 他為何還在做那份工作？工時長，薪水又少的可憐。

Ⓑ 他的老婆癌末，雙親又長期臥病在床。他有五個小孩要養，又欠一屁股債。儘管如此，他還是從容面對並不放棄。

Ⓐ 你去哪能找到這種韌性？

....

Ⓐ He sold all his possessions and gave all the proceeds to charity.

Ⓑ No way! He isn't rich, and yet he gives generously.

Ⓐ To top that, he's working full time to take care of kids at the local orphanage.

Ⓐ 他賣了所有的財物並全捐給了慈善單位。

Ⓑ 怎麼可能！他又不是很有錢，還這麼大方捐獻。

Ⓐ 不僅如此，他還全職在孤兒院裡照顧那些孩子。

....

Ⓐ Because of war, this couple lost contact with each other for over fifty years.

Ⓑ I heard they refused to give up hope of seeing each other again.

Ⓐ Yeah, it's amazing they could reunite after half a century.

Ⓐ 因為戰爭，這對情侶離散超過 50 年。

Ⓑ 我聽說他們拒絕放棄再次相聚的機會。

Ⓐ 對呀，過了半世紀還能重逢真是太驚人了。

Pathetic [pə`θɛtɪk]　adj. 可憐的；不足的；
【俚】乏味的
Take it in stride　ph. 從容面對
Tenacity [tɪ`næsətɪ]　n. 固執；不屈不饒；韌性

Proceeds [`prosidz]　n.【複】做某事或出售某物的收益
Reunite [ˌriju`naɪt]　vt. 再結合；再重聚

這樣用句型

2 喜怒哀樂

> **Where can you find** _____ **like** _____?

· a dedicated employee... him　你去哪找像他一樣認真付出的員工？

· another generous man... your father　你去哪找像你父親一樣大方的人？

· someone beautiful... your wife　你去哪找像你老婆一樣美麗的人？

· a dog... Snoopy　你去哪裡找像史奴比一樣的狗？

> **To top that,** _____.

· I'll run another 10 miles　不僅如此，我還會再多跑十哩路。

· she'll climb Mount Everest　不僅如此，她還要去攀登艾佛勒斯峰。

· he'll eat another porterhouse
不僅如此，他還要吃另外一客上等腰肉牛排。

· she has mansions all over Europe
不僅如此，她還在歐洲各地擁有豪宅。

> **They refused to give up hope of** _____.

- winning the lottery　他們拒絕放棄贏得樂透的希望。
- having another kid　他們拒絕放棄再生一個小孩的希望。
- getting pregnant　他們拒絕放棄懷孕的希望。
- migrating to Europe　他們拒絕放棄移民到歐洲的希望。

用這句話更厲害！

❶ I am so touched I am about to cry.
我感動的都要哭了。

❷ She was moved by the tear-jerking story.
她被感人的故事所感動。

❸ He is touched by her thoughtfulness.
他被她的貼心著想而感動。

❹ Her gesture of offering homeless people a warm meal impressed me.
她提供流浪漢熱食的舉動讓我印象深刻。

❺ They fought to hold back the tears upon seeing her selfless action.　看見她無私的行為，他們努力地忍住淚水。

❻ I cringe at movies with touchy-feely endings.
我有點怕過於情感化結局的電影。

❼ Her comments are very touching but the judge still refuses to exonerate her.
雖然他的評論非常感人，但是法官仍拒絕免除對她的指控。

❽ We are moved by fact that her charity organization campaigned to help thousands of homeless women.
我們被她幫助幾千個無家可歸的女人的慈善事業所感動。

❾ Her inspiring book truly touches my heart.
她所寫鼓舞人心的書真正感動了我。

❿ She is moved by the beautiful composition.
她被優美的文章所感動。

⓫ He's hoping that his girlfriend will be moved by fresh flowers. 他希望以鮮花感動他的女友。

⓬ She didn't feel moved because she felt that his gestures were contrived. 她並沒有被他感動因為覺得他的行為有點做作。

必背單字片語

☑ **Tearjerker** [ˋtɪrˌdʒɝˋkɚ] n. 賺人熱淚的電影或戲劇
He has volumes of tearjerkers in his movie collection.
他有好幾部賺人熱淚的電影收藏。

☑ **Homeless** [ˋhomlɪs] adj. 無家可歸的
This homeless man pushes a shopping cart aimlessly around the neighborhood.
這位流浪漢在鄰近街坊漫無目的地推著購物車。

☑ **Touchy-feely** [ˋtʌtʃɪˌfilɪ] adj. 過於情感化的
He unplugged the radio because it kept playing touchy-feely ballads.
他把收音機關掉因為電台一直撥放肉麻的樂曲。

☑ **Campaign** [kæmˋpen] vi. 從事運動
The union leaders are campaigning for better working conditons. 工會領導人為爭取改善工作條件而積極活動。

☑ **Composition** [ˌkɑmpəˋzɪʃən] n. 寫作；作曲；作品
I prefer classical compositions to the trash you hear on the radio.
比起電台裡聽到的垃圾，我比較喜歡古典樂曲。

☑ **Contrived** [kənˋtraɪvd] adj. 做作的；不自然的。
I find his politician's actions rather contrived and the speeches disingenuous.
我覺得這個政治家的行為還蠻做作的，言詞也很虛偽。

2 喜怒哀樂

Unit 16 好酷

這樣說英文

Ⓐ What a ride! I haven't had so much fun for a long time. Let's go again.

Ⓑ I thought you didn't like roller coaster rides but I guess I was mistaken.

Ⓐ Are you kidding me? This is so awesome!

Ⓐ 好好玩！我已經很久沒有玩的這麼過癮。讓我們再坐一次。

Ⓑ 我以為你不喜歡雲霄飛車，我想我錯了。

Ⓐ 開什麼玩笑？這很酷呢！

....

Ⓐ He has put on a suit, a silk tie, a pair of crocodile skin shoes and a pair of shades.

Ⓑ It sounds like he is trying to impress people by looking cool.

Ⓐ He looks ridiculous if you ask me.

Ⓐ 他穿上了西裝、絲質領帶、一雙鱷魚皮製的皮鞋和墨鏡。

Ⓑ 聽起來他好像試著讓人們留下他很酷的印象。

Ⓐ 我倒覺得他看起來很滑稽。

....

Ⓐ Come check out my new ride.

Ⓑ Oh my goodness! You bought that new luxury car we saw at the showroom. It's all tricked out with all the bells and whistles. Can I have a test drive?

Ⓐ Sure, when hell freezes over.

Ⓐ 來看我的新車。

Ⓑ 我的天呀！你買了我們去展示中心看到的那部新的豪華轎車。它配有全部最先進的設備。我能試開看看嗎？

Ⓐ 當然不行！

註 when hell freezes over 字面上是指當地獄結冰的那一天，因為基本上不會有那一天的到來，所以意指不可能的意思。

Vocabulary

Roller coaster   ph. 雲霄飛車
Shades [ʃedz]   n. 遮光物；太陽眼鏡
Ridiculous [rɪ`dɪkjələs]   adj. 可笑的；滑稽的

Tricked out   ph. 打扮；裝飾
Bells and whistles   ph. 花俏即能引人注目
的附加設備；先進的功能

這樣用句型

I thought ＿＿＿＿＿＿＿ but ＿＿＿＿＿＿＿.

· I could make it... I didn't   我以為我能做到，但我沒做到。

· she was the one... she wasn't   我以為她就是那個人，但她不是。

· the show was at three... it started at two
我以為表演三點開始，但它兩點就開始了。

· it was missing... it was in front of me all the while
我以為它不見了，結果它一直在我面前。

It sounds like ＿＿＿＿＿＿＿＿＿＿＿.

· you're going to jail   聽起來你要去坐牢了。

· she's got her eyes on you   聽起來她在注意著你。

· a real piano but it's actually a recording
這聽起來像是現場鋼琴演奏，但是它其實是錄音的。

· a screeching cat but it's really just me on the violin
這聽起來像是尖叫的貓，但其實在只是我在拉小提琴。

You ＿＿＿＿ that ＿＿＿＿ we saw ＿＿＿＿?

- asked... girl out whom... at the party
  你約了我們在派對上看到的那個女孩出去？
- dented... car... parked on his driveway
  你撞凹了停在他家門口的那部車？
- stole... diamond ring... at the jewelers
  你偷了我們在珠寶店看到的那指鑽戒？

用這句話更厲害！

1 I'm impressed that you can solve a Rubik's cube in less than a minute. 我覺得你能在一分鐘之內解開魔術方塊好厲害。

2 I got to fly first class to Europe for an unbelievably cheap price. That is so cool!
我買到一張超便宜去歐洲的頭等艙機票，真是太酷了！

3 She got me a fantastic-looking racing bike for my birthday.
我生日時她買了台超炫的競速單車給我。

4 This is an awesome cruise ship and I'm feeling lucky to be on it. 這是艘超酷的郵輪，而我能搭乘實在是太幸運了。

5 I have the fastest, meanest racing motorcycle in the whole neighborhood. 我有這個社區裡最快速、最好的競速摩托車。

6 You look absolutely wicked in that leather jacket and sunglasses. 你穿皮夾克和墨鏡看起來簡直酷極了。

7 I wouldn't line up to buy anything, even if they were cool new Apple products.
我不會為了買任何東西而去排隊，即便是很酷的全新蘋果商品。

8 My jaw dropped at the sight of his diamond encrusted iPhone. 我看他那台鑽石外殼的 iPhone 看得瞠目結舌。

9 Dude, it's uncool to treat your parents like trash.
小子，對待雙親如無物一點都不酷。

⑩ I think I look great in leather but girls think I just look preposterous.

我認為我穿皮革的衣服看起來很帥，但是女孩們覺得我看起來很可笑。

⑪ She can play two pianos with two hands simultaneously. How cool is that! 她能同時用兩隻手在兩台鋼琴上演奏，真是酷斃了！

必背單字片語

☑ **Rubik's cube** ph. 魔術方塊
I don't know how to solve the 9X9 Rubik's cube.
我不知道如何解開 9X9 魔術方塊。

- -

☑ **Unbelievably** [ˌʌnbɪˋlivəblɪ] adv. 非常驚人地
The price for a bag of popcorn is unbelievably expensive at the concession stand.
電影院的零食攤販賣的爆米花價錢貴得嚇人。

- -

☑ **Mean** [min] adj. 卑鄙；【美非正式】很好的
She is probably the rudest, meanest girl I have ever gone out with.
她大概是我曾經約會過的女孩中最沒禮貌也最壞的一個。

- -

☑ **Encrusted** [ɪnˋkrʌstɪd] adj. 帶有外殼的
Meat eaters love the new hotdog encrusted pepperoni pizza.
愛吃肉的老饕愛上新的用義大利臘腸比薩包起來的熱狗。

- -

☑ **Preposterous** [prɪˋpɑstərəs] adj. 荒謬的；可笑的
The company has a preposterous hiring policy that states that new recruits have absolutely no vacation days in their first year of employment.
公司有個可笑的雇用政策聲明新進員工第一年完全沒有休假。

Unit 17 運氣真好

這樣說英文

136

Ⓐ I can't believe he won two lotteries in a row!
Ⓑ His wife also won two lotteries in a row! What are the odds!
Ⓐ How incredibly lucky! I've never won anything in my life.

Ⓐ 我真不敢相信他連續贏了樂透兩次！
Ⓑ 他的老婆也連續贏了兩次。怎麼可能？
Ⓐ 真是超級幸運！我這輩子都沒贏過任何東西。

....

Ⓐ She's taking her finals tomorrow, so she's going to the temple to pray for good luck.
Ⓑ Didn't she flunk her exams multiple times?
Ⓐ Apparently she prays hard but she doesn't study at all.

Ⓐ 她明天有期末考，所以她要去廟裡拜拜祈求考運順利。
Ⓑ 她不是當掉好幾個考試嗎？
Ⓐ 很明顯的，她很努力祈求但從不讀書。

....

Ⓐ I have my lucky underwear on so I should be able to win the tournament.
Ⓑ Are you joking? What do boxers have to do with luck?
Ⓐ You should leave your rabbit's foot at home, then.

Ⓐ 我穿了幸運內褲，所以我應該能贏得比賽。
Ⓑ 開玩笑吧？內褲跟運氣有什麼關係？
Ⓐ 那你應該把你的兔腳留在家裡。（如果你不相信迷信的話）

> 註 Rabbit's foot（兔子的左後腳）被視為一種會帶來好運幸運符，是一種迷信，尤其盛行於北美洲的胡毒（hoodoo）文化。

Vocabulary

Odds [adz] n. （複）可能性；困難	Tournament [`tɝnəmənt] n. 比賽；錦標賽
Multiple [`mʌltəpl] adj. 多次數的；複合的	Boxer [`baksɚ] n. 四角褲

這樣用句型

> **How incredibly _____! I never _____.**

- rude... have encountered such insolence
  怎麼如此無禮！我從來沒遭遇這種無禮的待遇。

- fast... thought I would arrive so quickly
  怎麼這麼快！我從沒想過會這麼快到達。

- presumptuous... want to meet him again
  怎麼這麼傲慢！我再也不想見到他了。

- hedonistic... should have associated myself with her
  怎麼如此享樂主義！我應該不要再與她產生任何關聯。

> **Apparently, she _____ but _____.**

- lost her grip... she didn't fall into the ravine
  她明顯地無法掌控情勢，但並沒有掉進深淵。

- has many boyfriends... no soul mate
  她顯然有許多男友，但是沒有一個是性情相投。

- swerved to avoid the falling vase... fell inside the manhole instead
  她顯然急轉彎來避開掉下來的花盆，但卻掉進下水道施工洞中。

> **Are you joking? _____.**

- There are wolves coming after us　開玩笑嗎？野狼群正朝著我們追來？

- You are pregnant again　你在開玩笑嗎？妳又懷孕了。

② 喜怒哀樂

- You forgot your important interview　開玩笑嗎？你忘了去重要的面談。
- You stole money from the cash machine
開玩笑嗎？你從提款機那裏偷了錢？

用這句話更厲害！

1 I don't believe in luck or destiny.
我不相信運氣或命運。

2 I have a four-leaf clover which is supposed to bring me good luck.　我有一株能帶給我好運的四葉幸運草

3 What luck! I won NT2,000 in the scratch-and-win.
真幸運！我刮刮樂贏了新台幣兩千元！

4 I'm avoiding unlucky people because I think bad luck is contagious.　我會避開不幸的人因為我認為壞運是會傳染的。

5 Can you believe her luck? She won the lottery again!
你相信她的運氣嗎？她買的樂透又中獎了！

6 You are pushing your luck if you think you'll win again.
你如果認為你會再贏一次，你就是心存僥倖了。

註　push your luck 心存僥倖；luck out 運氣特別好；out of luck 運氣不好

7 She lucked-out and managed to acquire that luxury car at half price.　她運氣特別好，能以半價買到一台豪華轎車。

8 Any luck trying to get her to date you?
有機會試著約她出來跟你約會嗎？

9 Luck must be on my side because I did not encounter one single red traffic light on my way to work.
我走運了因為來上班時沿途沒有遇到紅燈。

10 To run a thriving business,I will need skills and a little luck.
要經營一個成功的事業，我需要技術和一些運氣。

11 Lady luck is smiling at me because I won a million NT at the casino.　幸運女神特別眷顧我因為我在賭場贏了一百萬台幣。

⑫ He has a lot of luck with the ladies because of his dashing good looks.　他的女人運很好因為他很英俊。

必背單字片語

☑ **Destiny** [ˈdɛstənɪ]　n. 命運
It is my destiny to be with you, my darling!
親愛的，跟你在一起是我的宿命！

☑ **Contagious** [kənˈtedʒəs]　adj. 傳染性的
Is bird flu a highly contagious disease?
禽流感是高傳染性的疾病嗎？

☑ **Acquire** [əˈkwaɪr]　vt. 獲得；取得
A big company acquired his business for a large sum.
大企業以一大筆錢取得他的生意。

☑ **Skill** [ˈskɪl]　n. 技術；技能
You have to develop your skills before anyone will hire you.
在別人願意僱用你之前你必須先發展你的技術。

☑ **Thriving** [ˈθraɪvɪŋ]　adj. 欣欣向榮的；成功的
The unemployment rate is down due to a thriving economy.
失業率因繁榮的經濟而下降。

☑ **Dashing** [ˈdæʃɪŋ]　adj. 時髦的；瀟灑的
The old lady likes to surround herself with dashing young men.
那位熟女喜歡和瀟灑的年輕男人在一起。

註 surround oneself with 和⋯為伍

Unit 18 期待

這樣說英文

Ⓐ They are looking forward to the excursion to the US.

Ⓑ I am not at all surprised of their excitement because they have been planning it for months.

Ⓐ Well, I look forward to some peace and quiet when they leave.

Ⓐ 他們很期待去美國旅行。

Ⓑ 他們那麼興奮我並不訝異因為他們已經計畫了好幾個月了。

Ⓐ 而我是期待等他們去的時候我的耳根子會清靜些。

⋯⋯⋯⋯⋯⋯⋯⋯⋯⋯⋯⋯⋯⋯⋯⋯⋯⋯⋯⋯⋯⋯⋯⋯⋯⋯⋯⋯⋯⋯⋯⋯⋯⋯

Ⓐ I must go do my hair, buy new shoes, makeup, and some perfume. I am going to put on my killer dress tonight.

Ⓑ Are you looking forward to a hot date this evening?

Ⓐ Actually, there are no guys because it's girls' night out.

Ⓐ 我必須去做頭髮、買新鞋、化妝品和香水。今晚我要穿那件約會必勝小戰袍。

Ⓑ 你似乎很期待今晚的豔遇？

Ⓐ 事實上，今晚沒有男人，因為是女孩們的聚會。

⋯⋯⋯⋯⋯⋯⋯⋯⋯⋯⋯⋯⋯⋯⋯⋯⋯⋯⋯⋯⋯⋯⋯⋯⋯⋯⋯⋯⋯⋯⋯⋯⋯⋯

Ⓐ I am really looking forward to my birthday.

Ⓑ Sweetie, I am envious of you. When you get to my age you want to be young again.

Ⓐ I get pimples and you get wrinkles, so that makes us even.

Ⓐ 我真的很期待生日的到來。

Ⓑ 親愛的，我真的很羨慕你。等你到了我這把年紀你會想再次變年輕。

Ⓐ 我長痘子，你長皺紋，所以我們平手。

Vocabulary

Excursion [ɪkˋskɝʒən]　n. 短途旅行　　Envious [ˋɛnvɪəs]　adj. 羨慕；忌妒

Excitement [ɪkˋsaɪtmənt]　n. 興奮；刺激　　Wrinkle [ˋrɪŋk!]　n. 皺紋

Killer dress　ph.【美俚】極有吸引力的洋裝

這樣用句型

> ### I am not surprised _____ because _____.

· by her good results... she has worked hard for a long time
我並不訝異她的好成果因為她努力了很長時間。

· at her tantrum... she is, after all, a spoilt brat
我並不訝異她的脾氣因為她究竟是個被寵壞的小孩。

· at all... I was expecting it　我完全不訝異因為我本來就預料到了。

> ### Actually, _____ because _____.

· I couldn't make it... I was busy cleaning my fridge
事實上我無法去，因為我忙著清理冰箱。

· she decided against it... she thought it wasn't worth her time
事實上她決定不要，因為覺得不值得花她的時間。

· it was cheap... he got a special discount from the manager
事實上那很便宜，因為他從經理那裡得到了特殊的折扣。

> ### I _____ and you _____ so that makes us even.

· get a dollar... get a dollar　我有一塊錢，你也有一塊錢，所以我們一樣。

· got kicked... got punched　我被踢而你被揍，所以我們互不相欠。

· get half... get half　你有一半而我有一半，所以我們均分。

② 喜怒哀樂

❶ I just can't wait to go to Disneyland!
我等不及去迪士尼了！

❷ I am so excited about tomorrow's wedding ceremony.
我很期待明天的婚禮。

❸ I dred the exam tomorrow because I haven't prepared for it yet.
我詛咒明天的考試因為我還沒準備好。

❹ He is reluctant to go to his dental appointment.
他實在不情願去看牙醫。

❺ She looks forward to hearing from the recruitment agency.
她期盼著工作介紹所的消息。

❻ The anticipation is killing me!
期待使我不舒服！

❼ I am eager to join the millionaire club.
等不及加入百萬富翁俱樂部。

❽ I look forward to tasting this exquisite wine.
我很期待品嚐高級葡萄酒。

❾ She was enthusiastic about going to her new school.
她對去新學校就讀感到很熱衷。

❿ I look forward to your downfall, you miserable pillock.
我等不及看到你失敗，你這個可憐的笨蛋。

⓫ I cringe just thinking about the torture I am about to endure.
想到我將承受的折磨使我退縮。

⓬ I can hardly contain my excitement.
我隱藏不了興奮的感覺。

必背單字片語

☑ **Ceremony** [`sɛrəˌmonɪ]　n. 儀式；典禮
Her jaw dropped when her fiancé announced that he is
calling off the engagement ceremony.
當她的未婚夫取消訂婚儀式時，她很訝異。

- -

☑ **Reluctant** [rɪ`lʌktənt]　adj. 不情願的
I am reluctant to marry her because she turned out to be
a social butterfly.
我不太想跟她結婚因為她其實是個交際花。

- -

☑ **Recruit** [rɪ`krut]　vt./n. 徵募；雇用；招募
We need fresh new recruits to energize the company.
我們需要為公司注入新血。

- -

☑ **Enthusiastic** [ɪnˌθjuzɪ`æstɪk]　adj. 熱心的；熱衷的
I am an enthusiastic supporter of animal rights.
我是維護動物權利的熱衷支持者。

- -

☑ **Torture** [`tɔrtʃɚ]　vt. 使精神上受折磨；使痛苦
Why do you torture me with your singing?
你為何要用歌聲折磨我？

2

喜怒哀樂

Unit 19 放鬆與祥和

這樣說英文

142

Ⓐ I need a vacation away from this hustle and bustle.

Ⓑ Where would you like to go? You look like you need some time off.

Ⓐ Somewhere relaxing like Bora Bora would be nice.

Ⓐ 我需要一個假期遠離擁擠與繁忙。

Ⓑ 你想去哪裡？你看起來像是需要一些休息。

Ⓐ 像大溪地博拉博拉島那樣放鬆的地方應該不錯。

⋯⋯⋯⋯⋯⋯⋯⋯⋯⋯⋯⋯⋯⋯⋯⋯⋯⋯⋯⋯⋯⋯⋯⋯⋯⋯

Ⓐ The view here is so serene; I could get used to the tranquility here.

Ⓑ I see this everyday so I get really bored.

Ⓐ Not me. Try living in New York City and you'll need ear plugs.

Ⓐ 這個景色好安詳，我能習慣這裡的平靜。

Ⓑ 我每天看，所以覺得很無聊。

Ⓐ 我可不會。去住紐約市看看，你將會需要耳塞。

⋯⋯⋯⋯⋯⋯⋯⋯⋯⋯⋯⋯⋯⋯⋯⋯⋯⋯⋯⋯⋯⋯⋯⋯⋯⋯

Ⓐ She likes visiting the spa to get some relaxation.

Ⓑ Oh that sounds nice! What does she do at the spa? Sauna? Massage?

Ⓐ She frequents the spa for hour-long foot reflexology sessions.

Ⓐ 她喜歡去水療館放鬆。

Ⓑ 喔，那聽起來不錯！她都去水療館做什麼療程？三溫暖？按摩？

Ⓐ 她常去水療館做一小時的腳底按摩。

Vocabulary

Hustle and bustle　ph. 擁擠吵雜
Serene [sə`rin]　adj. 安詳的；無雲的
Tranquility [træŋ`kwɪlətɪ]　n. 平靜

Frequent [`frikwənt]　vt. 常去
Reflexology [ˌriflɛk`salədʒɪ]　n. 按摩腳部
的反射療法

這樣用句型

143

> _____ like _____ would be nice.

- Something tasty... fried chicken　好吃的東西像是炸雞就不錯。
- Somewhere fun... the amusement park
  好玩的地方像遊樂場就不錯。
- Someone pretty... a magazine model
  漂亮的人像雜誌模特兒就不錯。
- Sometime... tomorrow　像是明天就不錯。
- Some way of travel... on a cruise ship　像坐郵輪那樣的旅遊應該不錯。

> The view here _____; I could _____.

- is spectacular... move here now　這裡的景色真壯觀，我現在可以就搬來。
- is appalling... just leave and never come back
  這裡的景色很可怕，我想離開並不再回來。
- is so ordinary... just die of boredom
  這裡的景色很普通，我無聊得要命。
- from this room cannot be beat... just unpack my bags now
  從這間房間看出去的景色無與倫比，我現在就想將行李拿出來。
- is a joke... tell the hotel reception off right now
  這裡的景觀真是個笑話，我現在就想去罵旅館的櫃台人員。

> She likes _____ to get _____.

- visiting dating websites... men's email addresses
  她喜歡到約會網站上取得男人們的電子信箱地址。

- using online messengers... in touch with her friends
  她喜歡用線上通訊程式來跟朋友們保持聯繫。

- yelling at people... attention　她喜歡叫罵他人來引起注意。

- travelling to Hong Kong... some shopping done　她喜歡到香港購物。

用這句話更厲害！

❶ Ah! There's nothing like some peace and quiet.
啊！沒有什麼事比得上平靜。

❷ It's so quiet here you can hear a pin drop.
這裡安靜到能聽到針掉下來的聲音。

❸ There is no way I can relax and rest in the proximity of the construction site.　我無法在建築工地附近放鬆休息。

❹ She is begging her son to shut up so she could do some work.　她拜託她兒子安靜點讓她能工作。

❺ The shattering vase broke the silence in the library.
花瓶破碎的聲音打破了圖書館裡的寂靜。

❻ The uneasy silence between them is deafening.
他們之間令人不安的寂靜震耳欲聾。

❼ To concentrate, you probably need to go somewhere quiet.
你可能需要到安靜一點的地方才能專心。

❽ How anyone can study in a boisterous setting like a fast food restaurant is beyond me.
我真的無法理解怎麼有人能在喧鬧的速食餐廳裡讀書。

❾ I am going to take off and relax at the end of the year.
我年底要休假去放鬆一下。

❿ The noise-cancelling headphones can provide you with some artificial quietness for a price.
削減噪音的耳機能使你付錢享有人造的安靜。

11 I can't even hear what I am thinking with this racket.
這樣的喧嚷我根本無法聽到自己在想什麼。

12 Are you at peace with your inner self?
你跟內心的自己和平共處嗎？

必背單字片語

☑ **In the proximity of** ph. 在...附近
There are many banks in the proximity of the commercial district.
在商業區附近有很多家銀行。

☑ **Shatter** [ˋʃætɚ] vi. 被砸碎；破滅
How dare you shatter my dream of becoming a beauty queen?
你怎麼能粉碎我當選美皇后的夢想？

☑ **Deafening** [ˋdɛfnɪŋ] a. 震耳欲聾的
The noise coming from the construction site is deafening.
施工基地那裡傳來的噪音震耳欲聾。

☑ **Concentrate** [ˋkɑnsɛn͵tret] vi. 集中；全神貫注；n. 濃縮液
She kept staring at the orange juice bottle because it says "concentrate".
她一直盯著柳橙汁瓶身看因為寫著「濃縮液」。

☑ **Boisterous** [ˋbɔɪstərəs] adj. 喧鬧的；活躍的
The boisterous crowd is cheering for their home team.
狂歡的人群為自己的主場隊伍歡呼。

☑ **Artificial** [͵ɑrtəˋfɪʃəl] adj. 人工的；人造的
The latest technology makes robots with artificial intelligence.
最新的科技能做出有人工智慧的機器人。

2 喜怒哀樂

203

Unit 20 好笑

這樣說英文

A I was laughing so hard I tripped and fell into the hole.
B I was laughing so hard I choked on my gum and gagged.
A He was laughing so hard looking at us he almost died of asphyxiation.

A 我大笑到跌進一個洞裡。
B 我大笑到噎到口香糖。
A 他看著我們大笑到差點窒息。

....

A Hahaha... It's so funny that I cannot stop laughing.
B What's so funny? What's tickling you?
A Sorry I cannot help it. Your new hair style looks so hilarious.

A 哈哈哈…太好笑了我笑的停不下來。
B 什麼事這麼好笑？什麼東西在逗你笑？
A 抱歉我無法控制。你的新髮型看起來真的很好笑。

....

A When I'm feeling down, I like to read or watch something funny to pick myself up.
B You mean like reading humorous comics, watching comedies and listening to funny talk shows?
A Exactly. And, like watching your car being towed while we're standing here talking.

A 當我情緒低落時，我喜歡看一些好笑的東西來振作自己。
B 你是指看好笑的漫畫、看喜劇、和聽好笑的談話節目嗎？
A 是的，還有類似站在這裡跟你說話並同時看著你的車子被拖走。

Vocabulary

Gag [gæg]　v. 窒息；作嘔
Asphyxiation [æsˌfɪksɪˋeʃən]　n. 窒息

Tickle [ˋtɪk!]　vt. 哈…癢；逗…大笑
Tow [to]　vt. 拖吊；拖曳

這樣用句型

I was ＿＿＿＿＿＿ so much I ＿＿＿＿＿＿.

- screaming... scared the bejesus out of everyone
  我尖叫得很大聲，大聲到把每個人嚇死。
- walking... wore out my shoes　我走太多路，走到自己的鞋都穿壞了。
- swearing... was making the army sergeant blush
  我罵很多髒話，罵到連軍隊的中士都不好意思。
- drinking... nicknamed myself Johnny Walker
  我喝很多酒，多到把自己取名叫「約翰走路」。
- talking... hurt my throat　我講太多話，多到傷到自己的喉嚨。

It's so ＿＿＿＿＿＿ that ＿＿＿＿＿＿.

- tasty... I cannot let it go to waste　這個太好吃，我不能浪費它。
- hot... she cannot sleep without air conditioning
  今天太熱，她無法不開冷氣睡覺。
- freaking obvious... she did it　這很明顯是她做的。
- yucky... even cockroaches wouldn't touch it
  這個太噁心，連蟑螂都不會想碰。
- exciting... she couldn't stop screaming　這個太刺激，她無法停止尖叫。

When I am feeling ＿＿＿＿, I like to ＿＿＿＿.

- hungry... raid the refridge
  當我感到飢餓時，我喜歡去翻冰箱（看有什麼東西可以吃）。

2 喜怒哀樂

205

- lonely... call my boyfriend　當我感到寂寞時，我喜歡打電話給男友。
- sleepy... take a nap　當我感到想睡時，我喜歡睡個午覺。
- bored... turn on the TV　當我感到無聊時，我喜歡打開電視。
- sad... talk to my mother　當我感到悲傷時，我喜歡跟我媽講話。

用這句話更厲害！

1 I laughed so hard I cried.　我笑到哭出來。

2 This is the funniest sitcom I have seen all year.
這是今年我看過最好笑的情境脫口秀。

3 The outcome was absolutely unexpected and insanely hilarious.　這個結局真是出乎意料而且愚蠢地好笑。

4 It felt as if somebody was tickling my ribs.
這感覺像是有人在搔我癢。

> 註　ribs 是肋骨的意思，tickle my ribs 就是像在肋骨兩側哈癢。

5 Somebody help me! I can't stop laughing! I can't breathe!
誰來救救我！我笑到停不下來了！我快窒息了！

6 I couldn't hold back the laughter and burst out loud.
我憋不住想笑就哈哈大笑了起來。

7 That humorous man made me laugh at my own shortcomings.
那個幽默的人讓我因為我自己的缺點而發笑。

8 How could a ridiculous yet funny thing like that happen to you?
這麼詭異卻好笑的事怎麼發生在你身上？

9 You have what it takes to be a comedian.
你有當搞笑藝人的天分。

10 I'm begging you: stop making me laugh!
我求求你：不要再讓我笑了！

⑪ Will you stop giggling? Dad is frowning at us!

你可以不要笑了嗎？爸爸在對我們皺眉頭了！

⑫ The comic's offensive humor was met with sporadic clapping and boos.

這本漫畫裡冒犯性的幽默得到了稀疏的掌聲及噓聲。

必背單字片語

☑ **Sitcom** [ˋsɪtˌkɑm]　abbr. (situation comedy 的縮寫) 情境喜劇
He spent his entire weekend watching sitcom reruns on cable.
他整個週末都在看第四台的情境喜劇的重播。

- -

☑ **Laughter** [ˋlæftɚ]　n. 笑；笑聲
The evil sound of his laughter is downright disturbing.
他笑聲中的邪惡令人十分不安。

- -

☑ **Humorous** [ˋhjumərəs]　adj. 幽默的；滑稽的
I prefer to spend time with humorous people.
我較喜歡跟幽默的人共處。

- -

☑ **Frown** [fraʊn]　vt. 皺眉
His decision to drop out of school made his parents frown.
他休學的決定使他的父母皺眉。

- -

☑ **Sporadic** [spəˋrædɪk]　adj. 分散的；偶爾發生的
We are going to have sporadic showers throughout the day.
今天整天會有零星的陣雨。

Unit 21 很棒

這樣說英文

148

Ⓐ Just look at the magnificent structure; I am in awe.
Ⓑ This bridge spans over 4,000 feet and is regarded as one of the wonders of the modern world.
Ⓐ I wonder if I can bungee jump off it.

Ⓐ 看看那個雄偉的橋樑，我對它心生敬畏。
Ⓑ 這座橋橫跨四千英呎，而且被認為是現代世界的奇景之一。
Ⓐ 不知我能否從這裡高空彈跳。

Ⓐ This is awesome! The humidity is low, the temperature is just right and there's a light, cool breeze.
Ⓑ It's quite a change from the wet nasty weather we had the past few days.
Ⓐ Let's go to the beach and enjoy the day.

Ⓐ 這真是太棒了！濕度低，溫度又剛好，還有清涼的微風。
Ⓑ 跟過去幾天溼答答的天氣差很大。
Ⓐ 我們去海邊享受這一天吧。

Ⓐ I won a trip to Europe in a lucky draw, and I can bring a friend.
Ⓑ That is marvelous! So when are we leaving?
Ⓐ Wait a minute. I never said you were coming along.

Ⓐ 我抽獎贏了一趟歐洲之旅，而且可以攜伴。
Ⓑ 太妙了！那我們何時出發？
Ⓐ 等一下，我從來沒說要帶你去。

Vocabulary

Magnificent [mæg`nɪfəsənt]　adj. 宏偉的
Bungee jump [`bʌndʒɪ ˌdʒʌmp]　v. 高空彈跳

Awesome [`ɔsəm]　adj.【非正式】很好的
Humidity [hju`mɪdətɪ]　n. 濕氣；濕度
Marvelous [`marvələs]　adj. 妙極了

這樣用句型

149

> **Just look at _____ ; I am in awe.**

· the spectacular rock formations　看看那壯觀的岩石構造；我心生敬畏。
· the size of the cruise ship　看看那艘郵輪的大小；我心生敬畏。
· this stunning work of art　看看那令人驚豔的藝術品；我心生敬畏。
· how tall the redwood tree is　看看這棵紅木有多麼高；我心生敬畏。
· how long the Great Wall of China is
　看看中國的長城有多麼長；我心生敬畏。

**②
喜怒哀樂**

> **Let's _____ and enjoy the day.**

· forget our troubles　忘記我們的煩心事並享受這一天吧。
· just ignore those hooligans　別理會那些惡棍並享受這一天吧。
· get some booze　痛飲一番並享受這一天吧。
· get off work early　早點下班並享受這一天吧。
· get out of the house　出門享受這一天吧。

> **Wait a minute. I never said _____ .**

· you could borrow my bike　等等，我從沒說過你能借用我的腳踏車。
· I was going out with you　等等，我從沒說過要跟你約會。
· my daughter can marry you　等等，我從沒說過我女兒能嫁給你。
· she could spend the night here　等等，我從沒說過她可以在這裡住一晚。
· I was giving you all my money　等等，我從沒說過要給你所有的錢。

用這句話更厲害！

1 What an exhilarating movie! I must go watch it again!
真是一部令人振奮的電影！我一定還要再看一次。

2 How awesome. My boss is going to give all of us a raise.
真不錯，我老闆要幫我們大家加薪。

3 I am so excited because I have been offered a scholarship to study in London.
我很興奮因為我拿到去倫敦留學的獎學金。

4 Our boss is probably the best manager I've ever met in my career.
我們的老闆可能是我職涯中遇過最棒的經理。

5 I was left with a huge sum of money. Super!
我繼承了一大筆錢。太棒了！

6 My wife gave me a sports car for my birthday. I am totally speechless.
我老婆送我一部跑車當生日禮物。我高興得說不出話來。

7 I am the greatest super hero who ever lived.
我是有史以來最厲害的超級英雄。

8 I spent the summer playing this great new video game.
我整個暑假都在玩這個新的超讚電玩。

9 I intend to achieve something great in my life.
我想要在有生之年完成很棒的事。

10 Let's give them a great biground of applause!
給他們熱烈的鼓掌吧！

11 She ate the ice cream with a great big grin.
她開心地吃著冰淇淋。

12 I love this succulent piece of T-bone.
我喜歡這份鮮味又多的丁骨牛排。

必背單字片語

☑ **Exhilarating** [ɪɡˋzɪləˌretɪŋ]　adj. 令人振奮的；使人高興的
I feel dizzy. I cannot take anymore exhilarating rollercoaster rides.
我感到好暈。我不能再坐令人嫉妒興奮的雲霄飛車了。

☑ **Raise** [rez]　n. 加薪
Instead of a raise, he got fired.
他沒有得到加薪，反而被解雇。

☑ **Scholarship** [ˋskɑləˌʃɪp]　n. 獎學金
He lost his scholarship after he failed all of his courses.
他當掉了所有的課之後，隨之失去了獎學金。

☑ **Applause** [əˋplɔz]　n. 鼓掌；喝采
The blinking 'Applause Now' sign is the audience's cue to clap.
閃爍的「請鼓掌」燈號是要觀眾們拍手的提示信號。

☑ **Grin** [grɪn]　v./n. 露齒的笑
Wipe that grin off your face! It's starting to annoy me.
不要再笑了！我已經開始生氣了。

☑ **Succulent** [ˋsʌkjələnt]　adj. 多汁的
Fruits in the right season tend to be sweet and succulent.
當季的水果通常很香甜多汁。

❷ 喜怒哀樂

Unit 22 樂意

這樣說英文

151

Ⓐ I cannot believe how she treats her boyfriend like her personal butler.
Ⓑ As long as he is willing, I don't see the problem.
Ⓐ I bet you wished you had a boyfriend like that!

Ⓐ 我不敢相信她如何把男友當成男僕使喚。
Ⓑ 只要她願意，我不認為有什麼問題。
Ⓐ 我打賭你也想要有個那樣的男友。

Ⓐ Are you willing to be with her in sickness and in health?
Ⓑ I will follow her to the ends of the earth, even if it kills me.
Ⓐ You're insane, but I proclaim you husband and wife.

Ⓐ 你願意跟她在一起，不論生老病苦？
Ⓑ 我將跟她到世界盡頭，就算是會把我害死。
Ⓐ 你真的瘋了，不過我還是宣布你們為丈夫和妻子。

Ⓐ It is my pleasure to have you as my guest in my humble home.
Ⓑ The pleasure is all mine. I think you are too modest; your house is humongous!
Ⓐ Really? Then you should see my mansion on my private island then.

Ⓐ 我很榮幸有您大駕光臨寒舍。
Ⓑ 榮幸之至。我覺得您太謙虛了，貴公館極為寬敞！
Ⓐ 真的嗎？那你應該去看看我在私人島嶼的豪宅。

Vocabulary

Butler [ˋbʌtlə] n. 男管家
Sickness [ˋsɪknɪs] n. 患病；疾病
Insane [ɪnˋsen] adj. 精神錯亂的；瘋狂的

Humble [ˋhʌmbl] adj. 謙遜的；卑微的；粗糙的
Humongous [hjuˋmʌŋgəs] adj. 【俚】巨大無比的

這樣用句型

> **I cannot believe (that)** _____ .

- he insulted my father in front of me
  我真不敢相信他在我面前辱罵我父親。
- he cut me off in traffic　我真不敢相信他超我的車。
- she smoked crack and got herself arrested
  我真不敢相信她抽大麻還被逮捕。
- they ran away from home and ended up in jail
  我真不敢相信他們逃家並且最後去坐牢。
- aliens are invading Taiwan　我不敢相信外星人正在侵略台灣。

> **Are you willing to** _____ ?

- lay your life down for your country　你願意為你的國家犧牲生命嗎？
- live with this nonsense for the rest of your life
  你願意荒謬地過一輩子嗎？
- accept the bribe and compromise your integrity
  你願意接受賄賂並背棄你的正直嗎？
- take his money and keep quiet　你願意拿他的錢了事嗎？
- work 20 hours a day and receive minimum wage
  你願意每天工作 20 個小時還拿最低工資嗎？

> **Really? Then you should** _____ .

- stop eating so much　真的嗎？那你應該不要再吃那麼多了。
- wake up early every day　真的嗎？那你應該每天早起。
- quit smoking and start living healthy
  真的嗎？那你應該戒菸並開始健康的生活。
- ignore all the criticism and press ahead
  真的嗎？那你應該忽視全部的批評並勇往直前。
- retaliate and show them who is the boss
  真的嗎？那你應該報復並讓他們知道誰才是老大。

用這句話更厲害！

❶ It is difficult, but for the sake of my kids I willingly work two jobs to support them.

雖然很困難，但是為了我的孩子，我情願做兩份工作來扶養他們。

❷ Are you willing to sacrifice yourself for your loved ones?

你願意為了所愛的人而犧牲自己嗎？

❸ I am happy to assist you in anyway I can.

我非常樂意給予你任何形式的幫助。

❹ He is hesitating to give his money to charity.

他對捐款給慈善單位有點猶豫。

❺ My partner and I are willing to sign this contract.

我跟我的合夥人非常樂意跟你簽署這個合約。

❻ It is my pleasure to see her suffer!　看她受苦是我的樂趣！

❼ I am delighted to travel first class even though it costs a small fortune.　搭乘頭等艙旅行雖然很昂貴，卻令我開心。

❽ I am eager and prepared to go to battle for you, my master!

我熱血沸騰並已準備好要為你去打仗了，主人。

❾ It is my pleasure to introduce you to this lovely young lady.

介紹你跟這位年輕貌美的小姐認識是我的榮幸。

❿ Her body is weak, but her spirit is strong and willing.

她的身體雖然虛弱，但是她的精神是強大並有意願的。

⑪ He is willing to tolerate your drivel because he loves you.

他之所以願意忍受你的蠢話是因為他愛你。

⑫ You cannot coerce me to do anything that I don't want to.

你無法強迫我做任何我不願意做的事情。

必背單字片語

☑ **Support** [sə`pɔrt]　v./n. 支撐；供給；扶養

She needs to be hooked on a life support system.

她需要被接上維生系統。

- -

☑ **Sacrifice** [`sækrə‚faɪs]　v. 犧牲；獻出

She sacrificed her life so that her children may live.

她犧牲她的生命讓孩子們活下去。

- -

☑ **Suffer** [`sʌfɚ]　v. 受苦；患病

I am suffering the consequences of not brushing my teeth properly.

我正在為了沒有正確刷牙而付出代價。

- -

☑ **Spirit** [`spɪrɪt]　n. 精神；心靈

Although she is unable to join us, she is here with us in spirit.

雖然她無法前來參與，但她的精神與我們同在。

- -

☑ **Tolerate** [`tɑlə‚ret]　vt. 忍受；容忍；容許

I cannot tolerate his arrogance so I slapped him.

我無法忍受他的狂妄而打了他一巴掌。

- -

☑ **Coerce** [ko`ɝs]　vt. 強制；迫使

The thugs coerced him into signing the agreement.

暴徒們迫使他要簽署協議。

2 喜怒哀樂

Unit 23 下定決心

Ⓐ I have made up mind to leave you!

Ⓑ But, we have been together for 10 years. Why are you leaving now?

Ⓐ Because you said I am indecisive. Well, this decision should convince you otherwise.

Ⓐ 我已經決定要離開你！

Ⓑ 但是，我們已經在一起十年了，為什麼現在離開？

Ⓐ 因為你說我優柔寡斷。所以這個決定應該可以說服你我並非如此。

......

Ⓐ I will sell everything I have, quit my job, move out of my apartment and go live in another city.

Ⓑ That's pretty drastic. What made you so determined?

Ⓐ The bank repossessed my car, I got fired, my landlord evicted me and my folks just asked me to move in with them.

Ⓐ 我將要變賣我所有的東西、辭去工作、搬出我的公寓並去另一個城市定居。

Ⓑ 這有點極端。什麼事使你如此決定？

Ⓐ 銀行查封了我的車、我被炒魷魚、我的房東把我趕出來，然後我爸媽要我搬回家跟他們一起住。

......

Ⓐ I don't know which way to go and I don't know what to do.

Ⓑ You should make up your mind and commit to your decision because you are not going anywhere with that mindset.

Ⓐ Make my decision for me then, so I can blame you if anything goes wrong.

Ⓐ 我不知道該往哪裡去，也不知道該做甚麼。

Ⓑ 你應該下定決心並忠於你的決定，因為你現在這樣無法成就任何事。

Ⓐ 那你幫我做決定好了。這樣如果出問題我可以怪在你頭上。

Vocabulary

Convince [kən`vɪns]　vt. 說服；使確信
Drastic [`dræstɪk]　adj. 激烈的；極端的
Folks [foks]　n. pl.【口】家屬，親屬；雙親；人們

Mindset [`maɪndsɛt]　n. 思維定式
Blame [blem]　vt./n. 責備；歸因於

這樣用句型

> But _____. Why _____?

- he hasn't gone home for days... are you keeping him in the office
  但是他已經好幾天沒回家了。你為何將他留在辦公室裡？
- I have finished my dinner... can't I leave the table
  但是我已經吃完晚餐了。我為何不能離開餐桌？
- I have given you all I have... don't you want to marry me
  但是我已經給妳我的全部。你為何還不跟我結婚？

> What made you _____?

- agree to his ridiculous demands　什麼促使你同意他無理的要求？
- hit his head with a frying pan　什麼促使你用平底鍋打他的頭？
- stuff your face with fried chicken in the middle of the night
  什麼促使你三更半夜狂吃炸雞？

> I don't _____ and I don't _____.

- ... agree with you... agree with him either　我並不認同你，也不認同他。

- ... know which guy to marry... know which guy to dump
  我不知道該跟哪個男孩結婚，也不知道該跟誰分手。

- ... see how I can afford a house... know what to do about it
  我不明白我如何能付的起這房子，而我也不知道該怎麼辦才好。

用這句話更厲害！

❶ He is determined to make his business a raving success.
他下決心要讓他的事業無比地成功。

❷ I cannot make up my mind because there are too many choices. 我無法決定，因為有太多選項。

❸ Opportunities slipped away because of his indecisiveness.
他的優柔寡斷造成許多機會流失。

❹ I have made a decision to be more decisive.
我決定要變的更堅決果斷。

❺ Don't run away from the responsibilities of making your own decisions. 不要推卸自己做決定的責任。

❻ If you don't make your own decisions, someone else will.
你若不自己做決定，別人會為你決定。

❼ I've made up my mind and there is no turning back.
我已經下定決心了，不會回頭了。

❽ We applaud his determination to finish the race.
我們為他堅持完成比賽而喝采。

❾ Hasty or popular decisions are not always the right ones.
太輕率或太受歡迎的決定不一定是對的。

❿ Would you wake up and go to work, or hit the snooze button and go back to sleep?
你會起床去工作還是賴床並睡回籠覺？

⓫ She could not make up her mind if she should have the salad or steak. 她不能決定該吃沙拉或是牛排。

⑫ Would you sacrifice one person to save two?
你會犧牲一人去救兩個人嗎？

必背單字片語

☑**Raving** [`revɪŋ]　adj. 瘋狂的；【口】非凡的；吹捧
All the boys were staring at that raving beauty.
所有的男孩都盯著那個非常漂亮的美人看。

☑**Turn back**　ph. 阻止；停止
You can always turn back when you find out that you are going down the wrong path.
當你發現你正朝著錯誤的路途走去時，你總是能夠回頭重來。

☑**Applaud** [ə`plɔd]　vt. 稱讚；向…喝采
I applaud his efforts to find a job in this difficult economy.
我稱讚他在經濟蕭條的時候找工作所做的努力。

☑**Hasty** [`hestɪ]　adj. 匆忙的；急忙的；輕率的
Being too hasty, he mistook his comic book for his business notes and rushed to the meeting carrying the 100th issue of Superman.
匆忙之下，沒有攜帶他的商務筆記，他反而誤拿了第 100 集的超人漫畫去開會。

☑**Snooze** [snuz]　vi. 打盹
He was fired because the boss found him snoozing in the pantry.
他被老闆抓到在茶水間內打盹而被解雇。

☑**Sacrifice** [`sækrəˌfaɪs]　vt. 犧牲
He sacrificed his career to spend more time with his family.
他為了花多一點時間陪家人而犧牲了他的職業生涯。

Unit 24 沮喪

這樣說英文

Ⓐ This is the worst day of my life; I got the pink slip and my wife is leaving me. What else could be worse?
Ⓑ Hey, look at the news. Isn't that your house on fire?
Ⓐ I just had to ask.

Ⓐ 這是我人生中最糟的一天；不僅拿到解雇通知，我老婆還離開我。還有甚麼比這個更糟？
Ⓑ 喂，看新聞正在報導，那個火災的地方不就是你家嗎？
Ⓐ 我幹嘛那麼多嘴。

Ⓐ I tend to have suicidal thoughts when bad things happen to me.
Ⓑ You need to think positively. Otherwise, there's some rope and a chair, a razor blade and a bottle of arsenic.
Ⓐ Ok you've made your point.

Ⓐ 當不好的事情發生時，我會有想自殺的傾向。
Ⓑ 你需要看開一點。不然，這裡有些繩子、椅子、刀片、和一瓶毒藥。
Ⓐ 好啦！我懂了。

Ⓐ Can someone help me please? I don't know what to do anymore.
Ⓑ You look unhappy. Why don't you go see a shrink and get some anti-depressants?
Ⓐ Wouldn't that make it worse?

Ⓐ 請問有人能幫幫我嗎？我不知道接下來該怎麼辦。
Ⓑ 你看起來很不快樂。你何不去看精神科醫師拿一些抗憂鬱的藥呢？
Ⓐ 那不是會使情況更糟嗎？

Vocabulary

Pink slip　ph.【口】停止僱用的通知
Suicide [`suə͵saɪd]　n. 自殺的行為
Arsenic [`ɑrsnɪk]　n. 砷、砒霜等毒藥。

Shrink [ʃrɪŋk]　n.【俚】精神科醫師
Anti-depressant [͵æntɪdɪ`prɛsənt]　n. 抗憂鬱劑

這樣用句型

> **This is the _____ ; I got _____.**

· best day of my life... a new job, a new car and I just married the girl of my dreams

  這是我人生中最好的一天，我有份新工作、一部新車，而且跟夢中情人結婚。

· worst date ever... a shock finding out that my girlfriend isn't a girl

  這是最糟的約會。發現我女友不是女人時真的嚇死我了。

· best job I've ever had... a nice salary, great benefits and six weeks of vacation

  這是最棒的工作。我薪水高、待遇好、又有六週的休假。

> **I tend to _____ when _____.**

· cry... I'm all alone　當我獨處時我會想哭泣。

· fart... I have had too much sweet potato

  當我吃太多地瓜時，我會想放屁。

· strip naked... the temperature gets too hot

  當氣溫太熱時，我會想脫光衣服。

> **You look _____. Why don't you _____?**

· happy... tell us why　你看起來很高興，何不告訴我們為何高興？

· like hell... go clean up　你看起來糟透了，何不去清理一下？

· like you could use some food... help yourself to some food in the fridge

  你似乎想吃東西，何不去冰箱看看有甚麼可以吃？

② 喜怒哀樂

用這句話更厲害！

159

❶ The gloomy weather made me miserable.
灰暗的天氣令我感到痛苦。

❷ I felt dejected because every publisher I asked had rejected my manuscript. 我因為每個出版商都拒絕我的稿子而感到沮喪。

❸ With an unemployment rate over 20% the economy cannot be anymore glum.
失業率高達 20%的經濟真是無比淒涼。

❹ The despondent man decided to pick himself up and try again.
這個沮喪的男人決定要振作起來再試一次。

❺ I think I have symptoms of Depression because I really want to commit suicide.
我想我有憂鬱症的症狀因為我很想自殺。

❻ He thinks that poverty as misery. 他認為貧窮就是一種不幸。

❼ I am so afraid because I have been out of work for years.
我很害怕因為我已經好幾年沒工作了。

❽ Stock prices are depressed due to the weak economy.
衰退的經濟使股價被壓低。

❾ In every life we have some trouble. When you worry you make it double. Don't worry be happy.
每個人的人生中都有挫折。當你擔憂時你就將它倍增。不要憂慮，請快樂起來吧。

❿ I found out my boyfriend was having secret romps with other men. 我發現我男友跟其他人秘密地喧鬧嘻笑。

⓫ You can cry about it, but make sure you pick yourself up and move on. 你可以大哭一場，但是一定要振作起來並繼續前進。

⓬ It's normal to experience stress but how you handle stress is what matters. 經歷壓力是正常的，但是重點是你如何處理它。

必背單字片語

☑ **Manuscript** [`mænjəˌskrɪpt]　　n. 手稿；原稿
They found ancient manuscripts when they were excavating the grounds.
他們在開挖地底時發現了古老的手稿。

☑ **Despondent** [dɪ`spɑndənt]　　adj. 沮喪的
He is despondent about the break-up, but eventually he will move on.
雖然他因為分手而沮喪，他終究還是會走出來的。

☑ **Misery** [`mɪzərɪ]　　n. 痛苦；不幸；【口】老發牢騷的人
I don't enjoy being around Tom, that old misery.
我不喜歡跟湯姆那種老愛發牢騷的人在一起。

☑ **Romp** [rɑmp]　　n. 嬉耍喧鬧；不費力地完成
The wild elephants are having a romp through the African plains.
野生大象在非洲大草原上玩耍。

☑ **Pick onerself up**　　ph. 振作起來
Successful people always pick themselves up after they have had a fall.
成功的人通常都在失敗之後自己振作起來。

☑ **Handle** [`hændl]　　vt. 處理；應付；駕馭
Do you know how to handle a raging bull with a piece of red clothe?
你知道如何用一塊紅布來應付發飆的公牛嗎？

2 喜怒哀樂

Unit 25　委屈

Ⓐ That car ran a red light and knocked me off my motorbike.
Ⓑ Are you ok? I think the car sped off with his horn blaring.
Ⓐ I'm a little bruised and shocked. Someone should get that road hog!

Ⓐ 那部車闖紅燈並把我從摩托車上撞飛。
Ⓑ 還好嗎？我想那部車加速開走了，還猛按喇叭。
Ⓐ 我是有點瘀青和受到驚嚇。應該要有人去把那個魯莽的駕駛攔下來。

Ⓐ He cheated on me and went out with three different girls!
Ⓑ What a jerk! You should just break up and find someone else who will respect you.
Ⓐ Actually, I'm seeing two other guys. Here are their photos. Which one do you think is better looking?

Ⓐ 他跟三個不同的女人劈腿！
Ⓑ 爛人！你應該跟他分手，另外找一個重視你的男友。
Ⓐ 事實上，我正在跟另外兩個交往。這是他們的照片。你覺得哪一個比較帥？

Ⓐ My boss deducted my pay for coming to work late although I was in the office until 3 AM the previous day.
Ⓑ That's just wrong. Did you take it up with the human resources manager?
Ⓐ I did, but he yelled at me for complaining.

Ⓐ 我老闆因為我遲到而扣我薪水，雖然前一天晚上我半夜三點才離開辦公室。
Ⓑ 那怎麼合理？你有去跟人事主管理論嗎？
Ⓐ 有呀，但是因為我的抱怨，他還對著我大吼大叫。

Vocabulary

Blare [blɛr]　vi. 發出響而刺耳的聲音
Road hog　ph. 自私的司機；魯莽的駕駛員
Cheat [tʃit]　vt. 欺騙；騙取

Deduct [dɪ`dʌkt]　vt. 扣除；刪減
Human resource　ph. 人力資源；人事部門

這樣用句型

Are you OK? _____?

· Do you need an ambulance　你還好嗎？需要幫你叫救護車嗎？
· Do you think you will be all right　你還好嗎？你覺得你能恢復嗎？
· Did you drink too much again　你還好嗎？你又喝太多了嗎？

Here are _____. Which _____?

· some ice cream and some cake ... do you prefer
　這裡有些冰淇淋和蛋糕，你想要吃哪一個？
· the beers we serve... would you like to sample
　這裡有我們準備的啤酒，你想要試喝哪一種？
· some of the flowers we sell here... do you want to buy
　這裡是一些我們賣的花，你想要買哪一個？

My boss _____ although _____.

· went on with the meeting... only two people came
　雖然只有兩個人出席，我的老闆照常舉行會議。

225

- gave us extra bonuses... business was bad
  雖然生意不好，我的老闆還是給我們額外的獎金。

- remained grumpy... the secretary tried to cheer him up
  雖然老闆的秘書試著要讓他開心，老闆還是很生氣。

用這句話更厲害！

162

❶ How could you do this to me?　你怎能這樣對我？

❷ I would not tolerate this kind of abuse any more. Pay me what you owe me or I will turn on you.
我再也不想受到這樣的虐待，付給我你欠我的錢不然我就報復。

❸ I cannot believe how prejudiced you are!
我真不敢相信你那麼有偏見！

❹ You know I love my dogs. Can you believe that I was arrested for animal abuse?
你知道我愛我的狗兒們。你相信我因為虐待動物而遭逮捕嗎？

❺ He abuses her physically and now she is filing for divorce.
他對她家暴，所以現在她正在訴請離婚。

❻ I am so fed-up with the unreasonable overtime hours.
我對這種不合理的加班時數已經忍無可忍。

❼ Two wrongs don't make a right, so don't seek revenge.
以牙還牙並不能息事，所以不要尋求報復。

❽ He is going to get you for fleecing him.
他以後會報復你對他的剝削。

❾ We should stand up and fight injustice.
我們應該站出來來打擊不公不義。

❿ I tried to rescue the stray dog but it turned around and bit me.　我試著拯救流浪狗，但他們居然回頭過來咬我。

⓫ My boss yelled at me for coming in late even though I worked overtime through the night.
我老闆為了我遲到而罵我，既使我整夜加班。

⑫ Somebody stole my wallet but the police chided me for been careless.　有人偷了我的錢包，但是警察居然責備我不小心。

必背單字片語

☑ **Turn** [tɜn]　vi. 轉向；變得；突然襲擊
The dog turned on its owner and bit him until he bled.
這隻狗突然襲擊牠的主人並將他咬到流血。

- -

☑ **Prejudice** [`prɛdʒədɪs]　vi. 懷有偏見；歧視
We should enact laws against prejudiced hiring practices.
我們應該立法禁止歧視性的僱用程序。

- -

☑ **Abuse** [ə`bjuz]　vt. 傷害；虐待
He abuses his little sister by hitting and kicking her constantly.
他一直對她妹妹施暴。

- -

☑ **Fed-up**　ph. 忍無可忍；感到厭煩
She is fed-up with his excuses and decided to teach him a lesson.
她已對他的藉口感到厭煩並決定給他一個教訓。

- -

☑ **Revenge** [rɪ`vɛndʒ]　vt./n. 報仇；報復
He had his revenge but he lived to regret it.
他報仇了但他終生後悔。

- -

☑ **Fleece** [flis]　n. 羊毛或絨毛織物；vt. 欺詐；剝削
That man in the purple fleece sweater fleeced me of a hundred quid.
那個穿著紫色絨織衫的男人騙了我一百鎊金幣。

2 喜怒哀樂

吵架

這樣說英文

163

Ⓐ She is quarreling with her husband about money.

Ⓑ Just yesterday I heard they were fighting over something else. In fact, they always have something to fight about.

Ⓐ I suppose you should never marry an argumentative woman unless you want to die young.

Ⓐ 她跟她丈夫為了錢而爭吵。

Ⓑ 昨天我才聽說他們為其它事情而吵。其實他們一直都在爭吵。

Ⓐ 我不認為你應該跟喜歡吵架的女人結婚，除非你想早死。

．．．

Ⓐ Come here right this instant, boy!

Ⓑ Ouch! Why did you pinch me, dad? I didn't do anything wrong.

Ⓐ That's just in case you did something wrong and I'm not there.

Ⓐ 兒子，你馬上給我過來！

Ⓑ 好痛！你幹嘛捏我啦，爸？我又沒做錯事。

Ⓐ 這只是以防萬一你做錯了什麼事而我剛好不在場。

．．．

Ⓐ Both sides started from a negotiation, went on to an argument then it deteriorated into a fistfight. Now, they are out to kill each other.

Ⓑ That's terrible behavior. They must be gangsters, right?

Ⓐ No, they are just members of parliament.

Ⓐ 雙方從協商開始，演變成爭執，然後惡化成拳打腳踢。現在，他們互相想把對方幹掉。

Ⓑ 好恐怖的行為，他們必定是幫派份子，對吧？

Ⓐ 喔，不是的。他們只是議會代表。

Vocabulary

Quarrel [`kwɔrəl]　vt./n. 爭吵；不合
Argumentative [ˌɑrgjə`mɛntətɪv]　adj. 爭辯的；好爭論的
Instant [`ɪnstənt]　n. 一刹那；頃刻

Deteriorate [dɪ`tɪrɪəˌret]　vi. 惡化；退化；品質或價值下降
Parliament [`pɑrləmənt]　n. 議會；國會

這樣用句型

> **I suppose you should never ＿＿＿ unless you ＿＿＿.**

· put crayons in the washer... want mom to beat the tar out of you
我不認為你應該放蠟筆進洗衣機，除非你想被你媽打死。

· borrow cars without permission... want to get arrested
我不認為你應該在沒有經過同意前就借走車，除非你想被逮捕。

· make racial jokes... want to get fired
我不認為你該開種族性的玩笑，除非你想被炒魷魚。

> **Both sides started ＿＿＿＿. Now they ＿＿＿＿.**

· cheering for their teams... are just hurling insults at each other
雙方開始為自己的隊伍加油。現在他們互相叫囂辱罵。

· drinking profusely... are in jail for disorderly conduct
雙方都開始牛飲，現在他們全因為酒後鬧事而被拘捕。

· pointing fingers at each other... are pointing guns at each other
雙方開始互相用手指指著對方，現在他們全都用槍指著彼此。

> **That's terrible behavior. ＿＿＿＿＿＿＿, right?**

- Their parents must be appalled
  真糟糕的行為。他們的家長應該會被嚇到吧？
- We should inform their guardians
  真糟糕的行為。我們應該通知他們的監護人吧？
- They should be sent straight to hell
  好恐怖的行為，他們應該直接下地獄，對吧？

用這句話更厲害！

1 Go pick on somebody your own size.
想找碴的話，去找個跟你差不多的人。

2 Stop yelling at me, I can hear you!
不用對著我大叫，我可以聽得到!

3 The two sisters bicker about whom their parents like more.
兩姊妹為了父母比較疼誰而鬥嘴。

4 I cannot fight this feeling of love for you any longer.
我無法再對抗我愛你的感覺。

5 Scientists argue that the universe started with a big bang.
科學家爭辯宇宙是由大爆炸而產生。

6 Arguing with the judge at your own trial is a really bad idea.
在自己的案件審理庭上與法官爭吵不是個明智之舉。

7 Do you want to start an argument, or do you want to resolve this dispute?　你想要跟我爭吵，還是要解決爭端？

8 He is trying to settle a squabble between him and his wife.
他試著要結束跟老婆之間的爭吵。

9 The fight ended up in a divorce with the husband paying alimony and child support.
他們之間的爭吵以離婚收場，男方支付贍養費和子女扶養費。

10 He argued with the police and got slapped with a heavy fine.
他跟警察起口角並被課徵非常高的罰金。

⓫ The old couple must abhor each other because they squabble about everything.

這對老夫婦一定彼此厭惡因為他們每件事都吵架。

必背單字片語

☑ **Pick on** ph.【口】找…的碴;挑選
The big kids liked to pick on little girls.
大孩子喜歡找小女生麻煩。

☑ **Bicker** [`bɪkɚ] v. 口角;爭吵
The siblings are bickering about how to split their inheritance.
兄弟姐妹間正在為了如何分遺產而爭吵。

☑ **Resolve** [rɪ`zɑlv] vt. 解決
How do you resolve an issue that involves multiple parties?
你該如何化解多方的爭議?

☑ **Settle** [`sɛtl] vt. 安排;決定;解決;結束;支付
They decided to settle the lawsuit out of court.
他們決定要法庭外和解。

☑ **Slap** [slæp] vt. 用手掌打;隨意放置;【口】對…起訴;課徵
He slapped the local newspaper with a lawsuit for slander.
他因為當地報社造謠中傷而對它提出告訴。

☑ **Abhor** [əb`hɔr] vt. 厭惡
I absolutely abhor the smell of durians.
我非常厭惡榴槤的氣味。

Unit 27 後悔

這樣說英文

166

Ⓐ I don't think you should have married her because she never did love you. Now she's gone off with another man.

Ⓑ You are right. I curse the day I set eyes on her. What should I do?

Ⓐ Go visit a marriage counselor or a lawyer.

Ⓐ 我向來都不認為你應該跟她結婚，因為她從未愛過你。現在她跟另一個男人跑了。

Ⓑ 你說的對。我詛咒看上她的那一天。我該怎麼辦呢？

Ⓐ 去找個婚姻諮詢師或是律師吧。

Ⓐ Oh why did I buy this car? It has broken down for the umpteenth time!

Ⓑ Didn't you say you bought it for a song?

Ⓐ Yes I did, and the car is spending more time in the garage than on the road.

Ⓐ 我到底買這部車幹嘛？它已經拋錨無數次了！

Ⓑ 你不是說你買的時候很便宜？

Ⓐ 是呀，而它在修車廠的時間比在路上還多。

Ⓐ I should have avoided going to the casino with you.

Ⓑ What do you mean? You had a good time, didn't you?

Ⓐ It was great until I lost all my money and my house. Now my wife is leaving me!

Ⓐ 我應該避免跟你去賭場的。

Ⓑ 什麼意思？你不是玩得很盡興？

Ⓐ 一切都很棒直到我輸掉所有的錢和房子。現在我老婆要離開我了！

Vocabulary

Curse [kɝs]　vt. 求上帝降禍；詛咒
Counselor [ˋkaʊnslɚ]　n. 法律顧問
Umpteen [ˋʌmpˋtin]　adj. 【口】無數的；很多的

For a song　ph.【口】以很低的價錢
Casino [kəˋsino]　n. 賭場

這樣用句型

I don't think you should ＿＿ anymore because ＿＿.

· eat so much... you're getting too fat
我不認為你該繼續吃這麼多因為你變得太胖了。

· drink... you're drunk 　我不認為你應該繼續喝因為你醉了。

· smoke... your teeth are all yellow
我不認為你該繼續抽菸因為你的牙齒都變黃了。

· sing... people are starting to hate you
我不認為你該繼續唱歌因為大家開始討厭妳了。

· smile at little children... you look frightful when you do
我不認為你該對小朋友微笑因為你這麼做的時候很嚇人。

Oh why did I ＿＿＿＿＿＿＿＿＿＿?

· wear dreadful clothes and make myself look awful
我為何要穿如此糟的衣服讓我自己不好看？

· quit school when I was young 　我為何年輕的時候要休學？

· eat everything on the table 　我為何吃完桌上的每樣食物？

· ignore my mother and run off with him
我為何沒聽我媽的勸而跟他私奔？

· stare at that ugly guy 　我為何凝視著那個醜男？

It was ＿＿＿＿＿＿ until ＿＿＿＿＿＿.

- ... great... you showed up　一切都很好直到你的出現。
- ... tasty... he added more salt　這個很好吃，直到他加了更多的鹽。
- ... a boring class... a beautiful girl walked in
  這堂課很無趣，直到那位漂亮女生走進來。
- ... a noisy party... the police arrived　這個派對很吵鬧，直到警察到來。
- ... a popular restaurant... they found cockroaches in the kitchen and shut it down
  這間餐廳很受歡迎，直到他們發現廚房內有蟑螂並被勒令停業。

用這句話更厲害！

168

1 I should not have fed my goldfish an entire can of fish food.
我不應該把整罐魚飼料餵給我的金魚。

2 I regret that your services are no longer needed.
我很遺憾不再需要你的服務了。

3 He regrets not studying and failing all his exams.
他很後悔沒有準備並當掉考試。

4 She was regretful for moving her mother to a nursing home.
她很後悔將她媽媽送進養老院。

5 He swore at the minister and almost immediately he regretted his action.　他咒罵牧師之後馬上對自己的行為感到後悔。

6 We regret to inform you that you are made redundant.
我們很遺憾的通知你被開除了。

7 If you marry him you will regret it for the rest of your life.
你如果跟他結婚將會後悔一輩子。

8 She expressed her regret at her friend's demise.
她對她朋友的死亡表示哀悼。

9 I have no regrets at all by getting rid of him.
我並不後悔離開他。

10 I have no qualms sending the fat boy to boot camp.
把胖小孩送去訓練營我並不會內疚。

⓫ He has misgivings about participating in the get-rich-quick scheme.

他對參與快速致富計畫感到有疑慮。

⓬ I feel sorry for not telling her all my true feelings.

我非常後悔沒能跟他講我真正的感受。

必背單字片語

☑ **Regret** [rɪ`grɛt]　vt./vi./n. 懊悔；遺憾；後悔
Her parents refused to show up at her wedding, and now they are regretting.
她的父母拒絕出席她的婚禮，而現在後悔了。

- -

☑ **Swear** [swɛr]　vi./vt. 發誓；咒罵
I swear I will never be lazy again. 我發誓不再懶散。

- -

☑ **Redundant** [rɪ`dʌndənt]　adj. 多餘的；累贅的
This essay is tiring to read because it is full of redundant sentences.
這篇論文很難讀因為都是贅述的句子。

- -

☑ **Demise** [dɪ`maɪz]　n. 死亡；終止
The evil monster is cackling at the superhero's demise.
邪惡的怪獸對超級英雄的死亡發出格格的笑聲。

- -

☑ **Qualm** [kwɔm]　n. 內疚；良心不安
I have qualms about winning the race unfairly.
我對以不公平的方式贏得比賽感到良心不安。

- -

☑ **Scheme** [skim]　n. 計畫；詭計
They carried out their diabolical scheme to steal from the old.
他們執行了一個邪惡的計畫來騙老人。

Unit 28 失望

這樣說英文

Ⓐ I was pretty disappointed about my trip to Europe. I did not get to do what I wanted to do, and yet I was exhausted.

Ⓑ Didn't you join the tour? I thought it would have been out of this world.

Ⓐ I sat on the bus from dawn 'til dusk, ate Chinese food for every meal and visited only souvenir shops. It would have been cheaper to photoshop myself onto postcards.

Ⓐ 我對這次的歐洲之旅非常失望。我並沒有做到我想做的，但是我快累翻了。

Ⓑ 你不是參加旅行團嗎？我還以為會不同凡響呢。

Ⓐ 我從早到晚坐在巴士裡面，每餐吃中國菜，然後只參觀紀念品店。我把自己修圖修進明信片裡可能更便宜。

Ⓐ My parents are really disappointed with my exam result.

Ⓑ That cannot be true because you have always been a straight-A student. Didn't you do well?

Ⓐ Well I got an 'A', but they were expecting an 'A+' so they think I'm slacking off.

Ⓐ 我爸媽對我的考試成績極為失望。

Ⓑ 這不可能，因為你一直是個成績優異的好學生。你沒考好嗎？

Ⓐ 我是拿到甲等，但他們期盼的是甲上，所以他們認為我退步了。

Ⓐ I waited all year for this movie, but it turned out to be such a bummer!

Ⓑ Everyone was raving about it. What made you say it was no good?

Ⓐ The movie had too many computer graphics in it and the storyline was so predictable. Watching paint dry would have been more exciting.

Ⓐ 我等了整年要看這部片子，結果真是令人失望！

Ⓑ 每個人都很喜歡這部片子，為何你說它不好？

Ⓐ 這部片子有太多電腦動畫，劇情太過墨守成規。看油漆變乾還比較刺激。

Vocabulary

Out of this world　ph. 不同凡響；【口】極好的
Slack off　ph. 懈怠；減緩；退步

Rave [rev]　vi. 狂熱稱讚；極力誇獎
Predictable [prɪˋdɪktəbl]　adj.【貶】墨守陳規的

這樣用句型

> Didn't you _____ ? I thought _____.

· quit... you had left the company
　你還沒辭職嗎？我還以為你已經離職了。

· go home... I saw you leave the party
　你還沒回家嗎？我還以為看到你離開派對了。

· marry him... he proposed to you
　你還沒嫁給他嗎？我還以為他已經向你求婚了。

> My _____ really _____ with my _____.

· mother is... satisfied... cooking　我媽對我的廚藝相當滿意。

· husband is... confused... childish behavior
　我先生對我幼稚的行為非常困惑。

· father was... upset... choice of boyfriends
　我父親對我選的男友非常苦惱。

> I waited _____ but _____.

- ... for him over here... he waited for me over there
  我在這裡等他，但他在那裡等我。
- ... for her reply... my patience ran out
  我等著她的回覆，但已經失去耐心。
- ... for only a minute... I got impatient and left
  我只等了一下子，但我不耐煩就離開了。

用這句話更厲害！

1 He was sorry he paid so much money for an expensive meal that was rather bland.
他很遺憾付了那麼多錢吃一頓淡而無味的大餐。

2 The new car did not meet his expectations.
這部新車沒有達到他的期望。

3 This new movie was a real let down.　這部新片真是令人失望。

4 The service in this five-star hotel is rather unsatisfactory.
這家五星級飯店的服務實在令人不滿意。

5 Words cannot express how utterly disappointed I am with the new leadership.
我對新領導的徹底失望不是言語能足以形容的。

6 This book is hyped up by the media, but its contents leave much to be desired.　這本書被媒體大肆宣傳，但其內容有待加強。

7 Her test scores fell short of the requirement for admission.
她的考試成績尚未達到被錄取入學的門檻。

8 The feeling of disappointment overcame her will to go on.
失望的情緒使她不想再繼續下去。

9 Dining here may be expensive but the service and the food do not disappoint.
這裡的餐點也許昂貴了些，但其服務和食物品質卻不負眾望。

10 He over-promised and under-delivered so customers wanted a refund.　他承諾的多於能做到的，所以顧客們想要退貨。

⑪ I am so frustrated with my exam results I want to go home and cry.　我對考試成績相當失望，我想回家大哭一場。

⑫ Mother says I am a disappointment to her. But, she is a disappointment to grandma too so I think we are even.
我媽說她對我很失望。但是，奶奶對她也是很失望，所以我們平手。

必背單字片語

☑ **Bland** [blænd]　adj. 淡而無味的；無刺激性的
Her cooking was rather bland so her husband enrolled her in a cooking class.
因為她煮的菜都淡而無味，所以她的先生幫她報名廚藝課。

☑ **Let down**　ph. 放下；鬆懈；令人失望的
Her work quality was a total let down at work.
她在公司的工作品質是令人完全失望的。

☑ **Utterly** [`ʌtɚlɪ]　adv. 徹底地；完全地
She married for money and became utterly miserable with her marriage.　她為了錢而結婚，結果婚姻變得相當不幸。

☑ **Hype** [haɪp]　vt./n.【俚】大肆宣傳；使興奮
I tend to skip any movie that has been hyped up by the media.　我傾向不去看那些被媒體大肆宣傳的電影。

☑ **Admission** [əd`mɪʃən]　n. 進入（學校）許可；入場券；錄用
What did you pay for admission to the football game?
這場足球賽的入場券你付多少錢？

☑ **Refund** [rɪ`fʌnd]　vi./n. 退還；償還／退款
These pants make my buttocks look big. I demand a refund.
這件褲子使我的屁股看起來很大，我想要退還。

② 喜怒哀樂

Unit 29 抱怨

這樣說英文

172

Ⓐ I'm quite cross because this computer keyboard has keys missing from it.
Ⓑ Your keyboard looks fine.
Ⓐ I assure you there are keys missing. The computer kept telling me to press any key but there is no "any" key.

Ⓐ 我很生氣因為這個電腦的鍵盤有缺掉幾個按鍵。
Ⓑ 你的鍵盤看起來很好。
Ⓐ 我確定有缺少按鍵。電腦一直叫我按任意鍵,但是就是沒有「任意」鍵。

....

Ⓐ Excuse me but your dog dug up my flowerbed. It's all ruined now. Look at my petunias!
Ⓑ Oh, I'm terribly sorry. Maybe you should mend it with my shovel, barrow and other garden tools you borrowed and never returned.
Ⓐ Eh, I don't like petunias that much anyway.

Ⓐ 喂,你的狗把我的花圃都挖壞了。整個都毀了。看看我的牽牛花!
Ⓑ 噢,真的很抱歉。也許你需要用我的鏟子、手推車以及其他你跟我借卻從沒還我的工具來整修。
Ⓐ 嗯,其實我也沒那麼喜歡牽牛花。

....

Ⓐ I am so lucky because my mother-in-law is such an angel.
Ⓑ Really? You are lucky because mine is still breathing.
Ⓐ You dolt! I meant she's nice, not dead.

Ⓐ 我很幸運因為我的婆婆是個天使。
Ⓑ 真的嗎?你很幸運因為我的還活著。
Ⓐ 笨蛋!我是說他人很好,不是已經死了。

Vocabulary

Cross [krɔs]　adj. 發怒的;生氣的
Ruin [`rʊɪn]　vi. 毀壞;變成廢墟

Mend [mɛnd]　vi./vt. 修理
Dolt [dolt]　n. 笨蛋;傻瓜

這樣用句型

> I'm quite _____ because _____.

- excited... I'm going on an Antarctic expedition
  我很興奮因為我要去南極探險。
- scared... I'm stuck on a deserted island
  我很害怕因為我困在無人島。
- disappointed... she stood me up
  我很失望因為她放我鴿子。

> Excuse me but _____.

- your kid is kicking my seat　喂，你小孩在踢我的椅子。
- I was here first　喂，我先來的。
- who are you　抱歉，你是誰？
- you were going to marry me, not him
  喂，是你要跟我結婚，不是他。
- didn't you say I could go on a vacation
  喂，你不是說我可以去度假嗎？

註 Excuse me 可以是「對不起」、「不好意思」、或是如果是不客氣的用法，就是「喂！」的意思。

> I'm so lucky _____.

- to have divorced her finally　我真幸運終於跟她離婚。

· to win the lottery　我很幸運贏得樂透。

· to catch the last train out of here　我很幸運趕上最後一班火車離開。

· to see Halley's comet　我很幸運看到哈雷彗星。

用這句話更厲害！

❶ I **demand** to see the manager right now!
我要求立刻見到經理！

❷ Why do bad things always happen to me?
為何壞事都發生在我身上？

❸ There's nothing good to eat around here.
這附近沒什麼好吃的。

❹ The old lady is grumbling because she feels she has been mistreated.　這老女人抱怨因為她覺得被虐待。

❺ Stop whining already and start on your homework.
別再發牢騷了，開始寫你的作業。

❻ The audience responded with groans when the star of the concert did not show up.
當演唱會的明星沒有出現時，觀眾一片嘆息。

❼ You need to be strong to take all the blame as a service representative in the complaint department.
你在客服部門當客服人員需要堅強地接受所有的指責。

❽ It's quite tiring to hear you air your grievances repeatedly.
聽你反覆放送你的不幸真的很累人。

❾ She is about to go insane listening to her mother's incessant complaints.　她聽她媽媽的抱怨聽到都快瘋了。

❿ He complained that he was given insufficient time to finish his work.　他抱怨沒有足夠的時間完成工作。

⓫ They let out a deep moan when they were ordered to hike 20 miles in the snow.
當他們被指派要在雪地中徒步 20 英哩時他們發了一堆牢騷。

⑫ Stop lamenting about your problem and do something about it!　別怨嘆你的問題，並且去解決它！

必背單字片語

☑ **Demand** [dɪ`mænd]　vt. 要求；需求
Her demands are not reasonable so I choose to ignore them.
她的要求不合理，所以我選擇不理會他們。

☑ **Whine** [hwaɪn]　vt./n. 發牢騷；哀號聲
The dog gave a whine when it was put into a cage.
小狗被關在籠子裡時發出哀嚎聲。

☑ **Representative** [rɛprɪ`zɛntətɪv]　n. 代表
The radical group sent a representative to attend a press conference.
激進團體派了一個代表參加記者會。

☑ **grievance** [`grivəns]　n. 不滿
For years he nursed a grievance against his math teacher.
這麼多年來，他一直對數學老師心懷不滿。

☑ **Incessant** [ɪn`sɛsnt]　adj. 持續不斷的
The incessant noise from upstairs is keeping me awake.
從樓上傳來持續不斷的噪音使我不能入睡。

☑ **Insufficient** [ˌɪnsə`fɪʃənt]　adj. 不足的
We will feel hungry later because we have insufficient supply of food.
我們等會兒會感到飢餓因為我們沒有足夠的食物。

Unit 30 困擾

這樣說英文

175

Ⓐ There is a creepy man standing right outside our apartment but I have no idea who he is. What should we do?

Ⓑ That could be my uncle from the countryside. He looks all filthy, though. He said he was coming for a visit but didn't specify when.

Ⓐ I thought he was some perpetrator. I almost went out there with a baseball bat.

Ⓐ 有一個可怕的男人站在我們公寓外面，但是我不知道他是誰。我們該怎麼辦？

Ⓑ 那可能是我從鄉下來的叔叔。但他看起來好髒亂。他說過要來看我，但是沒說確認甚麼時候。

Ⓐ 我還以為他是什麼壞人，差一點就拿球棒出去（趕人）了。

⋯⋯⋯⋯⋯⋯⋯⋯⋯⋯⋯⋯⋯⋯⋯⋯⋯⋯⋯⋯⋯⋯⋯⋯⋯

Ⓐ Where are my keys? Have you seen my car key? I must find it!

Ⓑ Was it with that pile of envelopes? I think I might have mistaken it for trash.

Ⓐ You knucklehead! I'm late for my date! Hurry, run after the dumpster truck!

Ⓐ 我的鑰匙呢？你有看到我的車鑰匙嗎？我必須找到它！

Ⓑ 它跟一疊信件放在一起嗎？我想我可能把它誤當垃圾丟了。

Ⓐ 你這個小傻瓜！我約會遲到了！趕快去追垃圾車！

⋯⋯⋯⋯⋯⋯⋯⋯⋯⋯⋯⋯⋯⋯⋯⋯⋯⋯⋯⋯⋯⋯⋯⋯⋯

Ⓐ My girlfriend wore a dress that made her look really fat but I couldn't tell her.

Ⓑ That's awkward. She would have beaten you to a pulp if you did, though.

Ⓐ Yes, I'm quite aware of that. What would you have done?

Ⓐ 我女友穿了一件讓她看起來很胖的洋裝，但我不能告訴她。

Ⓑ 真尷尬。如果你真的跟她說，她應該會狠狠地揍你一頓。

Ⓐ 是呀，我知道。如果是你會怎麼做？

註 beat one to a pulp 打癱某人；狠揍某人

244

Vocabulary

Creepy [`kripɪ] adj. 令人毛骨悚然的
Filthy [`fɪlθɪ] adj. 汙穢的；骯髒的
Knucklehead [`nʌkl͵hɛd] n.【美口】小傻瓜

Dumpster [`dʌmpstɚ] n. 大型垃圾裝卸卡車
Aware [ə`wɛr] adj. 知道的

這樣用句型

> **There is a _____ but I have no idea _____.**

- hair in my soup... how it got there
  我的湯裡有根頭髮，但我不知道它是怎麼掉進去的。

- spy amongst us... who it could be
  我們之間有個間諜，但是我不知道可能是誰。

- car in the garage... if there is any gas in it
  車庫裡有部車，但我不知道車裡有沒有油。

- gigantic fireball hurtling towards the earth... if Superman could save us this time
  有一團巨大的火球正往地球猛撲過來，但我不知道超人這次能否救得了我們。

> **I am _____ ! Hurry, _____.**

- having a diabetic fit... bring me my insulin
  我的糖尿病開始發作！趕快把我的胰島素針劑拿來。

- turning into a werewolf... tie me up
  我正在變成狼人！趕快把我綁起來。

- drowning... pull me out　我溺水了！趕快救我上岸。

- falling in love with a married woman... save me from a disastrous relationship
  我愛上了一個有夫之婦！趕快將我從這段孽緣中救出來。

> She would have _____ if you _____ .

- … knocked you unconscious… hadn't told her you were behind her
  她會把你打昏如果你沒告訴她你在她後面。

- … departed without you… hadn't arrived in time
  她不會等你就出發如果你沒有準時到達。

- … yelled at you… didn't meet your sales quota
  她會對你大吼如果你沒有達成銷售業績目標。

- … driven you nuts… didn't move out of the house
  她會把你逼瘋如果你沒有搬出家門。

用這句話更厲害！

177

❶ My head is spinning over this problem.
這個問題搞得我頭昏腦脹。

❷ This setback kept me up all night in bed.
這個挫折讓我整晚失眠。

❸ I struggle to find a solution to this issue.
我努力地找出問題的解決方案。

❹ I seek answers but they remain elusive.
我探索答案，但是還是無法理解它們。

❺ The police were confounded by how the thief escaped.
小偷是如何逃跑的使警察感到困惑。

❻ His explanation left me even more perplexed and incensed.
他的解釋使我更加困擾和憤怒。

❼ She was disturbed by his reclusive behavior and began avoiding him. 她對他孤僻的行為感到困擾，所以開始避開他。

❽ I am at the end of my rope with no way out of this conundrum.
我已經智窮力竭，還是無法度過這個難關。

❾ Should I marry for love or for money? This question has bothered me for a long time.

我應該為愛還是為錢結婚？這個問題困擾我很久了。

❿ Don't fret, because sometimes the solution presents itself.

別苦惱，因為有時答案會自己出現。

⓫ Damned if you do, damn if you don't.　你做也不是，不做也不是。

⓬ She breathed a sigh of relief when her problems were resolved.　當她的問題獲得解決時，她鬆了一口氣。

必背單字片語

☑ **Struggle** [`strʌgl̩]　vi. 掙扎；奮鬥；努力
She is struggling to feed all her children.
她為了撫養全部的小孩而奮鬥。

- -

☑ **Elusive** [ɪ`lusɪv]　adj. 難以理解的
The reason to the mysterious disappearance of his car remains elusive.
他的車子離奇消失的原因還是難以理解的。

- -

☑ **Confound** [kɑn`faʊnd]　vt. 出乎意料的行為使人困惑
The worsening economy confounded the optimistic analysts.
衰退的經濟困擾著抱持樂觀態度的經濟學家。

- -

☑ **Incense** [ɪn`sɛns]　vt. 激怒
Mother was incensed over your attempt to pull the tablecloth out from under the plates.
你企圖將桌巾從盤子下面抽出來的行為激怒了媽。

- -

☑ **Reclusive** [rɪ`klusɪv]　adj. 孤寂的
Reclusive people do not enjoy social activities.
孤僻的人不喜歡社交活動。

Unit 31 拒絕

這樣說英文

Ⓐ I told my boyfriend to take a hike. In fact, I told him we're through.

Ⓑ Oh boy! What did he do to you to deserve that?

Ⓐ He proposed to me in a stadium full of spectators. I can't take that kind of pressure so I rejected him.

Ⓐ 我叫我的男友滾蛋。其實，我跟他分手了。

Ⓑ 天哪！他對你做了什麼事要被那樣對待？

Ⓐ 他在擠滿觀眾的球場跟我求婚。我無法承受那樣的壓力所以我拒絕了他。

⋯⋯⋯⋯⋯⋯⋯⋯⋯⋯⋯⋯⋯⋯⋯⋯⋯⋯⋯⋯⋯⋯⋯⋯⋯

Ⓐ It's a letter from the university. I'm going to find out if I'm going to Harvard!

Ⓑ I didn't know you applied. Quick, open it and see what it says.

Ⓐ They rejected me. If you need me I'll be upstairs crying my eyes out.

Ⓐ 有一封從大學寄來的信。我要看看是否能進哈佛！

Ⓑ 我不知道你提出了申請。趕快，打開來看看裡面怎麼說。

Ⓐ 他們駁回我的申請。如果你要找我，我會在樓上大哭。

⋯⋯⋯⋯⋯⋯⋯⋯⋯⋯⋯⋯⋯⋯⋯⋯⋯⋯⋯⋯⋯⋯⋯⋯⋯

Ⓐ Won't you please go out with me? Come on, I implore you.

Ⓑ Get away from me. I wouldn't date you even if you were the last man on earth.

Ⓐ I know we're forty years apart, but age should not be a hindrance, right?

Ⓐ 你真的不跟我出去約會嗎？不要這樣啦，我求你了。

Ⓑ 走開。既使你是地球上最後一個男人我也不會跟你約會。

Ⓐ 我知道我們相差四十歲，但是年齡應該不是阻礙，對嗎？

Vocabulary

Take a hike　ph.【美口】滾開	Implore [ɪmˋplor]　vt. 懇求；哀求
Spectator [spɛkˋtetɚ]　n. 觀眾	Hindrance [ˋhɪndrəns]　n. 障礙

> **I can't take that kind of pressure so _____.**

- I started smoking　我無法承受那種壓力，所以我開始抽菸。
- I quit my job　我無法承受那種壓力，所以我辭去了工作。
- I divorced him　我無法承受那種壓力，所以我跟他離婚。
- I went berserk and punched him
  我無法承受那種壓力，所以我抓狂並打了他。
- I dropped out of college　我無法承受那種壓力，所以我退學。

> **Quick, _____it and _____.**

- poke... run　快一點，戳它一下並快跑。
- swallow... see if your headache goes away
  快一點，把它吞下去然後看你的頭痛會不會減緩。
- apply pressure on... stop the bleeding　快一點，用力壓住它來止血。
- kick... see if it's alive　快一點，踢它一下看它是否還活著。
- close... stop the zombies from coming in
  快一點，將它關上來防止殭屍進入。

> **Won't you _____ ? Come on, _____.**

- marry me... please marry me　你不嫁給我嗎？別這樣，請妳嫁給我。
- hire me... you know you need my help
  你不雇用我嗎？快吧，你知道你需要我的幫忙。

· lend me some cash... I really need money
你不借我一些錢嗎？別這樣，我真的需要錢。

· go away... stop bothering me　你不滾開嗎？快一點，別再煩我了。

· come look at my stamp collection... humor me
你不來看我的郵票收藏嗎？拜託，遷就我一下嘛。

用這句話更厲害！

❶ I refused to accept his insincere apology.
我拒絕接受他那沒誠意的道歉。

❷ She was refused entry to the posh restaurant because she wore shorts.　高級餐廳拒絕她進入因為她穿短褲。

❸ We reject the idea that the sun revolves around the earth.
我們否決了太陽繞著地球轉的理論。

❹ He refused to meet with the person who allegedly ran over his dog.　他拒絕跟那個疑似壓死他的狗的人見面。

❺ The rejects are proving everyone wrong by winning the championship.　落選者以贏得冠軍來證實每個人都錯了。

❻ There is a shoe store selling factory rejects for a song.
有一間賣超便宜的工廠次級品的鞋店。

❼ The union rejected a 30% pay cut proposal and went on strike.　工會拒絕裁減三成薪資的提案並策劃罷工。

❽ I was denied access to my email because someone has hacked my account and changed my password.
我無法讀取我的電子信箱因為有人盜用了我的帳號並改了我的密碼。

❾ He was embarrassed because his expensive supercar refused to start.　他很沒面子因為他的昂貴跑車不能發動。

❿ How do you reject a guy without hurting his ego?
你如何拒絕一個男人又不傷其自尊心？

⓫ I declined the invitation to give a speech at the graduation ceremony.　我回絕了在畢業典禮致詞的邀請。

必背單字片語

☑ **Insincere** [ˌɪnsɪnˋsɪr]　adj. 無誠意
He was insincere to help the orphans.
他並無誠意救濟孤兒。

- -

☑ **Posh** [pɑʃ]　adj.【口】奢侈的；第一流的
He lives in a very posh neighborhood but drives around in a lemon.
他住在非常有錢的地區卻開著一部爛車。

> 註　lemon 在此是俚語中指無價值的東西或瑕疵品，這個句子裡是指爛車。

☑ **Allegedly** [əˋlɛdʒɪdlɪ]　adv. 疑似地
She allegedly ran over the woman with her scooter but there weren't any witnesses around when it happened.
她疑似輾過一個女人和她的機車，但是發生的時候沒有目擊者在附近。

- -

☑ **Strike** [straɪk]　n. 罷工
The whole public transportation system came to a standstill because of a massive strike.
整個公共運輸系統因為大罷工而停擺。

- -

☑ **Embarrass** [ɪmˋbærəs]　vt. 使不好意思
She was embarrassed to find out that she had forgotten to pull the "XL Size" sticker off her pants.
她發現自己忘記將 XL Size 標籤貼紙從褲子上撕掉而感到不好意思。

❷ 喜怒哀樂

Unit 32 滿肚子火

這樣說英文

Ⓐ Get out of my way! You slowpokes shall stop and let me pass! (Honk)

Ⓑ You're going too fast. Slow down or else you're going to hit someone.

Ⓐ Be quiet! Roll down your window so I can give that driver a piece of my mind.

Ⓐ 讓開！你們這群慢郎中，停下來讓我過！（鳴喇叭聲）

Ⓑ 你開的太快了。慢一點，不然會撞到人。

Ⓐ 你閉嘴！把你的車窗搖下，我要去罵那個駕駛。

⋯⋯⋯⋯⋯⋯⋯⋯⋯⋯⋯⋯⋯⋯⋯⋯⋯⋯⋯⋯⋯⋯⋯⋯⋯⋯

Ⓐ Everyone get out of my way! I got a baseball bat and I'm going to bludgeon anyone who stops me!

Ⓑ Someone call the authorities! This mad man is smashing all the car windows! Help! Help!

Ⓐ That's right! I'm mad! I'm mad at society for humiliating me!

Ⓐ 你們每個人都讓開！我有一支球棒，所以我會攻擊任何阻止我的人！

Ⓑ 趕快去叫警察！這個瘋子正在把所有的車窗擊破。救命！救命！

Ⓐ 你說對了！我瘋了！我很生氣這個社會如此羞辱我！

⋯⋯⋯⋯⋯⋯⋯⋯⋯⋯⋯⋯⋯⋯⋯⋯⋯⋯⋯⋯⋯⋯⋯⋯⋯⋯

Ⓐ Just wait till I get my hands on her!! How dare she take my car without my permission!

Ⓑ But you have an old jalopy. It wouldn't matter if she scratched it, right?

Ⓐ No, you don't understand. I just bought a brand new car!

Ⓐ 等到我抓到她你就知道了！她膽敢沒有我的允許就把車開走！

Ⓑ 但是你的車是部過時的老爺車。如果她刮傷它應該沒關係，不是嗎？

Ⓐ 不是，你不知道，我剛剛買了部新車！

Vocabulary

Give sb. a piece of one's mind　ph. 責備某人；坦誠相告
Bludgeon [`blʌdʒən]　vt. 強迫；威脅；重擊
Authority [ə`θɔrətɪ]　n. 權；權力；職權
Jalopy [dʒə`lɑpɪ]　n. 過時的破舊汽車
Scratch [skrætʃ]　vt. 擦傷；抓；刮；去除；亂畫

這樣用句型

You are ＿＿＿＿. ＿＿＿＿ or else ＿＿＿＿.

- driving too slow.... Speed up... get a ticket for holding up traffic.
  你開車太慢了。開快一點，否則就會被開阻礙交通的罰單。

- working too hard... Get some rest... you'll die from overwork
  你工作太辛苦了。要多休息，不然會過勞死的。

- obviously lost. Ask for directions... go around in circles
  你很明顯迷路了。去問路，要不然會一直原地打轉。

Everyone ＿＿＿＿! I ＿＿＿＿.

- be careful... am coming through with a bucket of boiling water
  大家小心！我要提一桶滾水走過囉。

- be generous... am collecting funds for animal rights
  大家大方點！我正在為捍衛動物權利募款。

- please be quiet... cannot hear what the TV is saying
  大家請安靜！我聽不到電視機的報導。

Just wait until ＿＿＿＿.

- your father comes home
  等到你爸爸回家你就知道了！
- I'm done with my work and I'll join you

  等到我把工作做完我就會陪你。
- she gives you an answer before you jump to conclusions
  在你妄下結論前先等她給你答案。

用這句話更厲害！

❶ He gunned his engine and sped furiously across the junction.
  他火力全開並飆速開過十字路口。

❷ No way! Somebody is going to pay dearly for this!
  怎麼會這樣！一定要有人為這個付出代價。

❸ This is for what you did to me. Payback is a bitch, isn't it?
  這是回報你對我做的事。報應是殘酷的，不是嗎？

❹ Don't be so angry. Meditation can help you to control your emotions better.　別氣成這樣。冥想可以更有效的幫助你控制情緒。

❺ I am going to sue him for every last penny he has!
  我要把他告到破產！

❻ She is fuming because I tore a hole in her favorite dress.
  她很憤怒因為我把他最喜愛的洋裝弄破一個洞。

❼ Now you shall suffer the wrath of the gods!
  現在你應該遭受天譴！

❽ I am going to let him have it!　我要他好看！

註 let sb. have it 有著「就給某人吧」，但是在生氣時口頭上使用，卻有我要「收拾某人」或是「讓某人吃頓苦頭」的意思。

❾ Your dog dug up my flower bed and I am just livid.
  你的狗把我的花圃挖壞了，所以我非常生氣。

❿ I will forgive you only when hell freezes over!
  我永遠都不會原諒你的！

⑪ You can marry him over my dead body!

你想都別想要我答應你嫁給他！

必背單字片語

☑ **Furious** [`fjʊrɪəs]　adj. 大發雷霆；猛烈的
Trying desperately to hold it in, he pedaled furiously down the road towards the gas station bathroom.

拼命地試著忍住上廁所的感覺，他猛烈地踩著踏板騎向加油站的廁所。

☑ **Payback** [`pebæk]　n. 償付；歸還
You should use this charge card with a 1% cash payback.

你應該用這張有 1% 回饋金的信用卡。

☑ **Meditate** [`mɛdə,tet]　vi. 沉思
I spend two hours a day meditating and that helps me to think clearly.

我一天花兩小時沉思，這幫助我思路清晰。

☑ **Wrath** [ræθ]　n. 憤怒；【宗】天譴
I incurred my ex-girlfriend's wrath by spreading rumors about her new boyfriend.

我四處傳播前女友的新男友的謠言引發了她的憤怒。

☑ **Over my dead body**　ph. 除非我死了；免談
You can win the championship this year over my dead body.

你今年絕不可能贏得冠軍。

註 字面上的意思是「跨越我的屍體」，也就是說，我會拚死阻擋這件事情，要先等我死了這件事才有可能發生。

Unit 33 反駁

這樣說英文

Ⓐ I assure you she did not steal your money.

Ⓑ She is the only person here and my money is missing, so I am definite she is the thief.

Ⓐ According to the security video you dropped your wallet. Here, let me play it for you.

Ⓐ 我很確定她沒有偷你的錢。

Ⓑ 她是這裡唯一的一個人，然後我的錢不見了，所以我很確定她是小偷。

Ⓐ 監視器畫面顯示是你把錢包掉在地上。讓我播給你看。

- - - - - - - - - -

Ⓐ You really ought to refute his allegations if you want people to support you.

Ⓑ I think I have mustered enough courage to stand up to his accusations.

Ⓐ Good. Now go up to the stage and let him have it.

Ⓐ 你實在應該去反駁他對你的指控，如果你想要人們支持你。

Ⓑ 我想我已經鼓起足夠的勇氣去面對他的指控。

Ⓐ 那好，現在就上台去反駁他。

- - - - - - - - - -

Ⓐ You went out with my boyfriend last night, didn't you? You are an abominable witch!

Ⓑ I didn't pinch him from you in case you're wondering. He said he was going to leave you anyway.

Ⓐ That's not true! I'll break his neck if he did!

Ⓐ 你昨晚跟我男友出去對不對？你這個可惡的狐狸精！

Ⓑ 就算你感到懷疑，我也並沒有將他偷走。他說他反正要離開你了。

Ⓐ 那不是真的！如果他真的那樣說，我會把他碎屍萬段！

Vocabulary

Definite [`dɛfənɪt]　adj. 確切的；肯定的
Allegation [ˌælə`geʃən]　n. 斷言；辯解、主張
Muster [`mʌstə]　vt. 召集；鼓起（勇氣）

Abominable [ə`bɑmɪnəbəl]　adj. 可惡的；令人討厭的
Pinch [pɪntʃ]　vt.【俚】偷取；擅自拿取

這樣用句型

185

② 喜怒哀樂

> **She is the only person _____ so _____.**

- without a partner... I'll ask her to partner with me
  她是唯一一個沒有搭檔的人，所以我將請她跟我搭擋。

- I know in this town... I'll go ask her for help
  她是唯一一個熟悉這個城市的人，所以我將請她幫忙。

- who can defend us in court... hire her
  她是在法庭上唯一一個可以為我們辯護的人，所以雇用她。

> **You really ought to _____ if you want _____.**

- start running now... to escape the rampaging zombies
  你實在應該開始逃跑如果你想逃離到處破壞的殭屍。

- groom yourself better... to attract any girl
  你實在應該把自己打扮好一點如果你想吸引女生的注意。

- ask her out... her to be your date
  你實在該約她出去如果你想要她成為你的約會對象。

> **You _____, didn't you? You are _____!**

- drank all the booze and threw up... so wasted
  你把所有的酒喝光了並且吐了，對吧？你真的醉了！
- ran a red light... so going to get a ticket
  你闖紅燈了，對吧？你真的會拿到罰單！
- cheated on her... so busted
  你對她不忠，對吧？你失敗了！

用這句話更厲害！

186

1 I can neither confirm nor deny the accusations against me.
我既不能證實也無法否認對我的指控。

2 I swear to god I didn't do it and I can prove it.
我對天發誓不是我做的，而且我有證據。

3 I shall sue whoever hurls false allegations at me.
我會去控告任何不實指控我的人。

4 Do you expect me to respond to the humiliating accusations with wit and gracefulness?
你指望我以機智和風度翩翩的氣質去回應那些侮辱性的指控？

5 I had to go to court to refute all the fraudulent credit card charges. 我需要去法院反駁被詐騙的信用卡帳目。

6 My son did not cheat on his exam. His friend offered to let him copy the answer.
我兒子考試沒有作弊。他的朋友願意讓他抄答案的。

7 You should do more research and get your facts straight!
你應該多做些研究並將事實搞清楚！

8 She started it! I already told her not to play with fire.
她先開始的！我已經告訴她不要玩火了。

9 I remain innocent until proven guilty.
我在被證實有罪之前都是清白的。

10 She alleged that I had secretly read her diary but that is not possible because I am illiterate.
她指控我私底下偷看她的日記，但是那是不可能的。我不識字。

⓫ It is not my fault that we lost this account. Who would have thought they defaulted?

失去這個客戶不是我的錯。誰曾想過他們會違約？

⓬ I have nothing to do with this. She is just trying to frame me.

我與此事無關。她只是想陷害我。

必背單字片語

☑ **Deny** [dɪ`naɪ] vt. 否認
She won't deny the fact that she is lazy, but she won't change her ways either.

她不否認她很懶惰這個事實，但它也不會改變她的做法。

- -

☑ **Fraudulent** [`frɔdʒələnt] adj. 詐欺的；騙取的
How can you tell if you have just received a fraudulent phone call? 你如何能知道是否接到詐騙電話？

- -

☑ **Research** [rɪ`sɝtʃ] n. 研究
According to my research, you are probably a descendent of an ape. 根據我的研究，你可能是猿猴的後代。

- -

☑ **Guilty** [`gɪltɪ] adj. 有罪的；內疚
The girl feels guilty about not spending time with her parents when they were still alive.

這個女孩因為父母在世時沒有花時間陪伴他們而感到內疚。

- -

☑ **Illiterate** [ɪ`lɪtərɪt] adj./n. 不識字的；文盲
He is ashamed to admit that both he and his wife are illiterate. 他羞於承認他與妻子都是文盲。

- -

☑ **Frame** [frem] vt. 給…裝框；【俚】陷害；捏造
She framed her university diploma.

她將大學畢業證書裱框。

2
喜怒哀樂

259

Unit 34 猶豫

Ⓐ Yesterday I got a text message from you asking me about my credit card number.

Ⓑ I didn't ask you for anything. It sounds like a scam.

Ⓐ Oh no! At first I hesitated but I eventually texted over my ID number, credit card number, my ATM pin and the whole shebang.

Ⓐ 昨天我收到你的簡訊問我信用卡號。

Ⓑ 我沒問你,聽起來像是詐騙。

Ⓐ 天哪!原本我遲疑了一下,但是我還是把我的身分證號、信用卡號、還有我的提款卡密碼等全都傳過去了。

. . . .

Ⓐ Please marry me. If you don't, it would mean the end of our relationship.

Ⓑ Hmm. I am not sure. I want you to stick around but I want to see other people too.

Ⓐ Well, then I have no hesitation to call it quits.

Ⓐ 請嫁給我吧!如果你不願意,就表示我們要分手了。

Ⓑ 嗯,我不確定耶。我希望你在身邊,但是我也想跟其他人約會。

Ⓐ 那我會毫不猶豫的與你分手。

. . . .

Ⓐ What flavor would you like to try?

Ⓑ You have over a hundred flavors of ice cream! I am not sure which one I should taste first. Oh wait. I'm lactose intolerant.

Ⓐ In that case would you mind if I serve the customer behind you?

Ⓐ 你想試吃哪一個口味?

Ⓑ 你們有超過一百種口味的冰淇淋!我不太確定應該先從哪一個開始試吃。等等,我有乳糖不耐症。

Ⓐ 既然這樣,你介意我幫下一位顧客服務嗎?

這樣用句型

> **At first I _____ but I eventually _____.**

- wasn't sure... believed him　起先我並不確定，但我最後還是相信他。
- was going to slam the door on him... invited him in
  起先我還想讓他吃閉門羹，但我最後還是請他進來。
- couldn't believe him... did after listening to his explanation
  起先我本來不能相信他，但是我聽了他的解釋後還是相信他了。
- was freezing... warmed up with a good cup of coffee
  起先我凍僵了，但最後喝了杯香醇的咖啡恢復溫暖。

> **Please _____. If you don't, _____.**

- stay... I'll cry　請你留下來。不然我就要哭了。
- do as I say... I'll hit you with a frying pan
  請跟著我說的做，不然我就用平底鍋打你。
- ignore him... you'll fall for his tricks
  請不要理他，要不然你就會上他的當。
- drink plenty of water... you'll be dehydrated
  請多喝水，不然你會脫水。

2 喜怒哀樂

In that case, would you mind _____?

- if I took your seat　既然這樣，您是否介意我坐你的位子？
- giving up your concert ticket
  既然這樣，您介意放棄您的演唱會入場券嗎？
- coming back again tomorrow　既然這樣，您介意明天再跑一趟嗎？

用這句話更厲害！

189

❶ I don't know if I should go or stay.
我不知道是否該離開還是留下。

❷ Don't hesitate to contact me should you have any inquiries.
如果有任何問題請別猶豫與我聯繫。

❸ I am not sure if I needed to buy that extra computer.
我不確定是否需要多買那台電腦。

❹ I vacillate between this pretty girl and that gorgeous woman.
我在漂亮女孩和嫵媚女人間游移不定。

❺ Why are you so indecisive? Please make up your mind!
你為何猶豫不決？請趕快下定決心！

❻ I am unsure of which hors d'oeuvre to order.
我不知道該點哪一道開胃菜。

❼ Can you stop dithering and choose whom you want to marry?　你能不要再三心二意，快點選要娶誰好嗎？

❽ She couldn't decide so she bought everything in the store.
她無法決定，所以買下店內所有商品。

❾ He hesitated for a second and then started exchanging insults with the reporter.　他遲疑了一下然後開始與記者們互嗆。

❿ I could not decide which employee to fire so I fired them both.　我無法決定該解雇哪一位員工，所以就將兩個人都開除了。

⓫ They were uncertain about what to have for dinner so they ate nothing for the night.

他們不確定晚餐要吃什麼，所以他們整晚沒吃。

必背單字片語

☑ **Inquiry** [ɪn`kwaɪrɪ] n. 詢問；打聽；探索
Further inquiry suggests that she has been to Atlantic City with an unknown man.
更進一步的調查顯示她曾經跟一名未知的男子到過大西洋城。

- -

☑ **Vacillate** [`væsl͵et] vi. 躊躇（+between）
She vacillates between the designer shoe and a cheap knock-off.
她躊躇於設計師鞋款和便宜仿冒品。

- -

☑ **Indecisive** [͵ɪndɪ`saɪsɪv] adj. 優柔寡斷的
I cannot make up my mind if I liked people who are indecisive.
我無法決定是否喜歡優柔寡斷的人。

- -

☑ **hors d'oeuvre** ph.【法】（主菜前的）開胃小菜
They ordered strange sounding hors d'oeuvres from the menu. 他們點了菜單上聽起來很怪的開胃菜。

- -

☑ **Dither** [`dɪðɚ] vi. 躊躇；猶豫
He did not dither about his next course of action.
他不會猶豫下一步該怎麼做。

- -

☑ **Exchange** [ɪks`tʃendʒ] vt. 交換
She exchanged glances with the charming, handsome guy sitting by the piano.
她與坐在鋼琴旁的英俊男子眉來眼去。

Unit 35 吃驚

190

Ⓐ There was a twenty-car pile-up on the highway.

Ⓑ Oh no! Didn't your wife say she was taking the highway to work?

Ⓐ Yes, I was shocked. But, I got a bigger shock when I found out there was another man in the car with her.

Ⓐ 高速公路上發生了二十部車的連環車禍。

Ⓑ 喔不！你老婆不是說她要開高速公路去上班嗎？

Ⓐ 是呀，所以我嚇了一跳。不過當我發現車上還有另一個男人跟她在一起時我更震驚。

- -

Ⓐ Mom, I got arrested for shoplifting. I'm at the sheriff's office right now.

Ⓑ Oh no! Are you serious? Oh, I should have given you the money when you asked for it. I feel so bad.

Ⓐ Chill, mom. I'm just kidding. I'm just upstairs on my cellphone. Now, about that money...

Ⓐ 媽媽，我因為在店裡偷東西被逮捕。我現在在警長辦公室。

Ⓑ 喔不！你當真嗎？當時你跟我要錢的時候我應該給你一些才對。我真是難過。

Ⓐ 別緊張，媽，我是跟你開玩笑的。我只是在樓上用手機打給你。那至於錢的事...

- -

Ⓐ Call our kids and tell them we're getting a divorce.

Ⓑ I'm puzzled. We're not divorcing. Wouldn't that give them a shock for nothing?

Ⓐ Yes, but that'll make them fly home straightaway to see us.

Ⓐ 打電話跟我們的孩子說我們要離婚。

Ⓑ 我不懂。我們並沒有要離婚，這樣不是沒事去嚇唬他們嗎？

Ⓐ 對呀，但是那會使他們馬上飛回家來看我們。

Pile-up　ph.【非正式】多車相撞，連環撞車

Shoplift [`ʃɑpˏlɪft]　vt./vi. 冒充顧客在商店內偷竊（商品）

Sheriff [`ʃɛrəf]　n. 警長；郡長

Puzzled [pʌz!d]　adj. 困惑的；搞糊塗的

Straightaway [`stretəˏwe]　adv. 照直前進地；立即地

這樣用句型

Oh no! Did _____?

· you buy insurance from that conman　喔不！你向騙子買保險嗎？

· you burn the cooking　喔不！你把菜燒焦了嗎？

· he drive off the cliff　喔不！他開的車墜落山谷了嗎？

Are you serious? I should have _____.

· listened to your advice　你當真嗎？那我應該聽從你的建議。

· paid more attention to my surroundings
你當真嗎？那我應該更注意我周遭的人事物。

· regular health checkups　你當真嗎？那我應該定期去檢查。

Call _____ and _____.

· home... wish everyone well　打電話回家祝大家平安。

· the police... report the crime　打電話到警局報案。

· your girlfriend... break up with her　打電話給你女友分手。

用這句話更厲害！

1 Gasp! I am appalled at the chaos he caused!
我被他所造成的混亂嚇呆了！

2 There is no way a person can cause so much havoc.
沒有一個人能夠造成如此的浩劫。

3 The scientist administered electric shocks to the dog.
科學家對這隻狗施予電擊。

4 They like to waste time reading about shocking celebrity gossip.
他們喜歡浪費時間讀一些驚人的明星八卦。

5 I cannot believe how low this person stooped to get ahead.
我不能相信這個人為了超前而屈尊的這麼低。

6 Holy cow! I have never seen a two-headed bovine!
我的老天！我從未看過兩個頭的牛！

7 His divorce shocked him back into reality.
他的婚變使他震驚地重回現實。

8 He forgot his insulin shots and went into a diabetic shock.
他忘記打胰島素的針劑，結果糖尿病休克。

9 The shock jock got taken off the air for cracking racial jokes.
那位蓬亂的蘇格蘭佬的節目因為開種族玩笑而遭取消。

10 The President shocked the nation when he admitted having an affair with an intern.
當總統承認跟實習生有婚外情時震驚了全國。

11 The earthquake produced a devastating shockwave that leveled buildings.
地震所發出的破壞性震波夷平了許多建築物。

12 The bank tellers had a fright during the bank robbery.
銀行辦事員在銀行發生搶案時受到驚嚇。

必背單字片語

☑ **Chaos** [`keɑs]　n. 混亂
The ensuing chaos in the market guaranteed panic selling by investors.
跟隨而來的股市動盪必然會讓投資人急著拋售股票。

☑ **Havoc** [`hævək]　n. 浩劫；大混亂
The disease wreaked havoc on his immune system.
這個病破壞了他的免疫系統。

☑ **Administer** [əd`mɪnəstɚ]　vt. 經營；管理；給予
Doctors administered anesthesia before they cut him open.
醫師在幫他開刀前將他麻醉。

☑ **Stoop** [stup]　vi. 屈身；彎腰
She stooped over to pick up some trash and found a gold coin.
她彎腰下去撿垃圾而發現一枚金幣。

☑ **Shot** [ʃɑt]　n. 注射
The doctors jabbed him with multiple shots before he went on his jungle excursion.
在他去叢林探險之前，醫生們給他打了很多針。

☑ **Crack** [kræk]　vt.【口】說（笑話）
She likes a guy who can crack jokes spontaneously.
她喜歡能夠即興說笑話的男生。

2 喜怒哀樂

超有梗 日常英語 Talk Show　Daily English Talk Show

這樣說英文

Ⓐ Your boss is asking you to come in during the weekend and work extra hours.

Ⓑ I would rather poke my eyes out with a fork than listen to that old bag.

Ⓐ She's standing behind you.

Ⓐ 你老闆要求你週末進公司加班。

Ⓑ 我寧可把眼睛挖出來也不要聽那個老太婆的話。

Ⓐ 她現在就站在你後面。

註　old bag 字面上是舊包包的意思，但在這裡是指老女人或老太婆的意思。

Ⓐ That creep is trying to ask me out! Why do I attract all the wrong guys?

Ⓑ You have been complaining about being lonely. Maybe if you were less picky you would find someone.

Ⓐ I would rather go out with the abominable snowman.

Ⓐ 那個卑鄙小人要約我出去！為何我都吸引不速配的男人？

Ⓑ 你一向都抱怨孤獨一人。也許如果你不要那麼挑剔你會找到伴。

Ⓐ 我寧可跟傳說中的喜馬拉雅山雪人出去。

Ⓐ Would you go camping in the wilderness? It can be lovely being far away from civilization.

Ⓑ I'd rather lounge around in a 5-star hotel and sip champagne in a Jacuzzi than sleep in a tent and get bitten alive by bugs.

Ⓐ Phew. I was hoping you would say that. I can't stand camping either.

Ⓐ 你會去荒野露營嗎？到離文明很遠的地方可以很美好。

Ⓑ 與其睡在帳篷裡被蟲咬，我還寧可慵懶地在五星級飯店消磨時光、在按摩池中喝香檳。

Ⓐ 幸好你這麼說，我也不能忍受露營。

這樣用句型

②
喜怒哀樂

Your _____ is asking you to _____.

· mother... have lots of children　你媽要求你生很多小孩。

· roommate... stop snoring　你的室友要求你不要打呼。

· landlord... pay your rent　你的房東要求你付租金。

Maybe if you were _____ you would _____.

· more careful... have noticed the hole in the floor
也許如果你更小心，你會注意到地上的洞。

· more adventurous... enjoy your trip more
也許如果更有冒險精神，你會更享受你的旅行。

· less obnoxious... have more friends
也許如果你不那麼討人厭，你會有更多朋友。

I'd rather _____ than _____.

· kiss a monkey... you　我寧可親一隻猴子也不親你。

- have sushi... fried chicken　我寧可吃壽司也不要吃炸雞。
- be dead... work with you　我寧可死掉也不與你共事。

用這句話更厲害！

195

1 My preference is to sit next to the lavatory for convenience.
為了方便我較喜歡坐在與飛機上的洗手間相鄰的位置。

2 He prefers working from home than commuting two hours a day.　他寧可在家上班相較於每天通勤兩小時。

3 I'd rather attend an Ivy League school but I couldn't afford it.
我寧可去上常春藤盟校，但是我付不起學費。

4 He would prefer to sit right at the front but he was too cheap to pay for the seat.
他會比較喜歡坐在前排，但是他太小氣而不想付錢。

5 The spy rather dies a painful death than betrays his country.
間諜寧可死得痛苦也不願出賣自己的國家。

6 This is his preferred weapon in close combat.
這是他在近距離搏鬥時較喜歡使用的武器。

7 Since when did you favor trains over buses for your choice of transportation?
你什麼時候開始寧可選擇火車而不是公車來做為交通工具？

8 I prefer short hair over long, but my boyfriend prefers it the other way round.　我較喜歡短髮而不是長髮，但我男友卻是相反。

9 Would you like to charge it? Or, would you prefer to settle the payment with cash?
你要以信用卡支付嗎？還是你較想要用現金支付？

10 My wife would rather starve herself to death than to eat my cooking.　我老婆寧可餓死也不願意吃我煮的飯。

11 If you don't like your computer desktop wallpaper you can change it by clicking on the "preference" button.
如果你不喜歡你的電腦桌面的桌布，你可以到「選項」中去更換。

⑫ Would you prefer if I called or emailed you? Or would you rather if I texted you?

你較想要我打電話給你還是寄電郵？還是你想要我傳訊息給你？

必背單字片語

☑ **Lavatory** [ˋlævəˌtorɪ] n. 洗手間
Someone has disabled the smoke detector in the lavatory and locked himself in.
有人將廁所內的煙霧偵測器弄壞並將他自己反鎖在內。

☑ **Commute** [kəˋmjut] vi. 通勤
I like to listen to music when I commute between my apartment and the office.
我喜歡在通勤於住處和辦公室之間時聽音樂。

☑ **Betray** [bɪˋtre] vt. 背叛；出賣
You betrayed the company by selling our secrets to the competitor. 你將公司的商業機密賣給對手而出賣了公司。

☑ **Transportation** [ˌtrænspɚˋteʃən] n. 運輸；輸送
We require transportation capable of light speed to escape from the diabolical aliens
我們需要以光速行駛的交通工具來逃離邪惡的外星人。

☑ **Charge** [tʃɑrdʒ] v.【美】用信用卡付賬
He is going to have a shock when he realized his girlfriend charged her first class ticket to Hawaii on his card.
當他發現他女友用他的信用卡支付去夏威夷的頭等艙機票時，他將會嚇一跳。

☑ **Settle** [ˋsɛtl̩] vt. 解決；支付
He settled all his credit card bills after receiving his paycheck. 他拿到薪水後支付了所有的信用卡帳單。

Unit 37 完蛋了

Ⓐ I have an important job interview today and I don't want to be tardy.

Ⓑ I suggest you hurry because I forgot to tell you the clock ran out of batteries.

Ⓐ Are you kidding me? What time is it? Why didn't you tell me earlier?

Ⓐ 今天我有一個重要的工作面試，所以我不想遲到。

Ⓑ 那我建議你動作快一點，因為我忘了跟你說時鐘已經沒電了。

Ⓐ 你在開我玩笑嗎？現在幾點？為什麼你不早點告訴我？

. . . .

Ⓐ Can you step on it? I have a stomachache and I need to get home straightaway.

Ⓑ Looks like you have to hold it in because there's a massive jam in front of us.

Ⓐ Stop the cab and let me out here. Looks like I have to run like hell.

Ⓐ 你可以開快一點嗎？我肚子痛，而且需要馬上回家。

Ⓑ 看來你必須要忍住，因為前方有很長的塞車。

Ⓐ 將車停下來讓我下車。看來我必須拼命地跑。

. . . .

Ⓐ Here we are finally on our vacation to Europe. I trust you have turned all the lights and the stove off before we departed.

Ⓑ Oh no, I didn't. I thought you did. By the way, I assume you have the passports and tickets.

Ⓐ Oh no, I don't. I thought you have them.

Ⓐ 我們終於要去歐洲之旅的假期了。我相信你已經將燈和火爐的火都關掉了。

Ⓑ 糟糕，我以為你關掉了。順帶一提，我以為你拿了護照和機票。

Ⓐ 糟糕，我以為你拿了。

Vocabulary

Tardy [`tɑrdɪ]   adj. 遲到的
Run out   ph. 用完
Straightaway   adv. 立刻；馬上

Massive [`mæsɪv]   adj. 大規模的
Depart [dɪ`pɑrt]   vi. 出發

這樣用句型

> **I have _____ and I don't want _____.**

· an exam tomorrow... to fail it   我明天有考試，而且我不想當掉。

· three pets... anymore   我有三隻寵物，所以我不再想要了。

· debt up to my eyeballs... to take up another loan
我債台高築，所以我不想再貸款了。

> **I have _____ and I need to _____.**

· a headache... see a doctor   我頭痛所以我需要去看醫生。

· too many credit cards... cancel some of them
我有太多張信用卡，所以我需要取消幾張。

· smelly socks... wash them
我有雙臭臭的襪子，所以我需要將它們洗一洗。

> **Here we are _____.**

· alone at last   我們終於單獨在一起了。

· lost in the desert with no water   我們現在在沙漠裡迷路了又沒有水。

- drinking ourselves silly on a Monday afternoon
  我們在星期一下午喝得爛醉。

用這句話更厲害！

198

1 What do you mean there is no contingency plan? We are trapped in the middle of nowhere and our car ran out of gas!
你說沒有應變計劃是甚麼意思？我們被困在了無人煙的地方，而車子也沒油了！

2 Murphy's Law states that anything that can go wrong will go wrong.　莫非定律宣稱如果會出錯的事情就是會出錯。

3 He panicked and lost control of his bowels.
他一緊張就「挫屎」。

4 He looked like a deer caught in the headlights of a truck.
他看起來像是快被卡車撞到的鹿一般驚慌。

5 He gave a speech without realizing that his zipper was open.
他演講時並沒發現拉鍊大開。

6 She criticized her boss in an email and then sent it to her boss by mistake.
她在電郵上大肆批評她的老闆，然後誤寄了這封郵件到老闆的信箱。

7 He sent an urgent package to Taiwan but it was routed to Thailand instead.
他寄出了一個緊急的包裹到台灣，但它卻被轉到泰國去了。

8 She whispered sweet nothings to the person on the phone without realizing she had dialed the wrong number.
她輕聲地跟電話那頭的人說情話，卻不知自己撥錯號碼。

註 sweet nothings 情話

9 Goodness gracious! How can you draw a mustache on your dad's picture inside his passport?
我的老天！你怎麼能在你爸爸的護照裡面的照片上畫鬍子？

10 He mistook Tabasco hot sauce for tomato juice and gulped it down.　他誤認塔巴斯哥辣椒醬為番茄汁並把整瓶圇圇吞了下去。

⓫ What am I going to do? I bought my boyfriend an expensive present and accidentally charged it to my husband's credit card. He will kill me when he finds out.

我該怎麼辦才好？我買了個昂貴的禮物給小男友，並且意外地以老公的信用卡支付。他發現時會殺了我的。

⓬ I am doomed! I memorized the wrong chapters for the exam.　我死定了！我背錯要考試的章節了。

必背單字片語

☑ **Contingency** [kən`tɪndʒənsɪ]　n. 意外事故；偶然事件
Diesel generators are part of any hospital's power outage contingency plan.
柴油發電機是任何醫院預防停電的應急計畫的一部分。

- -

☑ **By mistake**　ph. 搞錯
My colleague took my bag by mistake, and inside the bag he found a lover letter written by his wife to me.
我同事誤拿了我的袋子，卻在袋子裡發現他老婆寫給我的一封情書。

- -

☑ **Panic** [`pænɪk]　vt. 恐慌
Don't panic unless you want to make matters worse.
不要驚慌，除非你想讓事情更糟。

- -

☑ **Route** [rut]　n. 路線 vi. 按特定路線發送（東西）
Which route are you going to take to the hospital?
你要走哪條路去醫院？

- -

☑ **Gulp** [gʌlp]　v. 快速吞下
He was so thirsty he drank that glass of ice cold water in one gulp.　他口渴到把那杯冰開水一口喝完。

> 註　take a gulp 喝一大口；in one gulp 一飲而盡

Unit 38 太超過了

這樣說英文

199

Ⓐ I'm going to eat this burger and then devour that plate of lasagna.

Ⓑ You've already eaten a roast chicken, ten sushi rolls, a loaf of bread and a whole cake. What are you, a bottomless pit?

Ⓐ You haven't touched your noodles. Are you going to eat that?

Ⓐ 我要將這個漢堡吃掉，然後吃光那盤千層麵。

Ⓑ 你已經吃了一隻雞、十條壽司、一條麵包和整個蛋糕。你是什麼，無底洞嗎？

Ⓐ 你還沒吃你的麵。你要吃嗎？（不要就給我）

....

Ⓐ I have a date with that attractive guy from the gym so I'll have to cancel our dinner appointment.

Ⓑ How do you keep track of all your boyfriends? This must be the sixth guy you're seeing this week.

Ⓐ I'm just increasing my chances of meeting Prince Charming. Better than sitting and moping at home, right?

Ⓐ 我要去跟在健身房認識的一個很帥的男生約會，所以我要取消我們的晚餐約會。

Ⓑ 你是怎麼記錄你所有的男友？這應該是這個禮拜約會的第六位男生了吧。

Ⓐ 我只是在增加我遇到白馬王子的機會。比坐在家裡悶悶不樂的好，對吧？

....

Ⓐ This summer he traveled to Spain, France and the UK. Then in fall, he'll head off to Canada for camping and Alaska for a cruise.

Ⓑ I can't believe it. How does he find the time and money to travel around like that?

Ⓐ He has a rich father, who spoils him silly with ridiculous sums of money. And oh, he's planning a trip to Australia for the winter. Want to tag along?

Ⓐ 這個暑假他去西班牙、法國、和英國旅遊，然後秋天他將去加拿大露營和去阿拉斯加坐郵輪。

🅑 真不敢相信。他哪來的時間和金錢這樣遊山玩水？

🅐 他有個把他寵壞並有一堆錢的富爸爸。還有喔，他計畫冬天去澳洲，想跟嗎？

Vocabulary

Devour [dɪ`vaʊr] vt. 狼吞虎嚥地吃；吃光

Bottomless pit ph. 無底洞

Prince Charming ph. 白馬王子；如意郎君

Cruise [kruz] n. 郵輪

Spoil [spɔɪl] vt. 寵壞（小孩）；毀壞

這樣用句型

You haven't _____. Are you going to _____?

- been honest with me... tell me the truth
  你還沒跟我坦承。你要告訴我事實嗎？

- traveled to Spain before... have your holiday there
  你以前還沒去過西班牙。你要去那裏度假嗎？

- kissed a girl before... kiss her　你以前還沒親過女生。你要親她嗎？

I have _____ so I'll have to _____.

- incontinence issues... wear a diaper
  我有失禁的問題，所以我必須穿紙尿褲。

- a schizophrenic mother... ignore everything silly she says
  我有個精神分裂的母親，所以我不理會她所說的每件傻事。

- had enough of you... stay as far away as I can from you
  我已經受夠你了，所以我要離你越遠越好。

He has a _____, who _____ with _____.

- mother... likes to interfere... his personal life
他有個喜歡干涉他私人生活的母親。

- boss... motivates the staff... empty promises of imaginary company stock options
他有一個以幻想的公司股權的空頭支票來激勵員工的老闆。

- girlfriend... is obsessed... her own reflection in the mirror
他有一個對鏡子裡的自己很著迷的女朋友。

用這句話更厲害！

❶ That's too much! He won the lottery three times in a row.
太超過了！他連續贏了三次樂透。

❷ How greedy can you get? How can you eat all the cakes from the buffet bar?
你怎麼那麼貪心？你怎麼能把自助餐檯上的蛋糕全吃完？

❸ Give them an inch and they'll take a mile.　得寸進尺。

❹ You're way out of line. I've had it!
你太過分了。我真是受夠了。

❺ In competitive eating events, we often see people eat inordinate amounts of food.
在大胃王競賽中，我們時常看到參賽者吃過度份量的食物。

❻ It is too ridiculous to swim in the lake in the middle of winter.
冬天在湖裡游泳實在太可笑。

❼ How can you make racial criticism in front of everyone?
你怎麼能在大家面前說有種族性的批評？

❽ Do you seriously expect me to drive 4 hours to a 30-minute meeting? That is absurd!
你真的期望我開車四個小時去參加一個三十分鐘的會議？那很荒謬！

❾ The billionaire has a toilet that is made out of pure gold.
這個億萬富翁有個以純金打造的馬桶。

必背單字片語

☑ **In a row**　ph. 連續
The football star scored three goals in a roll and led his team to victory.
這個足球明星連續進三球，帶領他的隊伍邁向勝利之路。

- -

☑ **Inordinate** [ɪn`ɔrdnɪt]　adj. 無節制的；過度的
This book has taken up an inordinate amount of time to write.
寫這本書佔用了太多時間。

- -

☑ **Ridiculous** [rɪ`dɪkjələs]　adj. 可笑的；荒唐的
Helen looks ridiculous in that pair of shades.
海倫戴這付墨鏡看起來很可笑。

- -

☑ **Absurd** [əb`sɝd]　adj. 不合理的；荒謬的
It is absurd to pay NT$500 an hour for parking at the countryside.
在鄉下停車需要付一小時新台幣五百元很不合理。

Unit 39　噁心

這樣說英文

202

Ⓐ Hello there handsome. Say, you haven't looked this good for a while. I just find you so irresistible!

Ⓑ Why are you in such repulsive lingerie? I am so grossed out right now.

Ⓐ That is so rude! You should learn to be more romantic.

Ⓐ 哈囉，英俊的小子。哎呀，你已經很久沒有看起來那麼帥了。我突然覺得你令人無法抗拒！

Ⓑ 你為何穿這麼使人反感的睡衣？我都快吐了。

Ⓐ 真是無禮！你應該學學如何更浪漫。

....

Ⓐ Your kid is so smart! What a genius! I bet he is going to Harvard.

Ⓑ What in the world are you talking about? He only recited the alphabet and he is only in kindergarten.

Ⓐ That's exactly my point, boss. Your son is just like you: smart, dashing and so successful at such a young age.

Ⓐ 你的小孩好聰明！真是個天才！我賭他一定進哈佛大學。

Ⓑ 你到底在說什麼？他只是背出英文字母，還有他現在還在讀幼稚園。

Ⓐ 老闆，這正是我的重點。你兒子跟你很像：聰明、帥氣並且這麼年輕就很成功。

....

Ⓐ Your mother is such a great cook! I love her chicken and mash, and her cake just melts in your mouth. My compliments to your mother; she should get a Michelin star.

Ⓑ You are kidding, right? The chicken is burnt, the mash too dry and the cake harder than a rock. They all look so gross!

Ⓐ I think your mother likes me because she is grinning form ear to ear.

Ⓐ 你媽的廚藝真好！我喜歡她煮的雞肉和薯泥，還有她做的蛋糕入口即化。我向你媽致敬，她應該得到米其林一顆星。

B 你在開玩笑，對吧？雞肉燒焦了、薯泥太乾了、還有蛋糕像石頭一樣硬。這些看起來都令人噁心。

A 我認為你媽喜歡我，因為笑得合不攏嘴。

註 grinning ear to ear，誇飾笑得嘴巴張很大代表很開心。

Vocabulary

Irresistible [ˌɪrɪˋzɪstəbl̩] adj. 富有吸引力的
Genius [ˋdʒinjəs] n. 天才
Recite [riˋsaɪt] vt. 背誦

Michelin Star ph. 法國米其林餐廳評比所給的星級
Grin [grɪn] vi. 露齒而笑

這樣用句型

203

> **Are you _____? Do you _____ ?**

· asking her out... want to infuriate her husband
  你要約她出去嗎？你想惹她先生大怒嗎？

· looking at the sun... want to go blind
  你對著太陽看嗎？你想要變瞎嗎？

· kicking sand in my face... want to take this outside
  你在羞辱我嗎？你想要到外面解決嗎？

註 kick sand in one's face 是個俚語，指的是 be mean to someone，有教訓某人或是羞辱某人的意思，而不是真的踢沙子到某人臉上喔！

> **Your _____ is such _____! I bet _____ .**

· sister... a snob... she only hangs out with the rich and the famous
  你姐姐真是個勢利眼的人！我猜想她只跟有錢有勢的人混在一起。

- brother... a jerk... nobody likes him
  你哥哥真是個古怪的人！我猜沒人喜歡他。
- boss... a cheapskate... he never gave you a raise
  你老闆真是個小氣鬼！我猜他從沒你加薪過。

用這句話更厲害！

❶ Brown nosing the boss seems like an effective way to get promoted.　對老闆拍馬屁似乎是個升遷的有效方式。

❷ This restaurant is so filthy and gross!
這家餐廳真是既髒亂又令人噁心！

❸ Unfortunately, your inability to brown-nose is holding you back in your career.　很不幸的，你不會拍馬屁讓你事業無法更上一層。

❹ I wonder what ulterior motives she may have with that saccharine sweet smile.
我很納悶她那故作多情的甜美微笑背後有什麼別有用心的動機。

❺ All the sweet talk means absolutely naught if words are not followed by action.
所有的甜言蜜語都沒有意義，如果之後沒有行動的話。

❻ Their public display of affection is attracting curious on-lookers.　他們眾目睽睽之下表現愛意吸引了好奇的旁觀者。

❼ This pizza crust looks all soggy and moldy. It's so disgusting. I wouldn't touch it if I were you.
這個比薩的餅皮看起來濕軟又有點發霉。真噁。如果我是你我不會去碰它。

❽ Look, the couple under the tree has been smooching away for hours.
看那裡，這對情侶已經在樹下摟抱親吻好幾個小時了（好肉麻呀）。

❾ That made me sick!　那讓我覺得很噁！

必背單字片語

☑ **Effective** [ɪ`fɛktɪv]　adj. 有效的
We must find an effective way to defend ourselves against global warming.
我們必須找到一個有效的方法對抗地球暖化。

☑ **Inability** [ˌɪnə`bɪlətɪ]　n. 無能；無力
His inability to fulfill her wishes has compromised his chance to marry her.
他無力滿足她的願望使他失去跟她結婚的機會。

☑ **Motive** [`motɪv]　n. 動機
What is his motive for committing the hideous crime?
他犯下駭人聽聞罪刑的動機為何？

☑ **Saccharine** [`sækəˌrin]　adj. 故作多情的；過甜的
Instead of sugar, he added a powdery substance with a saccharine taste into the cake mix.
他在蛋糕原料粉中加了甜度很高的粉狀物質來取代白糖。

☑ **Naught** [nɔt]　n. 無；不存在；【數】零 adj. 無用的
The sports car can go from naught to a hundred miles per hour in 5 seconds.
跑車能在五秒內從零加速到每小時一百英哩。

❷ 喜怒哀樂

Learn Smart! 038

超有梗的日常英語 Talk Show

口語與幽默感一起飆升

作　　者	陳紳誠、謝旻蓉
封面構成	高鍾琪
內頁構成	菩薩蠻電腦排版有限公司

發 行 人	周瑞德
企劃編輯	徐瑞璞
校　　對	劉俞青、陳欣慧
印　　製	世和印製企業有限公司
初　　版	2014 年 9 月
定　　價	新台幣 369 元
出　　版	倍斯特出版事業有限公司
電　　話	(02) 2351-2007
傳　　真	(02) 2351-0887
地　　址	100 台北市中正區福州街 1 號 10 樓之 2
E - m a i l	best.books.service@gmail.com

港澳地區總經銷	泛華發行代理有限公司
地　　　址	香港筲箕灣東旺道 3 號星島新聞集團大廈 3 樓
電　　　話	(852) 2798-2323
傳　　　真	(852) 2796-5471

國家圖書館出版品預行編目(CIP)資料

超有梗的日常英語 Talk Show：口語與幽默感一起飆升 /
陳紳誠, 謝旻蓉著. -- 初版. -- 臺北市：倍斯特, 2014.09
　面；　公分
ISBN 978-986-90883-1-2(平裝附光碟片)

1.英語 2.口語 3.會話

805.188　　　　　　　　　　　　103016120

Simply Learning, Simply Best!

Simply Learning, Simply Best!